"I'm afraid you've com here from…"

"Chicago."

"Chicago." Of course. Lots of wealthy industrialists in that fine city. Was there a shortage of acceptable men her age? Both sides of the war had lost significant numbers.

With the rush of adrenaline fading, he began to notice details about her. Miss Longstreet wasn't a classic beauty. Her features were too interesting. Slightly playful. It was the eyebrows, he decided. Sweeping over large, expressive eyes, the dark slashes formed a natural arch and were set in perpetual inquisitiveness.

No, it wasn't the brows. It was her unusually shaped mouth. Soft and pink, the top lip curved in a smooth arc above the full lower one. A tiny freckle hovered above it on the right. Definitely intriguing.

He blinked those thoughts away. Intriguing or not, the city girl wasn't staying.

Folding his arms across his chest, he delivered a glare that made most townsfolk quiver in their boots. "The trip was a waste, Miss Longstreet. I am not, nor will I ever be, in the market for a bride."

* * *

Cowboy Creek: Bringing mail-order brides, and new beginnings, to a Kansas boomtown

Want Ad Wedding—Cheryl St.John, April 2016
Special Delivery Baby—Sherri Shackelford, May 2016
Bride by Arrangement—Karen Kirst, June 2016

Karen Kirst was born and raised in East Tennessee near the Great Smoky Mountains. A lifelong lover of books, it wasn't until after college that she had the grand idea to write one herself. Now she divides her time between being a wife, homeschooling mom and romance writer. Her favorite pastimes are reading, visiting tearooms and watching romantic comedies.

Books by Karen Kirst

Love Inspired Historical

Cowboy Creek

Bride by Arrangement

Smoky Mountain Matches

The Reluctant Outlaw
The Bridal Swap
The Gift of Family
"Smoky Mountain Christmas"
His Mountain Miss
The Husband Hunt
Married by Christmas
From Boss to Bridegroom
The Bachelor's Homecoming
Reclaiming His Past

Visit the Author Profile page at Harlequin.com.

KAREN KIRST

Bride by Arrangement

HARLEQUIN® LOVE INSPIRED® HISTORICAL

Special thanks and acknowledgment to Karen Kirst
for her contribution to the Cowboy Creek miniseries.

Recycling programs
for this product may
not exist in your area.

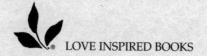

LOVE INSPIRED BOOKS

ISBN-13: 978-0-373-28363-7

Bride by Arrangement

www.Harlequin.com

Printed in U.S.A.

Let nothing be done through selfish ambition
or conceit, but in lowliness of mind
let each esteem others better than himself.
—*Philippians* 2:3

To Elen Matuszkova—
even though thousands of miles separate us,
you're still close to my heart. We love and miss you.

Many thanks to editor Elizabeth Mazer for
choosing to work with me again. It's been a
pleasure. And to my fellow authors in this
continuity, Cheryl St.John and Sherri Shackelford.
I've enjoyed working with you both.

Chapter One

Cowboy Creek, Kansas
June 1868

Noah Burgess wasn't cut out to be sheriff. He'd worn the badge less than three days and had already failed the town he'd helped found. Seemed one simple task—rounding up the Murdoch brothers and their band of outlaws, men who'd managed to relieve the bank of its gold and end Sheriff Davis's life—was beyond him.

Muscles stiff from long hours in the saddle, his shirt clinging to his sticky, sweat-slicked skin, he welcomed the sight of his homestead rising up from the sea of prairie grass. The steadfast sun painted everything in a butter-yellow haze. The one-and-a-half-story cabin wasn't grand or vast like his friends' houses. In fact, with its awkward roofline and porch awning dissecting the front facade, the home he'd designed and constructed was somewhat of an eyesore.

Unlike Daniel Gardner and Will Canfield, his best friends and cofounders of Cowboy Creek, he didn't plan on taking a wife and filling his home with offspring. His cabin may not impress folks, but it was practical. Kept him warm during the brutal prairie winters and cool enough during the summer months. Kept the rain and snow out. What critters managed to breach its walls the cat took care of.

He'd done a better job with the barn. Granted, he'd gone a tad overboard. The structure was large enough to house five wagons abreast and ten deep. Straight ahead, stately cottonwoods lining the creek bank blocked the frequent breezes sweeping across the undulating plains. Above him, a hawk's cry sliced the air, the bird's broad wings outstretched as it dipped and peaked searching for a meal.

The tight ball of tension between his ribs unraveled as his sorrel horse, Samson, carried him closer. This slice of Kansas granted him sanctuary and tenuous peace after years of fighting on chaotic battlefields and months of inescapable suffering in filthy field hospitals.

Ranching was in his blood. Working the land and tending livestock came naturally. Running thieves and outlaws to ground? Not a profession he'd ever aspired to.

Noah was headed for the barn when he noticed the cabin's front door ajar. Pulling up the reins, he slid out of the saddle and had his revolver unholstered by the time his boots hit the ground. His senses sharpened. The vegetable garden was undisturbed, and the fields dotted with shorthorn cattle revealed nothing unusual.

Multiple scenarios ran through his mind. Outlaws like the Murdochs wouldn't think twice about helping themselves to others' property. An unattended homestead presented the perfect pickings. Indians in these parts weren't too pleased with the locals, either, the needless slaughter of buffalo solely for their hides provoking some to violence.

His ears strained for unfamiliar sounds.

Jerking down the loading lever, he fumbled in his tiny cap box for the percussion cap. When he had it in place, he gently replaced the hammer. He could get off one good shot. Weapon outstretched, he eased the door open inch by inch. Narrow steps ascended into the loft. Perfect place for a body to hide. He scanned the half wall's top ledge. Farther in, the pie safe and hutch came into view, as did the Waterloo step-stove he'd ordered because it was the same kind his ma had used.

A chair creaked and Noah reacted.

He lunged into the room. "Make another move, and I'll shoot you where you stand…" He trailed off, jaw sagging. Had he entered the wrong house?

"Don't shoot! I can explain! I—I have a letter. From Will Canfield." A petite dark-haired woman standing on the other side of his table lifted an envelope in silent entreaty. Her jewel-adorned fingers trembled. "Are you Noah Burgess?"

At the mention of his friend's name, he slowly lowered his weapon. But his defensive instincts still surged through him. It was difficult to make sense of encountering a female in his home. Not an ordinary female, either. This one belonged on the finest streets of Paris, France or New York City. What she was doing in an isolated, male-dominated Kansas cow town he couldn't fathom.

From the polished boot tips peeking beneath her bell-shaped skirts, to the orderly perfection of her hair swept up and off her neck, she oozed sophistication. Elegance. She may as well have stepped from the pages of a child's fairy tale. He got an impression of creamy, rich fabric, dainty pink bows and skirts that formed a cascading cloud of perfect folds. A thin pink ribbon encircled her neck. Noah had no words for the hat atop her crown. Too small to provide shade, the ivory-colored contraption was drowning in pink and red bows.

She was dainty. Ethereal. And clearly lost.

When he didn't speak, she gestured limply to the ornate leather trunks stacked on either side of his bedroom door. "Mr. Canfield was supposed to meet us at the station. His porter arrived in his stead… Simon was his name.

He said something about a posse and outlaws." A delicate shudder shook her frame. "He said you wouldn't mind if we brought these inside. I do apologize for invading your home like this, but I had no idea when you would return, and it is June out there."

Her gaze roamed his face, her light brown eyes widening ever so slightly as they encountered his scars. It was like this every time. He braced himself for the inevitable disgust. Pity. Revulsion. Told himself again it didn't matter.

When her expression reflected nothing more than curiosity, irrational anger flooded him.

"What are you doing in my home?" he snapped. "How do you know Will?"

"I'm Constance Miller. I'm the bride Mr. Canfield sent for."

"Will's already got a wife."

Pink kissed her cheekbones. "Not for him. For you."

Shock nailed his boots to the floorboards. "Excuse me?"

"You are Mr. Burgess, are you not?"

She looked deliberately to the tintype photograph propped on the mantel. Three young, naive soldiers stood proudly in their freshly issued uniforms. He was in the middle, flanked on either side by men who had become like brothers, Daniel Gardner and Will Canfield. The same men who'd followed him out here as soon as the war ended. Men who'd pestered him to pitch in for the bride train and order one for himself.

His throat closed. *They wouldn't have.*

"That's my name," he forced past stiff lips.

"I was summoned to Cowboy Creek to be your bride." She was looking at him with encroaching desperation, silently imploring him to confirm her statement.

He closed his eyes and mentally pummeled his blockheaded friends. They'd stirred up a hornet's nest with this one. How many times had he told them he wasn't interested? Why couldn't they accept he was resigned to a solitary life?

"Your friend didn't tell you." The dismay coloring her tone snapped his eyes open. A sharp crease brought her brows together.

"I'm afraid not." Slipping off his worn Stetson, Noah hooked it on the chair and dipped his head toward the crumpled parchment. "May I?"

Miss Miller didn't appear inclined to approach him, so he laid his gun on the mantel to unload later and crossed to the square table, keeping it as a barrier between them. He took the envelope she extended across to him and slipped the letter free, aware of an undertone of vanilla. Was it coming from her? He'd expected garish perfume, not sweet subtlety.

The words scrawled in neat, succinct rows were indeed Will's. The handwriting was unmistakable. Heat climbed up his neck as he read the description of himself. His friend had embellished his finer traits while downplaying the disfigurement he'd earned during the battle of Little Round Top.

Tips of his ears burning, he stuffed it back inside and tossed it on the tabletop. "I'm afraid you've come all the way out here from…"

"Chicago."

"Chicago." Of course. Lots of wealthy industrialists in that fine city. So why hop a train out here? Was there a shortage of acceptable men her age back in the Midwest? Both sides of the war *had* lost significant numbers…

With the rush of adrenaline fading, he began to notice details about her. Miss Miller wasn't a classic beauty. Her features were too interesting. Slightly playful. It was the eyebrows, he decided. Sweeping over large, expressive eyes, the dark slashes formed a natural arch and were set in perpetual inquisitiveness.

No, it wasn't the brows. It was her unusually shaped mouth. Soft and pink, the top lip curved in a smooth arc above the full lower one. A tiny freckle hovered above it on the right. Definitely intriguing.

He blinked those thoughts away. Intriguing or not, the city girl wasn't staying.

Folding his arms across his chest, he delivered a glare that made most townsfolk quiver in their boots. "The trip was a waste, Miss Miller. I am not, nor will I ever be, in the market for a bride."

He hadn't been expecting her. Clearly. Grace Longstreet stared at the walnut gun handle angled on the mantel and swallowed tightly. Fear tasted coppery in her mouth. Guilt oozed through her veins like black sludge. If she didn't pull off this masquerade…

Her fingers curled into balls, causing her many rings to bite into her skin. Failure didn't bear thinking about. She must convince this intimidating homesteader of two essential facts—that her name was Constance Miller, and that he had a responsibility to marry her. There wasn't room for her conscience or pride. Her little girls' well-being hinged on the success of her subterfuge.

Sunlight streaming through the bare window set his fair hair ablaze and made his flinty gaze appear to radiate blue fire. Noah Burgess was a blond, blue-eyed Norse Viking clothed in cowboy gear. He had nothing in common with the men in her social circle, with their expensive suits, slicked-back hair and soft hands. This man lived and breathed the great outdoors. He was one with nature. Strong and virile. He wore a pale blue button-down shirt, tan vest, canvas trousers and brown leather boots caked with trail grit. A red-and-white bandanna was knotted around his neck. A powerful-looking man, his biceps and wide shoulders strained the fabric, folded as they were over a chiseled chest that narrowed to lean hips and thick, muscular legs.

She tried not to stare at the scars. Raised, uneven webs of pink skin fanned over his lower left jaw, extended under his ear and onto his neck, disappearing beneath his shirt collar. Grace wanted to ask what had hurt him. Mr. Canfield hadn't given her details, saying only that Mr. Burgess had sustained an injury in battle. But she'd sensed his recoil the first time she'd noticed them, and so she refrained.

Whatever the case, it didn't distract from his rugged presence. He possessed strong features. His mouth, set in a hard, straight line, looked as if it hadn't curved into a smile for quite some time.

When she'd discovered her cousin had agreed to come West and marry a complete stranger, Grace had seen only an opportunity to escape the city. She hadn't given a single thought to whom or what she'd find at the other end of the tracks. It wasn't until she and the girls were safely on the train, Chicago's skyline gradually fading into the distance, that she'd paused to consider the possible ramifications of her impulsiveness. Fact was, she didn't know anything about Constance's intended groom. Her cousin hadn't been able to tell her much. With no suitable marriage prospects in her impoverished neighborhood, the younger girl had been anticipating a fresh start, despite the inherent risks in such an undertaking. Grace had gifted her with a satisfactory sum for letting her switch places. Right about now, her cousin was undoubtedly searching for another eager groom in a different territory.

During the long, uncomfortable journey, Grace had contemplated the contents of Will Canfield's letter—Constance had read it to her enough times for her to have it memorized—and had been comforted by his description of Noah Burgess as an honorable man. She'd prayed a lot, too. With her soul

conflicted, she'd begged for God's understanding and forgiveness. What choice had she had, in the end?

Noah shifted, the silver badge over his heart glinting,
catching her eye for the first time.

"You're the sheriff?" she blurted, hard put to hide her
distress. There'd been no mention of it in Mr. Canfield's
letter. Then again, that gentleman had apparently left off
more than one piece of pertinent information.

Conning an ordinary homesteader was one thing. But
a lawman? Her already upset stomach tightened further
into hard knots.

"It's a recent development." His lips firmed. She couldn't
tell if he was perturbed with her, his own situation or both.
"Our former sheriff, Quincy Davis, was shot and killed several days ago. The town needed a replacement."

"I'm sorry for your loss."

Kneading his nape, he heaved a sigh. "Look, Miss Miller,
you've a right to be upset. My friends meant well. They'll
fix this. Will owns the Cattleman, Cowboy Creek's premier
hotel. You can stay there at his expense while you await the
return train to Chicago."

"But—"

"Don't worry about the cost of the ticket, either. It'll be
taken care of."

Grace grasped for the right words. "Have you ever considered your friends may be right?"

His hand slapped to his side. "I don't take your meaning, ma'am."

"Perhaps they see a need in your life you haven't yet
acknowledged. Why else would they do something so
outrageous as to arrange a marriage for you without your
consent?"

She could practically hear his teeth grinding together.
"Are you suggesting I don't know my own mind?"

Grace was accustomed to men's displeasure. She'd endured Ambrose's for five years. Ambrose was gone, however. If she had only herself to think about, she'd accept this mistake and walk away. But her daughters' future was at stake. Her brother-in-law, Frank, would do anything to make her his, including threatening to separate her from Jane and Abigail if she didn't comply with his wishes. She had to pursue her daughters' best interests, no matter if she had to get on her knees and beg this man to take her as his bride.

"I'm suggesting you give marriage to me some thought before you send me packing. I'm a proficient housekeeper." She indicated the cabin's clean but sparse interior. "I can sew. Cook. Surely you don't have time to prepare adequate meals with all your other responsibilities."

His expression frustratingly inscrutable, he raked her with his cool blue gaze. His clear dismissal threatened to deflate her already shaky self-confidence.

Humiliation licking her insides, she lifted her chin. "I may appear incompetent, but I assure you, Mr. Burgess, I know how to make myself useful."

He studied her a moment longer. "Go back to your pampered life in the city, Miss Miller. I don't know what sort of glamorous accounts you've read about life out here, but they ain't reality. One week on this homestead, and you'd be begging me to send you back."

Surely it was her appearance he was judging, not her, the woman. He didn't know her. Couldn't see her soul, her heart. "You're wrong. I can prove you're wrong."

A long-suffering sigh pulsed between his lips. "Let me be plain. It doesn't matter to me whether you're prairie material or not. I don't want a wife. I don't want you or any other woman." He jerked a thumb to the open doorway. "I've just come off a three-day search for a gang of outlaws. I'm tired and hungry, and I need to see to my horse. So if you'll excuse—"

Behind her, the bedroom door creaked open. "Momma?"

Grace froze. Exhausted from the interminable train ride, the girls had been drooping by the time they'd reached the homestead. She'd put them in the only bed in the house.

The intractable sheriff's focus shot past her, his eyes going wide. He blinked several times.

"You have a kid?"

"As a matter of fact, I have two."

Chapter Two

Kids? She had kids? "I thought it was *Miss* Miller."

"You assumed."

The ardor with which she'd spoken moments ago cooled, and Noah witnessed a mother's protective instincts surface. She beckoned to the little girls hovering in the doorway, a loving smile urging them not to be frightened. They had obviously been sleeping in his bed. Through the opening, he could see that the plain wool blanket atop his straw-stuffed mattress was creased.

Children were a rarity in these parts. As were females, which was precisely why Daniel, Will and the other businessmen had conspired to locate willing mail-order brides. The railroad terminus had boosted their itinerant population, but they needed families to grow this town.

Huddling close to their mother's side, they watched him wordlessly. Their dark brown hair and delicate features resembled hers. White aprons overlay their dresses, both solid navy blue, and frilly pantaloons were visible from the knee down. Sturdy round-toed shoes completed the outfits.

"Girls, this is the gentleman I told you about. Mr. Burgess owns this homestead. He's also the sheriff of Cowboy Creek." She ran a hand over the nearest one's rumpled sausage curls. "This is Abigail."

Big chocolate-brown eyes regarded him solemnly.

Constance reached over and touched the second one's shoulder. "And this is Jane."

Jane's bright blue eyes danced with curiosity. Her skin was a shade lighter than her sister's, and freckles were sprinkled liberally across her nose and cheeks.

"Pleased to meet you, sir," Jane offered.

Abigail kept silent. Circling her mother's waist with her tiny arms, she hid her face in the voluminous skirts.

"How old are they?"

"They recently celebrated their sixth birthday."

Twins. Not identical, but there could be no mistaking they were kin.

Noah's gaze skimmed Constance's petite but curvaceous frame. Back home in Virginia, a neighbor woman had died giving birth to twins. The babies had perished, as well. He'd overheard his ma saying how dangerous the business of birthing one child could be, much less two. And that woman had been several inches taller and larger boned than the one standing before him.

"Where's their father?"

"Passed on a year ago."

There wasn't a flicker of grief in Constance Miller's steady gaze. The girls didn't react, either, which told him they were either too young to grasp the permanency of death or they hadn't shared a close relationship with the man.

His interest grew. Why was she dead set on hitching herself to a complete stranger? Had he misjudged her financial status? For all he knew, the clothes and jewelry were all that was left of her late husband's wealth. She could be destitute. With small children depending on her, of course she'd be willing to marry anyone who struck her as decent.

Had she somehow discovered Noah's worth? The Union Pacific had paid him a small fortune for his original homestead because of its proximity to town and the terminus. He'd used a portion of that money to purchase this new tract of land farther outside town. The rest of it he'd placed in the bank for a rainy day.

The trio stood watching him, waiting for him to speak. His ire stirred anew. His friends had put him in an untenable position.

Snagging his hat, he settled it on his head. "I'm going to take care of my horse, then ready the wagon. You have about an hour before we leave for the hotel."

Ignoring the widow's quiet gasp, he pivoted and strode for the exit, not stopping when he heard her order the girls to remain inside. His boot heels thudded across the porch, grew muted when he reached the short grass. The early-summer heat closed around him. Looping Samson's reins around his palm, he scowled. She sure was desperate. Had to be if she was willing to overlook his disfigurement.

The day his gun exploded in his face, Noah's life had altered course. In those first days and weeks, he hadn't known whether or not he'd survive. The risk of infection had been great. As time passed and he began to heal, slowly and painfully, he'd had trouble coming to terms with his new appearance. It had taken even longer to accept that love and marriage were out of his reach. Who could love a freak like him?

These days, he steered clear of mirrors. He couldn't stomach the sight of the twisted, nightmarish flesh. How could he expect any woman to regard it day in and day out? He couldn't even grow a beard to hide the damage to his face.

The door clicked shut, and his hold on his temper slipped.

"Listen, lady, I'm sure you're accustomed to men doing your bidding, but this ain't Chicago. I—"

All of a sudden, she launched herself at him. "Wild animal," she exclaimed, seeking shelter behind him, her grip on his arms viselike.

Samson shifted uneasily. Noah dropped the reins and, bracing himself, searched for the source of her fear. When he spotted the rangy black wolf loping across the yard, golden eyes zeroed in on him, Noah's muscles relaxed.

"That's not a wild animal. That's Wolf. My pet."

Her grip loosened a hair, but she remained pressed against his back, using him as a shield against perceived danger. She peered around him. "That's no pet. That's a beast!"

To a city gal like Constance Miller, the Kansas prairie must seem like a wildly beautiful yet untamed land. Made sense she'd be alarmed at the thought of a wolf as one's pet.

Her vanilla scent enveloped him. Noah hadn't been this close to a female since before his enlistment. His ma had been liberal with hugs, much to his discomfiture, and his three younger sisters had begged him constantly for piggyback rides about the farm. As they were family, they didn't count.

Maneuvering around to face her, he gripped her shoulders and edged her back a step so he could concentrate. The top of her head came even with his throat. She had to tilt her chin up to meet his gaze, putting her loveliness on full display. Her eyes weren't an ordinary brown, he noted, but the hue of warm honey. Undeniable intelligence shone there. And indomitable spirit.

"Wolf won't hurt you. He's half wolf, half dog. I've raised him from a pup."

Her attention shifted beyond him. "He looks…"

"Intimidating. I know."

"I was going to say hungry for human flesh."

"I was just appointed sheriff," he informed her. "How would it look if I allowed a visitor to our fine town to be eaten on her first day?"

She didn't look convinced.

"Take my hand. I'll perform the introductions."

She stared at his outstretched hand for long moments before laying her palm against his. Noah sobered. Her skin was incredibly soft and warm, the sensation too agreeable for his peace of mind. He focused on how her jewelry felt unnatural and prevented their hands from fitting together.

Turning to greet his faithful companion, he signaled for him to stop with his outstretched hand. Wolf obeyed at once. Resting on his haunches, pink tongue lolling, he awaited their approach.

"He'll sense my fear and devour me," Constance muttered under her breath.

Noah fought a rare grin, astounded she could evoke humor in him when little else had these past years.

"Wolf, meet Constance." Moving their adjoined hands, he allowed the animal to sniff her. He could feel her stiffness, the jolt that shot through her the moment Wolf licked her fingers.

"That's his seal of approval," he murmured, studying her profile. "Ready to pet him?"

"Not yet."

That implied she was staying, and she most certainly wasn't.

Disengaging his hold, he pointed to the cabin. "You should wait inside while I get ready for our departure."

"Mr. Burgess, please… Won't you give us a chance?"

The entreaty in her expression was at odds with her dignified stance. Noah averted his face. Regret and frustration pulsed through him. "You don't want to build a life with the likes of me. Trust me on this."

Signaling for Wolf to follow, he fetched Samson and headed for the barn situated directly across from the cabin, a wide expanse of land between them. He didn't look to see whether or not she'd heeded his command.

* * *

What was she supposed to do now?

Grace remained where she stood as the sheriff and his *pet* disappeared into the mammoth barn. Her corset dug into her ribs. The numerous layers of undergarments and skirts were heavier and more cumbersome here on the plains. Was it because, amidst the city's brick and stone buildings, her view limited to whatever street she happened to be traveling down, she didn't have the crazy urge to throw out her arms and twirl in a circle and race through fields of tall grasses and wildflowers?

Cupping her hand over her eyes, she surveyed the endless prairie. The air here was fresh and earthy. After the hustle and bustle of the city, the quiet was somewhat unnerving. Her ears were accustomed to the clack of horses' hooves on cobbled streets, the shouts of vendors hawking their wares, the cadence of a dozen conversations. They weren't accustomed to nature's music…the breeze rustling through the grass stalks, birds' cheerful twittering, cattle calling to each other, insects buzzing.

Noah Burgess had carved out a mighty nice life for himself.

His rustic cabin, while not comparable to the Longstreet mansion, had its own charms. The barn and outbuildings appeared well constructed. In fact, the entire homestead looked as if it had been planned in a thoughtful, orderly manner.

Her daughters would flourish here. Grow strong beneath the Kansas sun. Learn to appreciate people based on their character, not their social standing or worldly possessions. Most important, they'd be out of her brother-in-law's reach. A sick feeling stole over Grace as Frank Longstreet's coldly handsome features swam in her memory. Frank coveted what had belonged to his brother, and now that Ambrose was gone, there was nothing standing in his way. He was determined to step into her late husband's shoes. Her feelings didn't matter. She and the girls were like some sort of trophy to him.

A large grasshopper landed on her outer skirt. Having only seen one on the pages of a book, she studied its fat green body for long minutes before urging it to land elsewhere. Scooping up the bulk of the stiff fabric with both hands, she pivoted and went inside, the opening not nearly wide enough for her dress. If she did succeed in becoming this homesteader's wife, she'd need a more practical wardrobe.

Why did her cousin's intended groom have to be the most stubborn man this side of the Mississippi River? Why couldn't she have been met by a man eager to end his solitude? If Frank ever managed to discover her whereabouts, a husband would help put an end to his relentless pursuit.

Mr. Burgess's refusal to even consider marriage complicated things.

Jane sat playing with her doll at the only table in the room. Like the chairs and kitchen furniture, it was constructed of rough timber. Had he crafted everything himself? The cabin walls were made of shaved logs, the spaces between filled with a mixture of clay and other materials. A loft area ran along the right side. She couldn't see what was up there because of the half wall running its length. The ceiling rafters soared high above her head, giving the living space an airy feeling. Or perhaps that was due to the limited amount of furnishings. There were only four chairs in the home, each seated around the table. The windows on either side of the massive stone fireplace didn't have curtains. Neither did the one in the kitchen.

This home—brown, boring and bare—was in desperate need of sprucing up. Grace moved to the mantel and ran a finger along the top edge. Dust coated the surface. She examined more closely a carved wooden replica of a plantation-style house. The craftsmanship was exquisite. Painted white with black shutters flanking the windows, there were four miniature columns along the veranda and chimneys flanking the roofline.

The sheriff had spoken with a slow drawl. Perhaps this was a memento to remind him of his family's home.

Picking up the tintype she'd seen earlier, she studied the sheriff's younger image. How handsome he'd looked in his uniform. Or was it his carefree expression that made him seem so different? There was a zest for life and adventure in his countenance that the real flesh-and-blood man lacked. The man she'd met carried the weight of the world on his shoulders.

What had he meant by what he'd said? Was he truly so traumatized by his changed appearance that he didn't feel worthy of marriage? The thought saddened her.

"Momma?"

Replacing the frame with care, she looked up and frowned. Abigail was reclining on the sheriff's bed again. Sweeping past Jane, she entered the bedroom and sat on the mattress edge, crinoline and skirts billowing about her.

"What's wrong, honey?"

"I don't feel well."

Grace tested the warmth of her forehead and cheek. Her skin was hot and flushed. Concern swept through her system. Her quieter daughter wasn't one to complain.

She smoothed her dark curls. "Does your head hurt? Or your tummy?"

"My head." Her deep brown eyes bore witness to her misery.

Grace smoothed the alarm from her face to avoid upsetting Abigail. "I'll get you a drink of water and a cold compress for your head. Perhaps Mr. Burgess has some tea on hand."

She called for Jane.

The chair scraped across the floorboards. Stopping at the foot of the bed, she clutched her porcelain doll to her chest. "Yes, ma'am?"

"Sit with your sister while I go and locate the well."

Leaving them in the spacious, utilitarian bedroom, she searched the kitchen for a water pail, discovering a dented tin one on a lower shelf of the long counter opposite the stove.

New worries brewed like a summer squall. Illness, especially in children, could turn deadly in a matter of hours. Did Cowboy Creek even have a qualified doctor? Residing on her mother-in-law's estate, they'd had access to the finest medical care in Chicago. Here, she was among strangers. She didn't know Noah Burgess well enough to guess whether he'd have compassion for a sick child or whether he'd force them to remove to the hotel as he'd stated, no matter the circumstances.

Father God, I know You're probably angry with me. Deception is not something You take lightly. I understand that. But I beg of You, please don't let this sickness be serious. Please let Noah be sympathetic.

She went outside again, and the heat struck her with more force this time. The air had gone still. She explored the yard and discovered the well behind the house, halfway between it and the stream. The procession of towering cottonwoods and the generous swath of shade they cast called to her, a sheltering oasis on the vast prairie. The entire time she was at the well, she expected to encounter the sheriff. But he was nowhere to be seen.

It wasn't until she was back inside, arranging a damp cloth on Abigail's forehead, that he finally showed.

His impatient stride carried him through the cabin. He hovered in the bedroom entrance, gloved hands braced on either side. "I've got the wagon out front. Do you have a preference for how the trunks are stowed?"

Straightening, Grace smoothed her hands down the front of her bodice, which seemed to have grown tighter with his arrival. He'd washed the grit from his face, and his hair was damp, rendering it a deeper hue, like pan-heated syrup.

"No preference."

Nodding, his light blue gaze touched on Abigail huddled beneath the blanket and Jane, who stood on the opposite side of the bed, her demeanor subdued. He inclined his head toward Abigail.

"Something wrong?"

Grace forced herself not to cow before his commanding presence. She wasn't a docile girl who shattered at a single unkind word or dark glare. Not anymore. She could handle his annoyance.

What if he's the type to act out his anger? a small voice prodded. Ambrose's impatience with her had mostly manifested itself in fuming tirades. Occasionally he'd taken her by the shoulders and shaken her until her neck ached and vision swam. Only once had he risen his hand to her.

Shutting out the unpleasant memories, she stiffened her spine. Sure, she wasn't exactly welcome in his home, but this development was out of her control. Besides, his friend had given him a glowing recommendation. One of the original town founders, Will Canfield was also a wealthy and powerful property owner. Surely he wouldn't have misrepresented the sheriff's sterling reputation.

"I believe she has a fever."

Pushing into the room, he came close and studied her daughter. "What are her symptoms?"

"Her head hurts, and her skin's dry and hot."

"Anything else?"

"Not yet."

His penetrating gaze lifted to Grace. "Has she been in contact with any sick folks?"

"I'm not aware of any. The train car was crowded, but no one displayed outward symptoms."

Noah's inspection was shrewd. Did he not believe her? *This* she wasn't lying about.

"What about you?" he asked abruptly. "And the other girl?"

He wasn't asking out of concern for their health, of course. They were a burden to him. A disruption in his ordered life, one he'd been on the verge of getting rid of.

"We're feeling fine."

A resigned sigh lifted his broad chest. Massaging the curve between his neck and shoulder, he said, "I can't take her to the hotel and risk exposing the other guests to whatever this is. You'll stay here until she improves."

Grace had to dig deep for gratitude. Her child was sick with who knew what, and all he was worried about were the fine people of Cowboy Creek.

Dipping her head to hide her true feelings, she said, "I appreciate your generosity of spirit, Mr. Burgess. We'll do our best to stay out of your way."

Chapter Three

The widow's words pricked Noah's conscience. Generous? Hah. Anxiety and frustration built inside like a cannon about to blow. Grinding his back teeth together, he studied the wee girl.

Her mussed curls were damp, and errant tendrils clung to her neck. She shivered a bit beneath the thick wool blanket. Not a good sign considering the air was hot and stagnant with the windows closed.

He had no idea how to help her. Children in general made him antsy. Sick children made him downright skittish. To his shock and dismay, numerous soldiers had had their wives and children join them. The women had cooked meals and washed and mended uniforms. The children had assisted in these chores, their eyes haunted by the gory sights and sounds of war. One small boy had gotten caught in the cross fire—killed instantly by a stray minié ball.

Noah had steered clear of the lot of them. They'd had no business being there.

Abigail whimpered. Constance adjusted the compress, murmuring reassuring words. Alarm punched him in his midsection. Whatever was ailing the little girl could be serious. And while he hadn't asked for their presence, they were under his protection for the time being.

"Want me to fetch the doctor?"

Constance's head snapped up. "There's one in Cowboy Creek? I wondered… Can you tell me about his reputation?"

"Doc Fletcher set up his practice several years ago. While I personally haven't needed his services, folks around here have nothing but good things to say about him."

Her lips pursed as she considered his words. "If she isn't improved by morning, then I think that would be best."

He saw the unease and fear beneath her brave facade. *She's far from home. Her expected groom has blasted her plans to pieces. And her daughter is ill. Of course she's afraid.*

As the urge to take her hand and reassure her fought its way to the surface, he backed up a step. Compassion was an unfamiliar emotion, one he'd thought the army had drilled out of him. "I'll return the wagon to the barn and rustle us up some supper."

"I can help. Show me what you want me to do."

"That won't be necessary."

Noah hadn't had a decent meal in days. He wasn't about to let a pampered socialite loose in his kitchen. Constance Miller probably didn't know the difference between a spatula and an egg beater.

Not giving her a chance to respond, he left the house and tended his team, all the while mentally forming a rebuke that would singe the hair on Will's and Daniel's heads. Constance and her daughters shouldn't be here. If Will hadn't butted his nose where it didn't belong, Noah would've been able to give the town's problems his full attention.

The bank heist wasn't his only concern. There'd been other unsolved crimes in recent weeks. Poisoned cattle. A sabotaged lumber delivery that had delayed construction of several important buildings. An invader in Will's private quarters at the Cattleman. The Murdoch brothers were a troublesome bunch, bent on getting rich off others' hard-earned money. But they weren't all that smart. Noah suspected someone else was behind the town's troubles. Someone with an agenda.

In the far-left corner, Wolf rested in the straw-strewn dirt, golden eyes tracking his jerky movements. Noah hung the bridles in the tack room.

"We've got a fresh set of problems, old boy. The chief one's name is Constance."

Wolf's pointy ears perked up.

"Can you believe she was scared of you?"

The animal's eyes closed as if in disbelief.

"Crazy, huh?"

Constance's reaction wasn't abnormal. Most folks kept their distance from Wolf, which suited Noah just fine. Since the wolf dog accompanied him most everywhere, it meant they kept their distance from Noah, as well.

He forked fresh hay in the horses' stalls. The damaged skin on his shoulder and upper chest protested the movements. Since his release from the hospital, he'd made a habit of applying honey mixed with lavender to keep the skin soft and supple. Skipping the past several days hadn't been a good idea.

"One of the twins is sick."

Wolf blinked.

"Hope it's nothing serious." Leaning his weight on the pitchfork, he stared out the double opening to the cabin framed by gently rolling plains. "I thought my scars would disgust them, but they didn't seem to notice."

He'd expected Constance to recoil as so many others had upon first seeing him. The first time it occurred had been days after his doctor proclaimed him on the mend and suspended the lead paint treatments. The coverings had been removed, and he'd been allowed a mirror to see his new appearance. Just as he'd been confronted with the monster he'd become, a wife or sister of one of the patients had passed by, taken one look at him and clapped her hand over her mouth. Her horror had seared itself onto his brain.

He'd thrown the mirror to the floor, smashing it to bits, and sunk into a soul-deep melancholy that had lasted for months. If not for Daniel and Will, he might never have left the sick ward.

Striding to the corner stall, he checked on his dairy cow. "Hey, Winnie."

Twisting her head, she gazed at him with molten brown eyes.

"I see Timothy was here this morning to give you relief."

He hadn't had to hire help until getting pinned sheriff. Daniel had suggested his employee's adolescent son, and Noah had taken his advice. It appeared the boy had done a decent job, but he'd check the springhouse to see if the milk had been stored properly.

The pangs in his stomach became audible. Pushing off the ledge, he left the barn and headed straight for the henhouse. His plans to dine at the Cowboy Café after settling the Millers at the hotel having been thwarted, he'd have to fix something fast and easy. Scrambled eggs and fried ham wouldn't take but a few minutes. There wasn't time to make biscuits, but he was sure the blue-eyed girl—Jean, was it?—would like flapjacks.

The thought of little girls and flapjacks had him thinking about his sisters. The three of them had argued over the best way to eat them. Lilly had preferred them smothered with butter and jam. Cara insisted on molasses. The youngest, Elizabeth, wouldn't eat them unless there were sausage links rolled up inside.

In the henhouse, he tried to push aside thoughts of his family and failed. Lilly, Cara and Elizabeth were no longer little girls. They were in their early twenties now, likely married with children. His parents would've aged considerably. Were they well? Struggling due to the South's defeat? He couldn't help wondering how his family had fared during the long years of fighting.

He could remedy that by writing them, but that last spectacular row with his father prevented him. That, and the fact he didn't wish them to know that he was a shadow of his former self, that his inner self was as twisted by the war as his outer appearance.

Quickly gathering the eggs into a basket he left hanging inside the henhouse door, he chose a container of milk from the springhouse and hurried to the cabin. He could imagine the widow's disdain over this simple meal. Oh, she wouldn't let it show. No doubt she'd had lessons on how to hide her true feelings. But the image of the refined lady tucking into a five-high stack of syrup-smothered flapjacks put a smirk on his face.

When he entered, Constance emerged from the bedroom, her expression shadowed.

"Abigail is asleep, and Jane is amusing herself with a picture book." Her skirts swayed and swished as she moved to meet him beside the counter he'd crafted. "Since you won't allow me to assist in the meal preparation, may I ready the place settings?"

Her formal speech matched her appearance. He indicated the wall behind him. "The plates and utensils are in the hutch."

She worked without speaking as he lit the fire inside the stove box and mixed the flapjack batter. Out of his peripheral vision, he noticed her frequent glances and wondered what was going on inside her head. He had little experience with females outside his family. He'd joined the army before he'd had the chance to properly court any of the local girls. His nurses had been kind and proficient, but they hadn't had the time or desire to socialize.

Having company in his home felt odd. Daniel and Will stopped by occasionally. Mostly they gave him space and waited for him to come to them.

Noah snagged the kettle from the row of shelves above the dry sink. "Do you drink coffee?"

"I never acquired a taste for it. Do you have any tea?"

"Tea's for ladies and little girls."

One flyaway brow arched, and he suspected she'd like to blast him with a tongue-lashing. Her composure fully intact, she said, "Milk will suffice." Approaching the counter, she laid her ringed hand on the container. The gaudy jewels sparkled. "Do you mind if I pour some for Jane and myself?"

"Be my guest."

Turning away, he procured a knife and, placing the ham slab on the plate, began to carve thick slices. He was acutely aware of her position in the room as she moved about. By the time he had the food ready to dish up, his skin prickled with tension and his appetite was long gone.

"Where would you like for us to sit?" She stood framed by the window, Jane—not Jean—beside her.

"Doesn't matter." He hated feeling flustered in his own home. The sooner this meal was over and he could make his escape, the better.

Constance chose the seat opposite his. The girl sat on his right.

Noah scooted his mug closer and cleared his throat. "I normally say grace in my head."

"Momma always offers the mealtime prayer." Jane looked from her mother to him.

Constance grimaced. "This isn't our home, sweetheart."

"He's gonna be our pa soon enough. You said so."

Jane's large, cornflower blue eyes pinned him to his chair. This was a fine barrel of pickles. "Let's get on with it," he groused at the woman across from him. "I've got an errand to tend to."

An errand he wasn't about to put off until tomorrow.

During the ride into town, Noah nursed his temper, the torturous meal replaying in his mind. His self-consciousness about his scar had trumped all else. Seated directly across from him, the widow had had a clear view. There'd been no-where to hide. So he'd ducked his head, tucked into his meal and done his best to ignore his uninvited guests.

Undulating fields gave way to the town proper. As his homestead was situated west of Cowboy Creek, he didn't have to traverse the main thoroughfare to reach Will and Tomasina's place. He traveled up Third Street. A handful of clapboard houses were interspersed between the businesses. Not as crowded in this section, but there was still a fair amount of activity as men went about their daily routines.

On his right, a reed-thin man wearing an apron was in his shop's entrance sweeping out debris. "Howdy, Sheriff!"

Seconds passed before Noah realized the man was ad-dressing him. *You're the sheriff now, remember?* Folks nor-mally didn't initiate conversation. They treated him with wary respect.

He belatedly touched a finger to his brim. The man's gaze slipped to Wolf trailing behind and, smile slipping, he turned and reentered his shop.

Similar exchanges were repeated as he proceeded along the dusty street. By the time Will's manor came into view, Noah's hand was tired from all the waving. He hadn't pur-sued this position. He'd been asked to fill Quincy Davis's spot after that man's untimely death. Some said it was because he was one of the founding members, and they trusted him to do right by the townsfolk. Noah suspected it had more to do with the wild tales of his battlefield ex-ploits that circulated about town. He didn't consider him-

self a hero. Sure, he'd had to work hard to dispel the stigma
of his Southern roots, to prove he was committed to the
Union's cause, but he hadn't done anything to warrant the
label of hero.

And while committed to keeping Cowboy Creek safe, he
wasn't prepared to involve himself in the social goings-on.

Guiding his sorrel onto Will's property, they followed the
grass-flattened path made by wagon deliveries. His friend's
new home was about 90 percent complete and promised to
be a stunning testament to Will's success. The front facade
was designed to impress. Thick white columns supported
a rounded rotunda high above. Arched windows lined the
bottom floor, while the second-floor windows were rect-
angular in shape. Behind the columns and above the front
entryway was a stone balcony. Open porches flanked both
ends of the central structure.

The sounds of hammers and men calling to each other
greeted him. The newlywed couple, who'd spent their first
few days as husband and wife on the trail of outlaws, had
decided to move in before the house was complete. Noah
didn't blame them. A hotel suite wasn't the place to begin
their new life together.

Still, the constant activity had to be irksome at times.

When no one answered his summons, he stalked around
the perimeter to where workmen were busy attaching pale-
hued brick to the rear wall. Scaffolding covered the entire
structure like a wooden spine. Behind the house, the lush,
tree-dotted lot backed up to the church, its spire reaching
for the blue expanse above.

Noah scanned the milling workers. They cast wary
glances at him and Wolf. Ignoring them, he spotted his
quarry standing apart from the activity. Slightly taller than
the other men, Will tended to be the finest-dressed gentleman around, his short brown hair covered by a smart derby
hat. The silver-handled cane he was rarely without had been

imported from Italy and was rumored to contain either a hidden blade or gun. Will had injured his leg in the same battle Noah had suffered his accident. He'd come close to being forced to having it amputated. Ignoring the doctor's warnings, Will had chosen to forego surgery and wait and see if the wound healed. The risk had paid off. With the cane, his limp was hardly noticeable.

Skirting a platform of bricks, Noah picked his way through the construction site. Will was in deep conversation with Gideon Kendricks, the Union Pacific's representative, in town to sell railroad stocks.

Gideon noticed his advance first and lifted his hand in a wave. Like Noah, the man hadn't changed out of his trail-dusted gear following their unsuccessful search. Will, on the other hand, had taken the time to clean up.

"Noah." Will's smile was rueful, but his brown eyes lacked contrition. "I've been expecting you." He nodded at Noah's companion. "Good day, Wolf."

His forehead pounded. "I would've been here sooner, but there was a complication."

Will looked intrigued. "What sort of complication?"

Noah cut his gaze toward Gidcon. While he'd grown to like the newcomer, he didn't want to air his business in front of him. "I think you'll agree it's a private matter."

Gideon smoothed a hand over his dirty-blond locks. "I'll take my leave."

"Wait." Will put a hand up. "Before you do, I believe Noah would be interested in hearing the latest news."

"What's that?"

"We've had word that Cowboy Creek is being considered for the county seat. A Webster County representative is coming to tour the town before deciding if we'll be in the running."

Gideon let loose a low whistle. "Sure would be a boon for your town."

"The temporary seat is in Ellsworth," Noah said, distracted from his purpose. "You know as well as I do they have the advantage."

"Their population has stalled in recent years." Will rested his weight on the silver handle. "Now that we're a prime destination for drovers and their longhorns, we're poised to expand our numbers significantly. If we're chosen, think of the tax benefits."

"A courthouse would be built here," Gideon added.

"What about crime? If the rep learns of our recent mishaps and our failure to discover the perpetrators, he'll move on to another terminus town."

"You're the new sheriff. Surely between you, Daniel and I, we can figure this out."

"I'll be glad to assist, as well." Gideon's gray eyes were serious.

"I never did thank you for joining the posse," Noah told him. Gideon wasn't a permanent resident and, as far as he knew, had no plans to become one. His loyalty was to himself and his employer, but he'd volunteered to help in their time of need.

The gentleman lifted a shoulder. "I don't like seeing good, honest people robbed of their money. I'm just sorry we didn't catch up to the scoundrels."

A sigh gusted out of Noah. "I hate to admit it, but I'm afraid they'll come back for more."

"If that's the case, I hope to be here when they do. They won't be so fortunate next time." Extending his hand, Gideon said, "I'll leave you both to your private discussion." A smile flashed as he shook their hands.

Noah remained silent until he was out of earshot.

Will lifted his cane toward the trees and grassy knolls. "Let's walk."

"Good idea, *Captain*," Noah quipped, deliberately meaning to irk the other man. Will hated any and all references to the war, refused to discuss the battle that had left him with a permanent limp. "Wouldn't want your employees to witness what's coming to you."

He grimaced but didn't voice his displeasure. "Simon told me about your mail-order bride and her daughters. To my credit, I didn't know about the children. Mrs. Miller didn't mention them in her letters. What do you think of her? Is she acceptable in the looks department? I've heard some ladies have the tendency to embellish facts."

Noah took his attention off the ground and glared at his friend. "How could you do it, Will? I told the two of you that I wasn't interested. I came home this afternoon and almost blasted the woman with my weapon!"

Will stopped and studied Noah with a smirk. "Not the best way to welcome a lady into your home, Noah."

"I want her gone."

The church bell chimed the six-o'clock hour. The clanging startled the meadowlarks in the slender oak nearest them. He watched them take flight.

"We simply wanted you to have what we have. Now that Daniel and I have found love, we don't want you to be alone."

"You don't see how arrogant that is?" His hand sliced the air. "To think you could pluck a random female from a mail-order-bride catalog and I would automatically fall in love with her?"

"Perhaps love was a poor choice of words. You could do with companionship though, Noah." Will's dark brown eyes were earnest. "The reason we took matters into our own hands is you're too stubborn to admit you're lonely. You don't want to end up like Gus and Old Horace, do you?"

He rolled his eyes at the mention of the town busybodies, who spent most every warm day with their bottoms glued to the mercantile's porch chairs, scrutinizing the townsfolk's comings and goings.

"If I do, that's my business. Not yours." Absent-mindedly exploring the uneven texture of his neck with his fingertips, he scuffed the ground with his boot heel.

Will plunged his fingers into his hair, an unusual show of impatience. "This preoccupation you have with your disfigurement is exasperating, you know that? So you're not perfect. So what? Neither am I." He motioned up and down his bum leg. "No one is. Sure, some women might be put off. Vain, shallow women. But there are some who wouldn't give it a second thought."

A multitude of emotions boiled inside him. Will clearly wasn't going to admit he was wrong. Spinning on his heel, Noah stalked in the direction they'd come, leaving the other man to gape after him.

"Noah! Hold on!"

Not slowing, he pressed his lips together, afraid to speak. Afraid he'd utter something foul and damaging. Perhaps something he might not be able to take back.

"We can sort this out."

He did halt then, tossing over his shoulder, "The complication I told you about? One of her daughters is ill. As soon as she's recovered, the three of them will be removing to your best suite. I'll have the bill sent to you."

Continuing on, he'd reached the work site when he caught sight of bright red curls. Tomasina waved and smiled in welcome. He managed to corral his upset long enough to tip his hat and nod in greeting.

"Noah. I didn't realize you'd stopped by." Her vivid green gaze slipped past him and landed on her husband. The love and affection shining there increased his upset. "Come inside for coffee."

Will caught up to them. Giving Noah a wide berth, he moved beside Tomasina and curved an arm about her waist, tugging her close. "Do as the lady says, my friend. We have more to discuss."

He'd observed their tendency to stick close by each other during the search for the Murdochs. As a former cattle driver and rodeo star, it hadn't been all that unusual for Tomasina to accompany them. Besides, she wasn't the type to stay home and miss out on the action. Good thing Will acknowledged that fact.

"Maybe another time."

"I'll hold you to it," she said with a saucy grin.

He made his way to where his horse grazed, Wolf loping behind him. He was happy that his friends had found their perfect mates, but he wasn't meant to have what they had. It wasn't just his scars, either. The breach with his family and the atrocities of war had hardened him. Noah didn't have it in him to please a woman.

Sooner or later, his friends were going to have to accept that.

Chapter Four

"This is our first night in our new home." Jane exuded excitement. "May we explore the ranch tomorrow?"

Praying for wisdom, Grace removed Noah's wool blanket from the bed and replaced it with a cheery quilt from her trunk. Pinwheels of yellow, purple and green spun against an ivory backdrop. The colors brightened the room.

"Perhaps. We'll have to wait and see how your sister is feeling."

"I'd like to see the chickens." She traced a pinwheel with her finger, her blue eyes dancing with anticipation. Eyes very much like her father's. "And the pigs. I wonder if Mr. Burgess has rabbits."

A curious child, Jane had an affinity for learning. In the estate's library, she'd spent hours scouring encyclopedias and nature tomes. The Kansas prairie must surely have captured her imagination.

Curling on her side, Jane tucked one hand beneath her cheek. "Where's Mr. Burgess going to sleep, Momma?"

"I'm not sure yet." She dimmed the lamp's flame. Shadows flickered in the room's corners. "We'll figure something out."

During his absence, curiosity had gotten the better of her, and she'd peeked into the loft. There wasn't a bed, unfortunately. Only a desk and chair, and wall-mounted shelves with books and cabinets with closed doors. The cabin lacked a sofa, so that wasn't an option.

"Are you ready to say your prayers?"

Yawning widely, Jane nodded. Grace began to kneel beside the bed before recalling this wasn't her bedroom suite in Chicago and there wasn't a plush rug to cushion her knees. The floor here was bare and in need of a good scrubbing. Perching on the mattress edge, she placed one hand on Jane and the other on Abigail.

"I'm going to pray for Abby."

"That's a wise idea."

During her heartfelt prayer, Grace couldn't take her gaze off her sick offspring. Abigail had rested fitfully throughout the evening. Even gotten sick once in a pail Grace had thought to bring into the bedroom. Thankfully, the sheriff hadn't been around to see it. He acted as if he'd never seen a child before.

His discomfiture during dinner had been obvious. There could be no question he wanted them gone at the first possible opportunity. Noah Burgess was a hard-nosed, implacable man. He wasn't going to change his mind. She'd had the fleeting idea to offer him money in exchange for his name and protection, but she'd dismissed it. He wasn't dumb. No ordinary mail-order bride would do such a thing.

The last thing she needed was to arouse a sheriff's suspicion. She'd tried explaining Frank's dastardly behavior to her mother-in-law, only to be ridiculed and accused of trying to make trouble. Helen Longstreet hadn't approved of Grace marrying her eldest son and had hinted that she'd married him to access his wealth and societal connections. Helen had refused to believe her younger son, Frank, would want her, too. Grace had been tolerated by her husband's mother and targeted by his brother.

Jane ended her petition with a sleepy "Amen," and Grace

realized her thoughts had strayed during the entire thing. Familiar guilt pinched her. Not only was she duping the sheriff and anyone else she might come into contact with, she'd had no choice but to instruct her girls to go along with her story. Surely that made her the worst mother of all time.

I'm sorry, God.

Her divine Father had carried her through many dark days, His comfort her sole source of strength when everyone around her had proved an enemy. He'd been a friend when she'd been friendless. Disappointing Him in this manner wore at Grace's soul.

Lord, if he'd agree to marry me, I could make things right. Once we've been married a little while, I can reveal the truth.

The outer door clicked, and the floorboards resounded with a heavy tread. Grace's pulse tripped nervously.

Leaning down, she dropped a kiss on Jane's cheek. "Sleep well, my love."

Already drifting, Jane wriggled deeper beneath the quilt. Grace extinguished the lamp. Closing the door behind her, she remained where she was, watching as Noah removed items from a sack and lined them up on the wooden counter.

He flicked her a glance. "How's the sick one?"

"Her name is Abigail."

His mouth tightening, he continued his task.

"She's about the same."

Holding up a sachet, he filled a kettle with water and set it on the stove. "Elderberry tea will help with the fever."

Surprised at his thoughtfulness, she advanced into the room, studying his efficient movements as he took kindling from a tin container in the corner and chucked it into the stove's firebox. While waiting for the water to heat, he unpacked the remaining items and put them in their proper places. He set an enamel mug on the counter.

"You must be exhausted," she said. "I can prepare the tea for Abigail."

He gave her another considering glance that screamed dismissal. "You're a guest in my home."

In other words, it was his kitchen and she wasn't welcome.

Grace tamped down her rising irritation. "I noticed we've taken over the only bed. And there's no sofa."

His arms folded across his broad chest, he kept his gaze trained on the kettle. "I'll sleep in the barn."

"With Wolf?"

He grunted.

"Where does he normally sleep?"

"By the fireplace."

"So we're not only displacing you, but your pet, as well."

He pierced her with his cold blue gaze. "It's temporary. I spoke to Will, and he's committed to making your stay at the Cattleman a comfortable one. As soon as your daughter is well, I'll check the train schedule for a return trip to Chicago."

Grace bit the inside of her cheek. Arguing with him would get her nowhere. She had to use what little time she had to show him the many ways her presence would make his life easier. If she wanted to stay in Cowboy Creek, she had to make herself indispensable.

"Mighty thoughtful of you to bring me breakfast, Sheriff."

Noah set his pail on Sheriff Davis's desk—his desk now—and cocked a single brow in Deputy Buck Hanley's direction. In his midtwenties, Hanley's upbeat and sometimes flippant attitude initially had Noah questioning Davis's decision to hire him. The more time he'd spent in his company, however, the more his positive traits became clear. Hanley was levelheaded and in possession of well-honed instincts vital for a lawman.

Noah balanced his battered Stetson on one of the chair's upright slats and, adjusting his gun belt, sat and began to remove the pail's items one by one. Wolf found a spot beside the desk to lounge in, his golden eyes assessing the lanky deputy.

While Hanley didn't act afraid of Wolf, he didn't approach him, either. His attempts to talk to the animal resulted in Wolf ignoring him.

Noah examined the row of cells to his left. Three cowboys were sprawled on cots, sleeping off the previous night's excitement. A whiff of stale cigars and sweat assaulted his nose.

He tossed Wolf a sausage. "Busy night?"

Hanley nodded. "Yep. Broke up a fight on the south end of town shortly after midnight. These three weren't keen on cooperating, so I offered them a place to sleep for the night."

"Any property damage?"

"Nah."

"Good work."

Noah turned his attention to his breakfast, one he should've been enjoying at his own table, his grandfather's Bible or a newspaper laid out in front of him. Instead, he was here, avoiding the widow and eager to be alone with his foul mood.

The younger man edged toward the door. "Well, I suppose I'll go on home and rest up for tonight's shift."

He didn't bother lifting his head. "You do that."

The glass pane in the door rattled and Hanley's footsteps faded. Sighing, Noah bit off half a boiled egg and offered the other half to Wolf. He surveyed the jail's interior. He hadn't spent much time here because his first days as sheriff had been spent chasing after the Murdochs. The interior boasted a high ceiling, rough-hewn walls decorated with maps, the American flag and wanted posters. Five cells lined the wall, facing the entrance door and windows flanking it, each with their own cot. The desk was made of oak and sported coffee-ring stains and a jagged gouge in the corner. He followed the gouge with his fingertip, wondering how it had gotten there, wondering how *he* had gotten *here*.

He should be tending his ranch and livestock. He'd never aspired to be a lawman. He'd experienced enough violence to last a lifetime. The war had altered him, not only his appearance, but his way of thinking. Mentally, he'd aged decades, his soul irreversibly tarnished by the atrocities he'd witnessed. He'd come to Kansas in search of a fresh start, away from the constant reminders of the state of their nation.

Abandoning his meal, he moved to the nearest window. The jail sat at the intersection of Eden and Second Street. At this early hour, the streets were mostly deserted. All was quiet in front of Will's hotel, as well, the curtains at the windows drawn. A clerk swept the boardwalk in front of Booker & Son general store. Across the street, an elderly man was knocking on the doctor's door.

Noah released a ragged breath. He was responsible for the residents of Cowboy Creek. The weight of that duty fully registered for the first time, and he almost lost his breakfast. His mind rebelled.

What had possessed him to accept the town leaders' request? Had to have been a moment of insanity, that's what.

An ungainly figure trundled around the corner, and Noah recognized the boot-maker's wife, Opal Godwin. Her determined air gave him pause.

He met her at the door. "Mrs. Godwin. What can I do for you?"

She stood in the doorway, one hand supporting the huge mound of her belly, her squinty brown eyes darting between him, Wolf and the prisoners. "I have an issue to discuss with you, Sheriff Burgess. Do you have time now?"

Noah motioned to the bench pushed beneath the window he'd been stationed at a moment ago. "Let's talk out here on the boardwalk."

The sun's rays slanted across their feet. The thick air indicated the day would be a muggy one. Opal carefully lowered herself onto the hard seat, trying unsuccessfully to find a comfortable position. The woman was due to have that baby any day. He prayed today was not that day.

"My husband and I, along with the other affected shop owners, want to know what you plan to do about our falsified deeds. Our livelihood is in jeopardy, Sheriff." Her severe hairstyle highlighted the shadows beneath her eyes. According to Daniel's wife, Leah, a midwife who had been consulting with Opal, the young woman had endured a challenging pregnancy. "If you don't fix this, we might lose our business. And then how would we provide for this baby?" Her voice wobbled, and through the unshed tears, he glimpsed expectation.

She and Amos, her husband, were counting on him to save their business. They all were.

His gut twisted.

Noah paced from the corner post to just past the jail entrance and back. The guns resting against either hip were heavy and cumbersome. He wasn't used to carrying firearms, especially with the no-gun policy imposed within the town limits. But as the sheriff, he was Cowboy Creek's appointed guardian. He had to be prepared to protect the residents, especially with the Murdoch gang running amok. Those scoundrels had already proved they were without conscience, going so far as to interrupt a church service and robbing the parishioners of their money and jewelry. He well remembered Leah's unhappiness over the loss of her wedding band.

On top of the chaos the brothers had wreaked, Noah had inherited a whole host of other sticky issues from his predecessor—the mystery of the falsified store deeds being one of them. Opal herself had discovered the forgery. Without an authentic deed, the bank wouldn't extend loans for new purchases.

"I'm going to review Sheriff Davis's notes on the matter, then I'm going to interview everyone involved again. See if I can dredge up new information."

She didn't appear impressed. "Would you be willing to meet with the shop owners to discuss your plans to rectify this situation?"

"Of course." He adopted a confidence he didn't feel. "Give me three days to complete the interviews. We'll meet at the Cattleman on Friday."

Opal was quiet a long moment. Then, with a jerky nod, she struggled to her feet, waving off his extended hand. "I'll pass the word along. I pray you'll have more success than Sheriff Davis did."

Noah watched her leave. He had some serious praying to do himself.

He spent the morning examining the contents of Davis's desk. His notes about the shop deeds were pathetically brief. Noah paid the land office a visit. While the gentleman working there was willing to assist in the investigation and gave Noah access to the office paperwork, he didn't have any useful information. Frustrated, Noah returned to the jail to find three cranky cowboys demanding water, food and their freedom. He listened to them whine for an hour before their fellow drovers arrived to pay the fine for disrupting the peace. Once they were gone, he made a list of all the shop owners he needed to interview. He stayed busy, yet the widow remained on the edge of his thoughts. He'd prepared enough breakfast for her and her daughters. But what would they do for lunch? Images of his cabin burn-

ing to the ground taunted him. No way did he want a mol-
lycoddled socialite tampering with his kitchen.

Ducking into the Cattleman, he sought out young
Simon, Will's hotel porter. Since Constance had already
met Simon, she wouldn't be alarmed to see him riding onto
the property. He arranged for the boy to pick up lunch from
the Cowboy Café and take it out to her, assuring the boy
the errand wouldn't get him in trouble with his boss. Will
was responsible for Constance's presence; he could spare
his employee for a couple of hours.

By the time five o'clock came around and another deputy, Timothy Watson, showed up to relieve him, Noah was
antsy to return to the ranch. As instructed, Simon had re-
ported back to him, saying that Mrs. Miller had seemed
surprised but pleased with the delivery. Simon hadn't seen
Abigail, which meant she must still be confined to bed. He'd
let slip something that had Noah worried. He'd said that
when he arrived, Constance had been busy cleaning the
cabin. The furniture, what little he had, had been pushed
against the wall and buckets of soapy water stationed about
the living room.

He didn't want her cleaning, didn't want her touching
his belongings.

What would a woman like her know about caring for a
home, anyway? From the looks of things, Constance Miller
and her girls had lived a life of extreme ease. No doubt she'd
paid people to cook and clean for them.

Saddling up, he pushed Samson faster than usual. Halfway between town and his spread, a small herd of buffalo
watched him ride past, shifting nervously at the sight of
Wolf loping after him. Wild turkeys scattered when he
thundered onto the worn-thin trail leading to his cabin. He
slowed when he caught sight of his vegetable garden. The
short rows had been weeded in his absence.

Dismounting, he mumbled a prayer for fortitude and

let himself inside. Noah's abrupt entrance startled the two occupants. The bowl in Constance's hands tipped precariously. Jane's initial surprise transformed into a welcoming smile. Bounding over to him, she took hold of his hand as if they were longtime friends.

"Sheriff, look what I picked for you."

Scrambling to make sense of several things at once, he allowed himself to be tugged over to the table, where the girl was chatting and waving her hand at the mason jar filled with a combination of orange, blue and yellow wildflowers.

"Aren't they pretty?" she finally asked, big blue eyes blinking up at him.

"Huh."

The floors were still damp from their scrubbing. Not a speck of dust littered the mantel. The windows sparkled, the clean glass admitting more light and allowing a clear view of the cottonwoods and the stream.

He registered the smell of grease and chicken the same moment he spotted a bucket of feathers in the kitchen corner. Leaving the girl, he prowled over to where Constance stood at the stove, her skin dewy with exertion and tendrils of chocolate-hued hair skimming her cheeks. Chin lifted, she stiffened with apprehension.

Noah plucked a feather that had gotten caught in the lace of her dress. "What did you do to my chickens?"

Chapter Five

The sheriff examined the feather, drawing it through his blunt fingertips, a look of incredulity on his face.

Grace floundered for a response. Because of his height, his hard, muscled chest filled her vision, as did the strong, tanned column of his throat, the warped flesh on the left side disappearing beneath his shirt collar. His body gave off the scent of honey and something floral, a unique combination.

Not knowing what to expect, she sent Jane outside to gather more flowers.

"Don't you like fried chicken?"

His gaze traveled from the feather to the platter on the counter, then to her. He tilted his head a fraction of an inch. His assessment made her conscious of her disheveled appearance. She'd donned her most basic skirt, navy with thin white stripes, and a coordinating blouse. She hadn't even bothered with a hoop skirt. After a full day of scrubbing floors, polishing windows, dusting surfaces and tending to Abigail, she was dirty and sweaty and exhausted to the point of light-headedness.

"Did you ask Simon to kill the bird for you?"

"Simon? No. I did it myself."

"And where," he drawled, his Southern inflection deepening, "did a woman like you learn to pluck and gut a chicken?"

Annoyance boosted her energy. "A woman like me?"

"A city woman. From the looks of things, you haven't had to fend for yourself in a very long time."

"I haven't always lived an advantageous life, Mr. Burgess. You're making assumptions again."

"You're right," he conceded. "I know very little about you."

"And I know only what your friend Mr. Canfield told me about *you*."

"It hardly matters, does it?"

Jane burst through the door, waving fresh blooms. "Are these enough, Momma? I'm hungry."

Noah put distance between them and, taking the bowl of green beans from her hands, placed it on the table. Jane put the flowers into the jar with the others, not a bit intimidated by the brooding sheriff. "There. That's better." Lifting the bouquet again, she said, "Smell them."

Looking disconcerted, he bent his head and sniffed. "Uh, they smell nice."

Jane smiled in satisfaction and touched a fingertip to one of the petals. "I like the yellow ones best. Momma said I could put some in Abigail's room later."

Grunting a noncommittal sound, Noah came back for the chicken. "How's your other daughter?"

Grace glanced at the closed bedroom door. "Abigail was sick several times during the night, but her fever has subsided." As she'd worked throughout the morning and afternoon, she'd talked to God, asking Him to ease her child's misery. A deep well of gratefulness overflowed inside her. "She's resting comfortably now."

"Good news."

Aware that his relief stemmed from an entirely different reason than hers, she helped him carry over the remaining dishes and chose the seat across from him. After a moment of awkwardness, it was decided that Jane would offer grace. When she thanked God for providing her and her sister with a new pa and asked that he be nicer than her first one, Grace wanted to sink through the floorboards. Her face aflame, she avoided the sheriff's perusal by focusing on filling Jane's plate.

She expected him to eat in grumpy silence as he had the evening before, so she started at the sound of his roughened voice.

"Did you make these buttered rolls?" He snatched a second one from the pan and bit into it.

"Jane and I baked them."

"They're delicious. Better than the ones the café serves." He pointed to the half-eaten chicken leg on his plate. "Tasty chicken, too. You're an excellent cook, Mrs. Miller."

Jane darted her a furtive look, one that broke Grace's heart. What kind of example was she setting for her children, urging them to go along with her lie? If Frank had accepted that she wasn't interested in being with him, they could've remained in Chicago. Granted, she would've found a different place to reside in. Living with her mother-in-law and a mansion full of bad memories had become too difficult to bear.

She lowered her fork and reached for her water glass. "I'm glad you like it."

"I helped prepare the dessert, too," Jane announced proudly.

He wiped his mouth with a cloth napkin. "Dessert?"

"Yes, sir." Her eyes twinkled, and her fat curls danced along her wide dress collar as she bounced in her seat. "Pound cake with berry preserves. We would've made an apple pie but couldn't find any cinnamon."

"I hope you don't mind we used your supplies. I will replace them."

"That's not necessary," he said gruffly. "I should've stuck around this morning and showed you where I keep the foodstuffs."

Grace thanked him for sending Simon out with lunch and lapsed into silence. Not one to sit still, Jane fidgeted and hummed as she ate. The behavior had irritated Ambrose's mother, Helen. Many times after a tortuous family meal, Helen had taken Grace aside to admonish her for allowing it. No amount of scolding or instruction had been successful, however. From birth, Jane had been the more energetic of her girls.

Now she watched the sheriff from beneath lowered lids to gauge his reaction. He didn't appear to notice or care. His eyes on his meal, he seemed preoccupied with whatever was going on inside his head. She glanced at the tintype resting on the mantel. Curiosity welled up inside her, taking her by surprise. What terrible experiences had he endured that had so altered him from that young man in the photo?

In Chicago's elite circles, she'd been shielded from much of the war's gruesome reality. It was only through her church's charitable work that she'd gotten any significant information. The tales she'd heard had shocked her. Reports of inadequate supplies and disease. Debilitating injuries. Soldiers committing horrific acts against innocents. Noah had lived the war day in and day out.

"That carved plantation house on the mantel. Is that a replica of your childhood home?"

His brow knitted. Not looking at the object in question, he nodded but didn't speak.

"Where is that exactly?"

His chest heaved with a sigh. "Virginia."

"You were a Union soldier though, right? I saw your uniform in the photo. How—"

"I don't like to discuss my family or the war." His features were shuttered in warning.

More questions arose in Grace's mind. Noah Burgess was a mystery, one that wouldn't be easy to solve. Not that he was about to give her a chance.

"Well, it's a beautiful piece. The craftsman is extremely talented."

"Thank you."

She stared at his bent head and then at his large, capable hands, unable to reconcile the intricacy and beauty of the house, the creativity and artistry required to produce it, with the tough, aloof man before her.

"*You* made it?"

His light blue eyes were guarded. "I like to create things in my free time. It's a skill I learned as an adolescent."

"I'd love to see your other pieces, if you have any."

His shrug was noncommittal.

Stunned by how badly she wanted to learn more about her host, she dropped the subject. When they'd finished dessert and Grace told Jane to assist her in cleaning up, he held up a hand. "I'll take care of it. But first, I'd like a word."

His expression warned she wasn't going to like what he had to say.

Leaving Jane to play with her miniature tea set and dolls, Grace accompanied him to the stream, where he showed her to a bench carved out of a massive tree trunk.

"Did you make this, too?"

He buried his hands in his pockets. "I come down here sometimes to read or think, and I needed a place to sit."

It was a nice shady spot with a view of the green fields stretching to the distant horizon. "You like to read?"

"That surprises you."

"Yes," she admitted.

"Because I'm a soldier or because I'm a Southerner?"

Grace shrugged, ashamed she'd judged him again. "You simply didn't strike me as the bookworm type."

He scowled. "It's a good thing we're not getting hitched. We have a bad habit of judging each other as lacking in one way or another."

Unable to sit still beneath his enigmatic gaze, Grace stood and crossed to his spot near the water's edge. Her plan was on the verge of collapsing.

"That's because this is an unusual situation. Given time, we'll learn each other's personalities."

He grasped her hand and lifted it for his inspection. "You're not wearing your rings."

"Th-they would've gotten in the way."

Noah examined her reddened palm, his hold surprisingly gentle. She was almost sorry when he released her.

"You shouldn't have overexerted yourself. While I appreciate the meal and the effort you put into cleaning my cabin, it doesn't change a thing. You're not staying."

Desperation shivered through her. "I thought you were an honorable man. Mr. Canfield clearly exaggerated your finer qualities."

A tiny vein at his temple throbbed. "My honor isn't in question here, Mrs. Miller. I never promised to marry you."

His body shifted into a warrior's stance and the anger practically spiraled off him. Okay, so questioning a former soldier's honor was a dumb thing to do.

Skewering her with a look, he demanded with narrowed eyes, "Why are you so determined to stay where you're not wanted?"

That hurt. More than it should. Grace didn't know him, and yet, he was another in a long line that didn't want her around.

Holding her deception close to her heart, she seized on the most obvious answer. "I came here in search of a better life for my girls."

"Cowboy Creek is short on women and long on marriage-minded men. If you're determined to stay, you'll have your pick of candidates. It's not personal. Before the war, I might've made a good husband and father, but I've changed." He touched the raised pink flesh on his jaw. "This isn't the worst of it. It's what you can't see that's truly horrific."

Grace thought he meant the physical scars beneath his shirt.

"I don't care about your scars." Normally, she wouldn't reveal private details of her life, but despair trumped pride. "I was married to a handsome man whose inner character rendered him ugly. I care about integrity. Loyalty. A good work ethic. Mr. Canfield wrote a glowing report of your character, Mr. Burgess. I desire that for my daughters."

"You misunderstand. I didn't mean what's under here, although my physical deformity would be difficult for any woman to accept." He rubbed his flattened palm over his shirt. "I meant what's in here." He tapped his heart first, then his temple. "The war changed me in ways I can't begin to describe. I don't trust like I used to. I don't hope. Don't believe in the basic goodness of human beings. I don't have the ability to make anyone happy."

The bleakness in his features robbed her of speech.

"Since your daughter is on the mend, I'll make the necessary arrangements for you to remove to the hotel tomorrow afternoon."

He walked away from her again, something he was rather good at.

For the second day in a row, Noah ate his breakfast at the jail. He wasn't happy about it, either. The early-dawn ride into town had passed in a blur. One of the Murdoch brothers could've swooped in and he wouldn't have known it until the last second. He'd lost his concentration and focus because of the comely young widow.

Constance Miller. Funny, the name Constance didn't really suit her.

Adjusting his gun belt, he smashed his Stetson on his head, ordered Wolf to stay put and left the jail.

Sticking around this morning would've been the polite thing to do. Constance and her daughters were his guests, unwelcome though they may be, and his ma had instilled good manners in him and his sisters. But he'd found himself growing captivated in the brief moments he'd spent with her. She was a woman of contrasts. Beneath that feminine, fragile exterior lay fire-purified strength and the determination of an approaching storm. What she'd managed to accomplish in one day both stunned and impressed him. Noah would never admit it, but hers was the best fried chicken he'd ever tasted, even better than his ma's. And that moist, dense cake bursting with flavor... His mouth watered thinking about it. He could get used to coming home to fine meals like that.

But would she ever get used to welcoming a man such as him?

Constance said she didn't mind the scars, but she'd spoken the words in haste. She would say anything to get him to agree to the marriage Will had promised her. Well, she could have her Cowboy-Creek husband—it just wasn't going to be him. She'd thank him later.

Noah was in the middle of the intersection on his way to the Cattleman when he recognized his friend Daniel Gardner. He and his new bride, Leah, were preparing to enter Booker & Son general store. Changing course, he lifted his hand and called Daniel's name.

They both turned at the same time. Leah's shining blond tresses rippled in the breeze. Her apricot dress was let out at the waist to showcase her expanding form. Thanks to Leah, Opal and the reverend's daughter, Hannah, their town's population was on its way up. More mail-order brides meant new families, cementing Cowboy Creek's future. Constance's impish countenance flashed in his mind. If she settled on one of their businessmen or ranchers, she'd likely add to the population, as well.

The thought felt like a hot poker plunged in his gut. Calling up his annoyance at Daniel's actions, he strode to meet the couple.

"Noah." Daniel's deep green eyes searched his, gauging his mood. "I was going to stop by the jail once we'd finished our shopping."

"Good morning, Noah." Leah glowed with good health, her smile a testament to the success of her and Daniel's union.

Will, Daniel and Leah had grown up together in Pennsylvania. She and Will had gotten engaged at a young age, but the distance during the war had taken its toll on the relationship. Leah ultimately married a Union officer and moved away, so discovering she was on their first bride train had shocked both men. Even more of a shock was the fact she was widowed and expecting a baby. Wanting to provide a stable, secure life for her, Daniel had hidden the feelings he'd never declared behind an offer of a marriage based on friendship.

Fortunately for his friend, love had blossomed between the two. It was that love and happy marital state that surely must've prompted Daniel to go against Noah's wishes and do the unthinkable.

"I went to your office about an hour ago," he told Daniel. "They said you hadn't come in today."

Fiddling with her earbob, Leah blushed. "That was my fault. I needed my husband at home this morning."

The smile Daniel bestowed on her spoke of a happiness Noah could only dream of.

"Why don't you go on in while I speak to Noah? I'll join you in a bit."

Nodding, she balanced her weight against his arm and, leaning into him, planted a kiss on his cheek. "See you later, darling. And you, Noah."

"Take it easy, Leah."

By silent agreement, they moved along Second Street until they came to the deserted churchyard. This side street wasn't as busy as the main thoroughfare. Through the wooded area behind the church building, the roof of Will and Tomasina's house was visible.

"I saw Will yesterday." Seeking out the shade of a sixty-foot-tall box elder tree, Daniel removed his derby hat and dusted off the crown. A hank of chestnut hair slipped into his eyes, and he impatiently shoved it aside. As owner of the stockyards, he favored cowboy attire. Today, however, he was dressed like Will, in a fine brown suit and polished boots. "He told me about the widow and her daughters. What's she like?"

"That's your first question?" Noah demanded, throwing his hands wide. "I thought your first would be to ask how I'm coping with this latest problem in a long string of them. One I didn't ask for and didn't see coming. I never dreamed my closest friends would go behind my back and do something so underhanded."

Daniel looked disconcerted. "We didn't do it to add to your burdens. Our goal was to force you out of this ridiculous solitude you've consigned yourself to."

"It's not ridiculous," he ground out. "You know why I've chosen this life."

"I was in the war, too, remember?" he said quietly. "Man or woman, adult or child, I'm not convinced you'd find anyone in this nation who came through it unaffected. That doesn't mean you have to give up on life. You're as worthy of happiness as the rest of us, Noah."

"I don't agree. The way I feel inside… I'm a different man than I used to be."

"Different doesn't necessarily mean worse."

They would never have like minds on the subject. "I wish you and Will had discussed your scheme with me before you acted. This woman you've brought here has her mind set on staying. She's convinced our town will prove a fine setting in which to raise her young daughters."

"Is she not someone you can envision building a life with?"

Noah tilted his head back and stared at the knotty branches and matte undersides of the leaves suspended from them.

"I don't believe we'd get along," he said.

"How do you figure?" One dark brow quirked up.

"We have the bad habit of making assumptions about each other."

A stout, hairy man emerged from the hardware store across the street, a sack swinging from his right hand. He smiled when he saw them, revealing tobacco-stained teeth. "Howdy, Sheriff! Fine day to be alive, ain't it?"

Noah lifted a hand in acknowledgment, catching sight of the grin Daniel tried to hide.

"I pin on a badge and suddenly folks feel it's their duty to speak to me." He scowled.

"It's a nice change from how things used to be. You started this town. No reason you shouldn't interact with the grateful residents."

"*We* started this town. I'm happy to leave the mingling to you and Will."

"Back to the widow Miller. How did she react to your scars?"

"Didn't seem to mind. The girls, either." He squinted at Daniel. "Don't get that look."

"What look?"

"The dopey one that makes you look like you're seven," he shot back, wondering where his anger had gone. Maybe if they'd meant it as a joke or as a way to hurt him, he could've nursed his ire. But it had been a misguided attempt to improve his life. "I'm not marrying Constance. In fact, I was on my way to the hotel to secure her a suite. Will's largest and finest, as he'll be footing the bill."

He started walking through the grass toward the dusty street. Daniel blocked his retreat.

"Whoa. Are you sure that's such a good idea?"

"It's the logical choice."

"Tell me what she looks like," the other man prodded. "Is she pretty?"

"Pretty isn't the right word. She's like an exotic bloom that needs an awful lot of care and attention."

Daniel's gaze intensified. "An exotic bloom, huh?"

The tips of his ears burned. "Why does it matter?"

"You don't remember the crush of men at the train station the day Leah and the others arrived? The locals are starved for female companionship. If you put Mrs. Miller up at the Cattleman, she'll be accosted by marriage-minded men, not all of them worthy of a woman's hand."

"Not my problem." Sidestepping him, Noah continued walking.

"You're refusing to marry her." Daniel spoke to his back. "In doing so, you're putting her and her daughters at risk. Do you not feel an ounce of responsibility toward them?"

Noah halted, his gaze on the bustling traffic ahead—wagons, single riders and pedestrians. Clusters of crude, rowdy cowboys whistling and gesturing to Pippa Neely, one of the original mail-order brides and the town's resident actress, as she traversed the boardwalk.

Daniel came abreast of him. "It'd be a shame if she chose the wrong sort of man. You'd be forced to see the evidence of her poor choice for the rest of your life."

Noah ground his teeth. He couldn't deny that if he found out she or the twins were being mistreated, he'd wind up locked in a cell for beating the guy within an inch of his life. "There's another possibility."

Settling his derby on his head, Daniel waited.

"She might fancy a drover," Noah pointed out. "She wouldn't be sticking around then."

"That defeats our purpose. We want to grow Cowboy Creek, not provide brides for itinerant cowboys."

He threw up in his hands in frustration. "What do you propose I do?"

"Allow her to stay at your place until the three of us— you, me and Will—help her make a wise and proper choice."

Noah snorted. "She's not the sort of woman to be led about. Despite her helpless appearance, Constance knows her own mind."

"We won't make her choice for her. We'll simply be advising her on her suitors' characters and reputations."

He closed his eyes, wishing he could rewind time a couple of days. "Fine," he growled. "They can stay for the time being."

"Do you want Will and I there when you explain things?"

"Oh, no. It's best if you leave the explaining to me."

Chapter Six

Noah had just finished brushing Samson down that evening when Jane skipped into the barn.

"Hi, Wolfie," she crooned, her dark sausage curls quivering. Skirts swishing, she marched past the wolf dog and over to where Noah was replacing the brush in the tack room. "Hi, Sheriff. Or should I call you Pa?"

Pa? He spun around and peered down into her freckled face. It took a whole lot of effort not to gape at the pint-size child. "Uh, Sheriff will do for now."

How was it that her ma was frightened silly of his pet and this little squirt wasn't fazed? And how come she wasn't intimidated by him when a majority of the townsfolk had refused to interact with him prior to this sheriff gig?

Jane considered this and nodded, her blue eyes twinkling. "Sheriff, Momma sent me in here to fetch you for supper."

"She did, huh?"

"Yes, sir. We're having ham, greens, pickled beets—" her nose scrunched on that one "—and more rolls like we had yesterday. Momma said that since you liked them, we should make them again."

"Is that so?" He strode to the entrance, and she hopped along beside him. Noah felt tongue-tied in her presence.

He wasn't used to seeing kids, much less engaging in conversation with one. "Did you make dessert?"

She nodded emphatically. "Molasses cookies. Momma says there aren't many supplies here, so we have to make do with what we have and be thankful for what the good Lord has provided."

Noah would have to rectify that if Constance agreed to his plan.

"How's Amelia today?"

She tossed him an imperious look that put him in mind of her mother. "My sister's name is *Abigail*."

"Oh, right."

Bursting into the cabin ahead of him, Jane announced his presence. He stopped on the threshold, jolted anew by the presence of other people. Every single day for several years he'd come home to an empty cabin and a quiet that at times had mocked his decision to be alone. Now it wasn't empty or quiet, and he was having trouble adjusting.

Constance was at the stove, flushed and beautifully disheveled, the fixings for their evening meal crowding the counter. Her hair was even messier this evening than last, and he wondered if she was missing Chicago already.

His gaze slipped to the dark-haired, brown-eyed girl in the rocking chair beside the fireplace. Dressed in a ruffled nightgown, she sat with her legs tucked beneath her. Her loose hair hung in limp strands. She looked a lot less miserable than before, but she hadn't lost her wariness of him. He shifted his stance and, whipping off his hat, held it against his chest. Words lodged in his throat. What would his fellow Union soldiers say if they knew he'd allowed a tiny child to fluster him?

The tang of vinegary greens and salty meat hung in the air. In the center of his table sat a fresh batch of those rolls that melted like pillows of buttery goodness in his mouth.

This was one aspect of having a wife that Noah could get used to really quick.

Wiping her hands with a towel, Constance smoothed her hand over her hair and came around the counter, her deportment a testament to her social standing and privilege.

"After our conversation last evening, I was expecting you earlier today."

Noah's chest squeezed with a funny sort of wistfulness. No one had expected him home or cared what time he arrived for a very long time. No one had fixed particular dishes with him in mind, either.

"Let's speak outside."

Hanging his hat on the coat stand, he waited for her to follow. After instructing the girls to stay away from the hot stove, she joined him. He motioned to one of the rocking chairs. She sank into it, her skirts sighing into place, her head seeking rest against the slats.

"I have a proposal to make."

Her head jerked back up.

He held his hands up in a gesture of innocence. "Not that kind of proposal."

Her honeyed gaze studied him a moment before sliding to the fields and grazing cattle.

"You're determined to stay in Cowboy Creek," he said.

"I am."

"And you're not looking to marry for love."

Her disdainful expression aroused his curiosity. He'd assumed most females strove for that elusive emotion. "I thought that was what I was doing the first time I got married. I was proved wrong. All I want now is stability and security for my girls. I want someone who will be kind to them. Take an interest in their raising."

He recalled Jane's prayer. "Did your husband treat them poorly? Or you?"

"As you're not to be my husband, I'm going to choose not to answer that."

Oddly disappointed, Noah paced to the nearest post and, lifting his arm, propped a hand against it. Constance had spoken of what her daughters needed, but what about her needs?

Constance pushed out of the chair. "The food's getting cold." Maintaining her distance, she lifted her chin. "What is this proposal you mentioned?"

"I think it's best you remain here while searching for a husband."

Her winged brows swooped upward. "I thought you wanted me to stay in the hotel."

"Our town's population is predominately male. We're working to change that by bringing in bride trains, but we've a ways yet to go. A woman such as yourself will be inundated with a passel of prospective grooms."

"You mean a city woman with no knowledge of being a rancher's wife?"

His mouth grew dry. He wasn't about to admit it was her beauty and grace that had him worried. "For these men, any woman of marriageable age will do."

Her sooty lashes swept down, but not before he glimpsed a despondency that made his scars burn as if they were fresh and raw. His assumption that the wealthy widow must be endowed with a healthy sense of self-worth had been wrong. Imagine that.

He knew nothing about this woman. And he found himself wanting to know everything. A dangerous prospect.

"Will, Daniel and I can help guide you in your decision. We know which men are dependable, hardworking and honorable, and which ones we wouldn't trust to take care of a dog."

"We've determined you don't want anything to do with

me or my girls." She stared at where their boots nearly touched. "Why do you care who we wind up with?"

Because Daniel was right. While Noah had no part in bringing her here, he felt responsible for her. He wouldn't know peace if she made a regrettable choice.

"Just because I look like a stone-hearted beast doesn't mean I lack sentiment. I would never forgive myself if you wound up with a man who mistreated you or the girls."

Her startled gaze whipped to his, her lower lip trembling. "I don't think you look like a beast. Nor do I believe you've a heart of stone. You may have changed greatly from that man in the photograph, but the war and your injuries didn't strip your humanity away."

Noah couldn't speak. There was something in her voice and in her gaze that transported him back years, to the innocent, hopeful dreamer he had once been. A man with a bright future ahead of him. A man who'd counted on being a husband and father someday.

"You've been snooping through my house?" He seized on the bitterness and anger that had been his faithful companions since the day he woke up in a field hospital. No way could he allow former dreams to live again. Love. Family. Intimacy. It wasn't possible.

She flinched. "No! I wouldn't! The tintype is on the mantel, out there for anyone to see."

Noah turned away, rubbing the uneven flesh detectable beneath his shirt. Having her underfoot was going to be tougher than he'd thought. "I'll fetch the tub and water for your baths."

"What about supper?"

"I'll eat later." His stomach growled in defiance. "Make a list of everything you need. I'll go to the mercantile first thing in the morning."

Walking away was difficult when his conscience was insisting he apologize.

* * *

Shaking with emotion, Grace watched him disappear into the barn. She couldn't decide if she'd rather shake him, slap him or hold him. The man infuriated her. Snooping through his house… Honestly? But he also struck a chord of compassion deep inside.

The man was as prickly as a cactus. While his behavior screamed *stay away*, his pure blue eyes told another story. Loneliness stalked him, devouring him from the inside out. When was the last time someone held his hand? Hugged him? Kissed his cheek?

Her first instinct had been to call after him that she hadn't agreed to stay. As always, the danger Frank posed directed her actions. Staying here with the sheriff, all the while knowing she was a burden, was not ideal. It would be safer here than at a public hotel, however. Her brother-in-law wasn't one to give up without a fight. When Frank Longstreet wanted something, he went after it with cold-blooded ruthlessness. The hunt thrilled him. More than once through the years, she'd seen him set his sights on unavailable women. Engaged women. Married women. He employed his charming assault, wearing them down until he triumphed and then casting them aside, uncaring that their lives and reputations were wrecked.

The fact that Ambrose was his brother had held Frank mostly at bay throughout her marriage. In the year since his passing, Frank had steadily intensified his campaign to win her. He claimed he wanted to actually marry her. He expected her to be overjoyed. Refusing him had been the easy part. Grace knew that by fleeing Chicago, she'd become prey to his predator. She could only hope she'd covered their tracks well enough.

She wasn't sure exactly what he'd do if he found them.

Tamping down her worries, she rejoined the girls and called them to the table, not interested in eating herself.

Her anxiety over Frank and her ongoing deception had her stomach twisted in knots most days. She was determined to keep up her strength, however. The girls were dependent on her for everything. A pang of longing for her church family hit her. While few were aware of her private struggles, she knew she could depend on them for support if she but asked.

Grace was putting milk glasses at the place settings when Noah reentered, hefting a huge copper tub. His shoulder and arm muscles strained as he maneuvered it into place near the work counter.

Jane left her seat to run over to him. "Is that for us?"

"Sure is." Choosing a wide pail from beneath the counter, he strode for the door.

"Aren't you going to eat with us, Sheriff?"

Jane's confusion was understandable. Grace wasn't sure how to explain the circumstances—that Noah didn't want to marry her or anyone else, had no interest in being a father and was only allowing them to stay to assuage his conscience.

He twisted around, his expression unreadable. "I've got to fetch water for your bath."

Seeing her daughter's crestfallen expression, Grace waved a hand over the table's contents. "The meal's hot. It won't taste nearly as good lukewarm."

Reluctance stamped on his features, he set the pail on the floor and came to the table. Jane scooted into her chair beside him and clasped his big hand. "It's your turn to say grace."

He blinked at her, disconcerted by her outgoing manner, before bowing his head. Grace closed her eyes as his husky voice washed over her.

"And thank You, Lord, for allowing Alexandra to feel better," he said at the end. "Amen."

All three females stared at him. Jane piped up. "Her name is A-bi-gail."

Noah's gaze slid to Abigail, whose head was bent, a curtain of dark hair obscuring her face, and nodded solemnly. "Right."

His lips twitched. In the process of smoothing a napkin over her lap, Grace's fingers stilled. He was *teasing* them? The hardened ex-soldier who never smiled harbored humor somewhere behind that thundercloud demeanor?

Unsettled, she blindly spooned portions onto the girls' plates before filling her own.

"Have you ever been to Chicago?" Jane asked.

"Can't say that I have."

"It's huge."

"It's loud." Abigail spoke to Noah for the first time.

He paused midchew, his startled gaze sliding to Grace's for a split second before returning to Abigail's. "It's not loud here."

Nibbling on her roll, Abigail stared at the slightly drooping bouquet inches from her plate.

"Men sell flowers on the streets. Newspapers and candied nuts, too." Jane swallowed a bite of ham. "Momma took us to a fair one time, and there was a man drawing pictures of people for money. She paid him to do mine and Abigail's. We hung them in our bedroom because Grandmother didn't approve."

Grace attempted to mask her unease. She'd emphasized the importance of not telling anyone her real identity. But they were only six years old. How easily the truth could slip out by accident.

Before she could change the subject, Jane spoke again. "Our bedroom was much, much bigger than this cabin."

Noah's brows hitched up. "That sounds like a very big room." To Abigail, he said, "Aurora, did you have lots of toys in your room?"

Grace wasn't surprised that she didn't correct him. It

took time for her quieter daughter to warm to strangers, much less assert herself. "I miss Pepper."

"Who's Pepper?"

"Our pet rabbit," Jane answered for her, a habit Grace had tried to correct. "Momma wouldn't let us bring him. She said he'd miss his home in the garden shed."

They'd left most of their belongings at the estate. She hadn't wanted to alert the staff of their impending departure. The night before their train left, Grace had taken advantage of the Longstreets' absence—they'd attended a social function hosted by a business associate—and had hurriedly packed as many trunks as she'd dared, taking only the essentials.

The girls' rabbit had been the least of her worries. Now that they'd made their escape, she recognized how difficult leaving their home, friends and pets must be for them.

Abigail placed the last bit of roll on her plate and turned big sad eyes to Grace. "May I be excused?"

If she hadn't been ill, Grace would insist she finish her meal. "Of course. I'll save your plate in case you get hungry later."

"Yes, ma'am."

Unsurprisingly, Jane chattered throughout the meal. Noah didn't seem to mind, although Grace caught him wearing a nonplussed expression from time to time. She found herself hiding a smile. Who would've imagined the big tough sheriff with a wild beast for a companion and the guts to face down dangerous criminals would be thrown off balance by an innocent child?

There was more to Noah Burgess than the many titles he wore—Union soldier, rancher, town founder, sheriff. There were unmined layers and complexities that made up the man. A part of her mourned the fact she wouldn't be allowed to learn his depths. She was certain there'd be surprises along the way, some challenging, some heart-breaking, some perhaps even delightful.

She'd never know, would she?

Because she wasn't going to be his wife. She was going to be some other Cowboy Creek resident's wife. And he'd be alone again, exactly how he preferred it.

Chapter Seven

Noah couldn't sleep. The animals were restless. The straw in the hayloft was prickly and made his nose itch, and there was no breeze to stir the air inside the big structure.

He descended the ladder and, ordering Wolf to stay put, left his temporary sleeping quarters and walked through the darkness to the house. His boots whispered in the grass. Crickets chirped. The stream's lazy trickle was a comforting sound. A single light shone in the window. Good. That meant a quick trip to his loft office wouldn't disturb anyone.

Drawing nearer, he detected Constance's outline in a rocking chair. His steps slowed as his heart sped up. The woman made him uncomfortably aware of his isolation. Made him question his choice to be alone.

When she noticed his approach, she started to stand.

"Don't get up on account of me," he said. "I came to fetch something from the office. Will I disturb the girls if I go in?"

Resettling, her elegant hands clutched her housecoat collar at the neck. "They're sound sleepers. You won't disturb them."

Her light vanilla scent wafted toward him. He inhaled, trying not to stare at her thick mane of hair held back by a slim ribbon. The simple style made her look more like an adolescent girl than a mother of two.

"I'll just be a moment."

Hurrying inside, he noted the cleanliness of his home before climbing the ladder and locating his desired item. Out on the porch, he hesitated. He sensed a loneliness in her that mirrored his own.

"Is there anything I can get you?"

"No, thank you." She pointed to the short, fat book in his hand. "You read when you can't sleep?"

"It relaxes me."

Some of his fellow soldiers had ribbed him about his penchant for reading, saying reading wasn't a manly pastime. But the handful of books he'd been able to procure during his time on the battlefield had given him a blessed respite from the horror around him. "Do you like to read?"

She presented her profile to him, contemplating the prairie's inky darkness. "I can't read."

Noah dropped into the vacant rocker and processed the reluctant admission. While this was not uncommon, he'd pegged Constance Miller as an educated woman. Her wealth and position granted her access to the finest schools and universities.

"Your family didn't approve of women being educated?"

"It's not that." She sighed. "I've yearned to read ever since I was a small girl. No matter what I try, however, my mind can't make sense of the letters on the page."

"But you read Will's letter."

"No. Con—" She stopped, flustered, before going on. "I mean, my friend read it to me several times. I memorized it."

"I see. You know, Reverend Taggart's daughter, Hannah, has a similar problem with numbers. I wonder if it's related."

"I haven't met anyone else with my particular issue. My

husband found it difficult to accept." Bitterness coated her tone. "My inability to read was a huge source of embarrassment for Ambrose. He hired a multitude of tutors, but none were able to help. He finally declared I was too dumb to learn and made me swear not to tell anyone outside the family my shameful secret."

Noah's fingers curled into tight fists. The mental composite he was piecing together of Ambrose Miller was not a pretty one. "I'm sorry you had to endure that."

What else had she endured? She'd intimated her marriage hadn't been all she'd hoped. How bad had it gotten? Foreign emotion gripped him. He was seized with the desire to go to battle for this woman, to combat her enemies, to shield her from life's trials and tribulations no matter what the personal cost.

The unexpectedness and novelty of such bewildering emotion primed him to flee her presence. His body didn't respond to his mind's command. Instead of escaping to the barn, he remained in his seat, drinking in every detail about her.

"Would you like for me to read to you?"

Chapter Eight

The tentative question hung in the night air. Grace was speechless. Her own husband hadn't offered. Not once. For this forbidding stranger, a tough-as-nails sheriff who barely knew her, to have compassion on her plight brought tears to her eyes.

What had compelled her to admit her deficiency? Her inability to read had been a point of frustration and humiliation since childhood. Noah already viewed her as lacking. Adding to his poor opinion hadn't been the wisest move. What if he spread this information and prospective grooms shared Ambrose's opinion?

"That's fine if you're not interested. Just thought I'd ask—"

"I am interested," she blurted, sensing his imminent retreat. "I'm surprised, that's all. No one besides my daughters has ever read to me."

"Anyone with good sense can see you're an intelligent woman," he muttered with a trace of anger. "You shouldn't be made to feel lesser because of your issue."

Noah Burgess was angry at her dead husband. Angry on her behalf. Containing her astonishment, she strove for a casual tone. "What's the book about?"

"Our government and constitution."

Grace tried to mask her dismay. She wasn't certain she could stay awake for that.

"Oh. That sounds...interesting."

The husky chuckle rumbling through his chest caught her off guard. She stared at the half smile curving his sculpted mouth. He almost resembled that young man in the photograph.

"I was joking. It's *Oliver Twist* by Charles Dickens."

She found herself smiling back at him. "An improvement over laws and procedures, to be sure."

"Have you heard the story before?"

"I've heard *of* it. But I don't know the story. My girls haven't advanced to that level yet."

"I'll be right back."

His movements efficient and fluid, he went inside and returned with a kerosene lamp that he set on a small, roughly constructed table. The light glinted off his blond hair, streaking it with gold. He looked slightly less forbidding than usual. His sheriff's badge and vest were nowhere to be seen, his wheat-colored shirt was open at the neck and his undershirt visible.

Opening the book, he turned to the first chapter and began to read. At first Grace focused on the cadence of his words, the honeyed ebb and flow of his resonant voice. It wasn't long before she got swept up in the story and was whisked away on an imaginary adventure. With the soothing night air wrapping her in its embrace, the scents of grass and sunbaked earth mixing with traces of mint, she closed her eyes and pictured the story's setting and the colorful characters he described. When his voice trailed off some time later and the cover snapped closed, she experienced a sharp pang of disappointment.

She wanted so badly to ask if he'd continue the story tomorrow. But she'd stopped asking for things for herself a long time ago—the repeated rejections had been too hurtful—and focused on looking after the girls' needs. Ambrose hadn't loved anyone but himself. However, he'd purposed to keep his girls respectable in his social circles. Grace had learned to play on his pride in order to benefit them.

Standing, she pushed the heavy fall of her hair behind her shoulder and touched a hand to the march of buttons down the front of her housecoat. A feeling of vulnerability invaded her. Certainly the isolated setting and late hour contributed to it, as did her casual dress. More concerning was the fact he was now privy to her greatest weakness.

"I enjoyed the book very much. I appreciate you taking the time to read aloud when you'd clearly intended to read alone."

"Tomorrow night I'll have a glass of water with me." Standing, he cupped his throat. "My throat's too dry to keep going."

Joy leaped in her chest. "You don't mind?"

"Nah." He looked sheepish. "When my younger sisters were little, I used to read them to sleep every night. I never admitted how much I liked it. I'd gripe and complain to my ma when all the while I was as eager for story time as the girls."

"How many sisters do you have?" Grace found it difficult to picture him as a young boy with a family.

"Three." His expression grew distant, a sad furrow drawing his brows together. "Lilly, Cara and Elizabeth. All in their early twenties by now."

She wondered what they were like, if they were blonde and blue-eyed like their brother. "You must already be an uncle, then."

Noah jerked his startled gaze to hers. This shouldn't be a novel notion. Something wasn't right.

"When was the last time you saw them?"

"Since before I left for Pennsylvania to join the Union army."

Many years ago, then. "You haven't been in contact with your sisters, have you? What about your parents?"

His frown deepened, and the marred skin on his jaw stretched thin. His mood went as black as the night, and yet, though keenly aware of his size and strength, she did not feel threatened.

"This isn't a good idea," he said.

"What isn't?"

"Sharing our pasts. Personal information. We're not engaged to be married. Pretty soon you'll be married to someone else, and you and I will have limited contact with each other."

The regret squeezing her heart didn't make sense. She had no ties to the sheriff. She'd known him less than a week.

But you trust him, don't you?

Grace was confident Noah would never hurt her or the twins. If they were part of his family, he'd do anything to protect them. He'd provide for them. Maybe he'd even do things to bring them happiness…like reading to a grown woman who couldn't do it for herself. He might not be effusive in his welcome, he might keep people at a distance, but behind the badge Noah's heart beat pure and true.

While he and his friends intended to guide her to a good second choice, she couldn't be sure exactly what type of man she'd be marrying.

"I have a request."

Noah shifted his stance, clasping the book firmly by his side. "Name it."

"I don't wish to rush into a decision. I would like some time to gauge my potential husband's character for myself."

His brows shot up. "You were ready to marry me sight unseen."

"I trusted Mr. Canfield's account. You're one of the original town founders and highly respected. I'm not angling to stay with you until Christmas." Surprise crept over his features. "A few weeks will suffice. And if you can't stomach our presence that long, we'll move to the hotel at my expense."

"Take the time you need. Will, Daniel and I will make good on our promise. We won't let you make a mistake."

"You can't guarantee me a good marriage, Sheriff. Not unless you're willing to marry me yourself."

A muscle ticked in his jaw. "My decision's been made."

"Then the best you can do is pray God leads me to the right man."

Spinning on her heel, Grace escaped into the house, leaving him to stew on her words for once.

"She's the reason I couldn't sleep." Noah jabbed a finger toward the house the following morning. "This is why being alone is for the best. No one's around to stir up the past."

Wolf cocked his head, his golden stare seeming to commiserate with him.

Dreams of his sisters had plagued him throughout the night. In his mind, they were the same age as the year he'd left Virginia. Constance had reminded him that they hadn't remained unchanged. Lilly, Cara and Elizabeth were young women now, most likely married with children. He probably had nieces and nephews. Blood kin he'd never met.

Homesickness stole over him, a yearning to see his family stronger than it had been in years. Constance's fault, of course.

Noah flicked straw from his shirt. "I'm too old to be sleeping in barn lofts, I tell you that." Not that he had a choice. Couldn't very well expect the widow and her daughters to bunk with the livestock.

He strode into the yard, lugging a full pail of milk. The first rays of sun scattered across the pastures, setting the dewdrops to sparkling. A robin called to its mate. The temperature was still in the pleasant range.

Inside the house, he was greeted by an anxious-looking Jane. Her hair wasn't in its usual style, and she was wearing her nightclothes. Noah glanced at the closed bedroom door as he lifted the pail to the counter.

"Everything all right?"

Twisting her hands together, she quickly shook her head. "Momma's sick."

Alarm worked its way through his body. Not bothering to knock, he entered the bedroom, his focus on the dark-haired woman beneath the covers.

"Sheriff." She struggled to sit up. "I didn't realize how late it was."

"I'm still not used to being called that," he muttered, moving to her side.

"Mr. Burgess—"

"Noah," he corrected, noting Abigail hovering on the far side. "Jane said you're ill. What are your symptoms?"

"It's nothing." Pushing the quilt off her seemed to leach her of strength.

He put his hand to her forehead. The heat confirmed his suspicions. "It's not nothing. You have a fever."

"I don't get sick."

Her protestations might've been comical if not for her obvious suffering. Her hair was a tangle about her slim form. Her skin was pallid and clammy, her lips almost white.

"Everyone gets sick at some time or another in their lives." Gently, he placed his hands on her shoulders and nudged her against the pillow.

"I'm sorry."

Noah paused in replacing the quilt. "Why would you apologize for something you have no control over?"

A small voice answered from the doorway behind him.

"Momma apologized to our father a lot. He used to yell at her."

His gaze shot to Constance, whose trembling lower lip was at odds with her jutting chin. "Let's not discuss that with strangers, Jane."

Jane moved to take his hand. "Mr. Noah isn't a stranger, Momma." She lifted her face. "You're not going to fuss at her, are you?"

The innocent trust in her blue eyes gutted him. "No, I'm not." Crouching to her level, he pushed aside the anger swelling once more at a faceless man. Noah was glad Ambrose Miller wasn't able to hurt them anymore. "Your ma is going to need a lot of rest today. Will you help me take care of her?"

"Yes, sir."

He squeezed her hand. "The first thing I'd like for you to do is fetch a washrag from the kitchen."

When she'd gone, his gaze settled on the quieter twin. "Amy, bring me that hairbrush, will you?"

Abigail obediently did as he asked, maintaining ample space between them when handing him the brush. He wondered how long it would take for her to work up the courage to correct him about her name.

"Did you know I used to brush and braid my little sisters' hair?"

Sucking on her lower lip, she watched him with solemn eyes.

"Well, I did. I know how to be gentle."

Seeking reassurance from her ma, who nodded and smiled tremulously, Abigail turned and presented him with her back. He brushed the clean strands and plaited them into a tidy braid and tied a ribbon around the end.

"All finished. Go look at yourself in the mirror and check my work."

She fetched an ornate mirror that belonged to Constance and studied herself from different angles.

"How'd I do?"

His reward was a shy smile that made his spirits soar like a hawk on an updraft.

Jane returned with the cloth. Setting it aside, Noah braided her hair as well, and then sent them both to set out the dishes and utensils. Constance tracked his movements with her gaze. Her hands clutched at the quilt, and he noticed she was once again wearing those gaudy rings that screamed money and advantage. He wet the cloth, wrung out the excess water and laid it across her forehead.

A grateful sound sighed out of her as her sooty lashes lifted. "If you'll take care of breakfast, I'll see to lunch."

Noah shoved his hands deep in his pockets to resist smoothing her hair away from her face. "I'm afraid you won't be leaving this bed today. Maybe not tomorrow, either. Seems to me you've contracted whatever sickness Abigail had."

Her dry lips parted. "But your sheriff's duties—"

"I've got a pair of deputies who can oversee things for me. I'll run into town after breakfast and check in with them. Then I'll swing by the general store. Did you have time to make a list?"

"I'm inconveniencing you." She frowned. "More than I have already. The girls…"

"Will be fine. I may even take them into town with me so you can have peace and quiet."

Her winged brows rose. "You would do that?"

He wasn't jumping at the bit to escort twin six-year-olds to town, but Constance needed sleep in order to recuperate.

A tremor shook her petite frame. He couldn't resist sitting on the mattress and laying his palm against her cheek. To check her fever again, he reassured himself. Her skin was silky soft, smooth as a flower petal. Sleek strands of hair brushed his knuckles. She held herself very still, blinking up at him in silent inquiry, and he got the impression she hadn't been on the receiving end of kindness very often.

"I hope he suffered when he died," he growled. "I know that makes me a terrible person, but it's the truth."

Her forehead bunched before clearing a second later. "Ambrose perished in a train accident. His skull was crushed. That's the only detail I was given."

Noah fixed the displaced cloth. *God forgive me. I can't help how I feel.*

Jerking a nod, he removed his hand and stood, wishing he could stay and keep her company. "Is there anything I can get you? Dry toast? Tea?"

"Tea would be nice."

He was at the door when she whispered, "Noah?"

He twisted around at the sound of his given name on her lips. "Yeah?"

"Thank you."

Her eyes were bright with gratitude he didn't deserve. Not only had he repeatedly told her he didn't want her, he was pawning her off on another man, a stranger who may or may not put her and the girls' needs above his own.

Careful, Burgess. You're starting to care.

Constance hadn't wanted him, specifically. She'd answered a bride-wanted letter as a way to get out of Chicago and provide a better life for the girls. It didn't matter who she ultimately married, he told himself firmly, as long as he was a God-fearing man who'd treat her right.

The sooner she found that man, the sooner she'd move out. She'd cease to be Noah's concern and his life could finally return to normal.

Chapter Nine

"Sheriff Burgess." D. B. Burrows, editor of the *Herald*, eyed the girls flanking Noah with a touch of incredulity. "I'd heard reports you'd acquired a new family but didn't believe them until this very moment." Smoothing his thatch of raven hair and mutton-chop sideburns, the man searched the store aisles. "Is their mother with you? I'd like to meet the lady who managed to catch your fancy."

The muscles of Noah's upper back went taut. He'd never cottoned to the newspaper editor. For a man who'd seemed eager to make Cowboy Creek his new home, the gentleman spent a lot of time disparaging the town and its leaders, including Noah and his friends. He tended to publish splashy articles highlighting crime and other negative events while downplaying the good. Some folks liked stirring up trouble, and Noah figured D.B. for one of them.

The patrons stopped what they were doing to stare. Not surprising. He supposed seeing him—the town loner—with a pair of adorable little girls would be unusual.

"Mrs. Miller didn't accompany us today." Bending to the girls' level, he pointed to the shiny jars on the counter. "Go on over and pick yourselves out a piece of penny candy."

"Yes, sir!" Jane grabbed Abigail's hand and led her to the main counter.

Folks watched and whispered. Did they notice their off-center braids and the oatmeal stain on Abigail's collar? The pantaloons visible below their knees were creased, and the sashes about their waists weren't tied to Constance's standards. Not that she'd noticed. She'd drifted off to sleep before they'd left the cabin. Noah had gone in to bid her goodbye and heard her soft breathing. She'd looked so different from that first day, when her hair had been in an elegant, formal style and she'd worn an outfit that would probably cost him a month's salary. That day, she'd been prepared to take on the world. Today, she hadn't possessed the strength to get out of bed. His fool heart had gone mushy with sympathy and the strong desire to comfort her.

"You may as well know that Mrs. Miller and I are not to be wed. There was a misunderstanding. She will be choosing a husband from among Cowboy Creek's bachelors."

D.B. arched a single bushy brow. "Is that so?"

To D.B., no bit of news was off-limits. Noah watched the man reach for his pad and pencil only to check his actions. The arrival of Prudence Haywood, one of the original mail-order brides, saved Noah from having to rebuff the nosy editor.

"Are you ready to go? We have work to do."

After a cursory glance in his direction, the petite, curvy auburn-haired woman ignored Noah. Her manner didn't line up with that of a subordinate employee. Prudence had procured work at the newspaper shortly after her arrival and was frequently in D.B.'s company. Some had conjectured the two were romantically linked. There was no evidence to support it, however.

Irritation surged in D.B.'s eyes. "Not just yet." He turned to Noah, this time removing his pad and pencil. "How is your investigation on the fake property deeds coming along? Any new information?"

Aware their conversation was being monitored by practi-

cally everyone in the store, Noah said, "Why don't you stop
by the jail first thing tomorrow morning? You can conduct
your interview there."

"Does that mean you don't have anything of importance to share?" D.B. glanced at Prudence, who was fiddling with the brooch at her neck, a nervous habit of hers.
"And what about the invasion of Will Canfield's suite at
the Cattleman? Any developments on that?"

A vein in his temple throbbed. Noah didn't have answers and the editor was like a bloodhound hunting a fox.
He could probably sense Noah's unease.

D.B. pressed closer, his pencil poised above the paper.
"At least answer me this—is it true Cowboy Creek is being
considered for the county seat?"

"Yes, it's true."

Something flickered in his expression that set off an
alert. He didn't appear pleased at the news. Why would
that be?

Prudence touched her boss's sleeve. "We really must
go. You and the sheriff can discuss business tomorrow."

"Fine." Slipping the pad into his suit jacket pocket, he
gave the girls a last considering glance. "You won't allow
personal issues to prevent you from making our meeting,
will you, Sheriff?"

"Absolutely not."

"Good."

The pair exited the general store, rudely blocking Pippa
Neely from entering.

"What, no apology?" the exuberant actress called after
them. With a loud huff, the ginger-haired young woman
swept past the garden tools and stopped in front of him
with a flurry of skirts.

"Sheriff Burgess. How are you…" She trailed off, shock
mixed with utter delight at the sight of Jane and Abigail
approaching. They each held a fat peppermint stick in one

hand. "Well, I do believe my eyes must be deceiving me! I had no idea such sweet little things inhabited Cowboy Creek."

Noah introduced them. "Girls, Miss Neely is an actress. She performs at the opera house."

They appeared awestruck by Pippa's appearance. Her jade green outfit rivaled Constance's clothes in quality and beauty. The satiny fabric shimmered in the light every time she shifted. The sequined hat atop her chignon had multiple black feathers protruding from it.

"How do you do, ma'am." Jane elbowed her open-mouthed sister.

Abigail snapped her jaw shut. "Hello."

Pippa clasped her hands together. "Oh, they are enchanting, Sheriff. Do you think their mother would allow them to perform?" Before he could answer, she propped her hands on her knees and peered at them. "Do either of you dance? Sing? Act?"

Jane smiled. "We like to sing."

"Wonderful." Pippa nodded. "I must speak to your mother as soon as possible. The residents of this town will be bowled over by a pair of singing twins. Imagine the headlines!" Tilting Jane's chin up, she examined her face. "I can see you wearing a magnificent gown of royal blue satin." Touching the crown of Abigail's head, she mused, "And you would look stunning in bright yellow, like a black-eyed Susan."

Abigail blinked at her.

Noah was impatient to get their shopping done and return home. It wasn't the girls giving him fits—it was the adults!

"We'll have to continue this conversation another time, Miss Neely. I've a long list of supplies to gather before heading home."

"Of course." Straightening, she questioned him with

her warm hazel eyes. "Would it be all right if I paid their mother a visit?"

"Maybe next week." Constance would surely be feeling better by then.

"Wonderful."

"Let's go, girls," he said. "Don't want to keep your ma waiting."

Grace's head hurt. Her body couldn't decide if it was hot or cold, which meant she was constantly fiddling with the covers. Her stomach was unsettled. Thankfully she'd been able to keep down the toast she'd had that morning and the thin broth Noah had prepared for lunch. Being sick was bad enough without further humiliating herself.

She hadn't been bedridden since her pregnancy. While the estate staff had been attentive, her husband and mother-in-law had failed to show her compassion. They'd made her feel guilty for her weakness. That experience made her even more aware of the fact she was burdening her host.

"Say good-night to your ma. Then it's off to bed." Noah's firm voice drifted in from the kitchen.

After seeing to the care of energetic children, she'd expected the single man to be harried and impatient for the day to end. His demeanor didn't reflect such sentiment, however. Either he was more compassionate than she'd given him credit for or he was pretending to be for her sake.

Jane and Abigail bounded into the room. Their faces had been washed of grit, their hair brushed free of tangles. He appeared in the doorway, his blue gaze intent on her. Folding his arms, he propped a shoulder against the frame in a deceptively relaxed pose. He wasn't relaxed. His guard had been in place since the day he discovered them here.

Jane hopped on the bed. The motion didn't do her stomach any favors.

"Did I tell you about Miss Neely's hat?"

Grace tried to look interested and hide her scowl. Ever since the girls had returned, they'd regaled her with details about the beautiful, *single* actress. An ugly emotion an awful lot like jealousy had fueled her fever. Utterly ridiculous considering she had no claim on Noah.

I don't care that his eyes make me long to see the ocean and compare the hues. I don't care that his blond hair shines like the sun. I don't care that his touch is so gentle, so at odds with his fierce appearance, that it makes me crave what he isn't willing to give.

"She said I would look amazing in yellow." Abigail's remark hinted at the awe reflected in her face. What all had this woman said to them?

Cold washed over her once again, and she tugged the quilt up to her neck, the scents of lavender and honey like a warm embrace. Not scents she'd normally associate with a man.

Straightening, Noah advanced into the room, his large body shrinking the space. "I fixed a pallet near the fireplace so they won't disturb you tonight."

"Thank you. For everything."

He shrugged, his fingers probing the scarred flesh on his neck, something he seemed to do without conscious thought. "It was no trouble."

Grace appreciated that he was trying to spare her feelings. For a man who'd chosen to live alone and had no interest in creating a family, caring for a sick woman and two young girls had to be irritating at best. And yet, he hadn't complained. He'd assumed the duties of caretaker, one who was sympathetic and efficient. Noah Burgess was someone who willingly set his own needs aside in order to meet those of the people around him.

A verse from Philippians came to mind. *Let nothing be done through selfish ambition or conceit, but in lowliness of mind, let each esteem others as better than himself.* She imagined he'd been that way on the battlefield. A soldier determined to give his best, his all, to those serving at his side.

She allowed herself to scrutinize the marred flesh on his jaw and the place above his collar, wishing she felt free to ask how it had happened.

Noah noticed and scowled, the skin about his eyes tightening. "Time for bed, girls."

Grace forced her gaze to the various fabrics making up the quilt, sad that he assumed she was repelled by his injury. Sad, too, that he used his appearance as an excuse to keep others at arm's length.

Jane rushed over and took his hand, dark hair swinging as she tilted her head way back. "Will you tell us a bedtime story?"

Grace waited for his refusal, bemused by Jane's actions. Neither of her daughters had felt the freedom to approach Ambrose. Her husband had maintained a neat, polished appearance even at home, dressing in well-cut suits, his black hair cut short, and his mustache and goatee meticulously trimmed. A handsome man with cold eyes, he hadn't been nearly as intimidating as the Viking sheriff.

"I don't know any," he finally said.

"You could tell us how you acquired Wolf," Grace said, not looking at him.

"Yes," Jane exclaimed. "Please, Mr. Noah?"

"All right." He waved toward the bed. "Have a seat." Retrieving a chair from the other room, he spun it and straddled the seat. "I didn't always live in this spot."

"You didn't?" Abigail said, her brow creasing.

"Nope. When I came to this area, I chose land close to where the railroad station is now. When the railroad company chose Cowboy Creek as a terminus, they needed my land to lay tracks on."

"Didn't you want to stay?" Jane said.

"I put a lot of labor, sweat and tears into that homestead,

so yeah, I was reluctant to leave. But they offered me a good sum. And anyway, I hadn't ever aimed to live in the middle of the hustle and bustle of town. I craved peace and quiet." He appeared lost in thought for a minute. "About a week after I finished the cabin, I was out by the stream and heard a pathetic little howl. There in the weeds, I found Wolf wet and shivering and hungry. He was small enough to fit in the palms of my hands." He cupped his hands together to show them.

"Where were his parents?" Grace said, trying to picture the great, lumbering beast as a pup.

"I found his mother the next day…a large dog. Black like Wolf, but her eyes were dark brown. She didn't make it."

"How sad." Jane hugged her bent knees to her chest.

"I never saw the wolf who sired him. Probably passed through this area and kept on moving."

Abigail yawned and Noah pointed to the door. "Get in your pallet, ladies. I'll be there in a minute to turn down the lamps."

Both girls obeyed without question, kissing Grace on the cheek before scampering out.

Exhaustion weighed her down, but she wasn't ready to see him go.

"I feel horrible for taking your bedroom. Are you getting any sleep in the hayloft? It must be smelly and loud with the animals."

He rested one hand on the footboard. Without his gun belt and badge, he looked like a regular rancher. A handsome, well-built man of the land.

"The barn's not bad. The animals bed down for the night, so they don't bother me. At least there are walls and a roof to shelter me from the weather. I wasn't so fortunate during the war."

"Why did you join the Union?"

His eyes darkened. "You should get some rest."

"I slept this afternoon." Using the pillows as a support, she clasped her hands on her middle. "I'm tired but not sleepy."

And I long to know more about you, as forbidden as that is.

Noah paced to the window and stared at the night-cloaked prairie for so long she thought he wouldn't answer. It was a personal question, after all, and those were off-limits.

"My family built their wealth on the backs of slaves. While my father and his overseer treated them well, I couldn't justify owning another human being. We went to church every Sunday in our shiny conveyances, dressed in our expensive clothes and acting as if we were model Christians. The older I got, the harder it was for me to swallow the hypocrisy."

"So you left?"

"Not before challenging my father. I told him I would help him make our business work without the slaves." Kneading the ridge of his shoulder, he shook his head. "He was livid."

"When you couldn't change his way of thinking, you decided to fight for your beliefs."

He grimaced. "I wasn't welcomed with open arms."

Grace wasn't surprised. Living in Chicago, she'd heard her fellow citizens espousing hatred of the South as a whole entity. "You had to prove yourself worthy."

He turned to look at her. "I don't regret any of it. If I hadn't gone to Pennsylvania, I never would've met Will and Daniel."

A man of principle, Noah had been willing to sacrifice his relationship with his family in the pursuit of justice and equality. He'd been willing to sacrifice his very life. Just like thousands of others.

"Is the rift with your father the reason you aren't in regular contact with your family?"

"Regular contact?" He snorted. "I haven't spoken to them since the day I walked out."

Shock rippled through her. "You didn't write to inform them of your injury? You left them to worry and wonder whether or not you made it through the war alive?" She hadn't suspected him capable of such coldness. His poor mother...

The vein in his neck throbbed. "You have no right to question me. You don't know me or my circumstances." He stalked toward the open door.

"You claim you're not stone-hearted," she blurted, crumpling the quilt in her fists, "but your refusal to provide your parents with answers says otherwise."

"You've overstepped the line, Constance," he growled.

Grace. My name is Grace, she longed to shout. She wished to hear him call her by her true name. Just once.

"If you had children of your own, you'd understand my dismay."

"I don't. And I never will." He loomed like an immovable mountain. "I hope and pray you don't think that by hanging around you'll somehow change my mind. I didn't send for you, remember? I didn't ask for this."

Grace fought the sickness rising up, desperate not to be ill in front of him. Sweat beaded on her forehead. "You insisted we stay here, remember? *You*."

He faltered, forehead bunching as he examined her more closely. "You need a wet washrag? Some tea?"

"No," she whispered, seeking out the pail. "Please go."

Spinning on his heel, he left the room. Grace scrambled out of the bed to kneel on the unforgiving wood planks, reaching the pail without a moment to spare. She jerked when she felt masculine fingers skimming her shoulder and gingerly easing her unbound hair out of the way.

"Go away."

"Not going to happen." Gone was the accusation, in its

place tenderness she'd never received from her husband. She felt like crying.

Her stomach heaved again. Oh, the misery. "I don't want you to see me like this," she gasped.

"Shh," he soothed, handing her a damp cloth.

Burying her face in it, she relished the cool sensation. He waited without speaking, his hand warm on her upper back where he held her hair in place, until she was ready to return to the bed. Righting the covers about her, he folded the cloth and placed it on her forehead.

"I apologize for upsetting you."

Grace squeezed her eyes shut against the sight of him. Part of her reveled in his presence. The other rational part knew this scene would bring her fresh humiliation in the morning.

"It's fine. I'm fine."

"If you need me during the night—"

"I won't. Good night, Sheriff."

Not Noah. The less he was Noah to her and the more he was simply the town sheriff, the safer her heart.

"Good night."

He left her then, stopping in the main room to dampen the lamps and say a word to the girls before exiting the cabin. Only when she was certain he was gone did she let the tears fall.

Chapter Ten

He was an insensitive boor. The fact hadn't bothered him until two nights ago when he'd pushed Constance to her limit, angry more with himself than her because she'd spoken the truth. His fury over his father's refusal to even consider a different way of doing things, the hurt his spiteful accusations had inflicted, had festered throughout his absence. That last altercation had become fixed in Noah's mind. Not once had he considered his father's attitude might have changed. Nor had he given thought to his mother's anguish, his sisters' concern.

It had only been about his convictions, his drive to prove he was worthy of the blue uniform, and later, his injury, recovery and the ramifications of his disfigurement.

Until two nights ago, he hadn't allowed himself to think what his loved ones might've endured during the war. Those Southern homes that hadn't been used to house soldiers had been torched. If their owners were found in residence, sometimes they were granted mercy. Other times they were shot on sight. The women on the other hand... Noah's gut clenched at the gruesome images.

Dear God, I should've been praying for their protection instead of nursing my wounded pride. I'm sorry. I've been so selfish.

His horse crested a small ridge and sped up when the barn came into view. Nearing the cabin, Noah saw Constance and the girls out by the trees. Pulling up on the reins, he dismounted and strode to join them, not happy that the anxiety that had dogged him the entire day vanished now that he had them in his sights.

Constance had made herself comfortable on the carved bench, fabric piled in her lap and needle poised midair. She wore a plain dove-gray skirt—no sign of the hoopskirt she'd arrived in—and a powder blue blouse that mirrored the sky above. Her hair streamed to the middle of her back, pearl pins securing the locks at either temple, streaks of caramel visible in the light of day.

Sure would help matters if she wasn't so pretty, he thought ruefully.

Coming around the bench, he noticed her lingering pallor and worried she wasn't getting enough rest after her ordeal. She'd remained in bed only until lunch yesterday, when she'd joined him in the kitchen and insisted on helping clean up the dishes.

"Hey."

She looked up, her delicate features reflecting surprise. "Sheriff. I wasn't expecting you until supper. Are you hungry?"

She'd stopped using his given name. The distance it put between them was for the best, but he missed hearing her say it. Besides her, only Will, Daniel and their wives called him Noah. To everyone else in Cowboy Creek, he was Sheriff Burgess.

"No. I had a late lunch at the café." What was supposed to have been a simple meal had turned into an ordeal. Word had spread about Constance seeking a husband, and every few bites a lonely cowboy would stop by his table and ask after her. He'd wound up with a bad case of indigestion.

Tugging off his gloves, he said, "Mind if I sit?"

She glanced at the empty space beside her and scooted to make room. "Go ahead."

He sat and stretched his legs out, crossing them at the ankles and letting the gloves flop onto the space between them. A lazy, mint-scented breeze stirred her skirts. Water trickled between the banks, and the flutter of birds' wings rustled the nearest cottonwood. Tenuous peace invaded him, chasing away the frustrations of the day, and he was afraid that it wasn't the setting responsible but the woman at his side.

"Why do I smell mint?" Her needle dipped and lifted, the thin white thread stretching through the air.

"American germander. A member of the mint family. It grows wild in these fields."

"It's nice."

He pointed to the cluster of purple flowers visible on the far side of the stream. "See those? That's bee balm, useful for treating any number of ailments."

From this angle, he could see her unusually shaped mouth and the freckle above it. The urge to trace the contours of those peach-hued lips overtook him. Curling his fingers into fists, he was relieved to see Jane and Abigail rushing over.

"Mr. Noah!" Jane was panting, her cheeks flushed with excitement. "We found a turtle!"

"It has red eyes!" Abigail added. She'd lost a bit of her shyness since he'd spent the day taking care of them.

"Did you name him?" he asked, unable to suppress a smile. Something about these girls brought out the boyish playfulness he'd thought he'd lost years ago.

"No." Jane frowned. "We should think of one."

"Benedict," he suggested.

Her face scrunched.

"Wilbur?"

"Uh-uh."

Abigail held out her hands. "There's dirt under my fingernails, Momma."

"That's not the only place you have dirt," Constance remarked wryly.

Indeed, both girls' aprons bore signs of their play. He was surprised that Constance didn't reprimand them. The pampered socialite he'd assumed her to be would have. But she wasn't pampered or snobbish or idle. And out here, she wasn't a socialite.

Jane grabbed her sister's hand. "Let's go before he gets away."

Holding hands, the girls raced to their spot downstream.

"They love being outdoors," she said, a note of satisfaction twined with wistfulness in her voice. "The fresh air. The wide-open spaces. Being in nature. It's good for them."

"Without their sausage curls and your fancy clothes, the three of you could almost pass as native Kansans."

The multiple rings on her fingers destroyed the illusion. They looked cumbersome and out of place. He wanted to ask why she insisted on wearing them but refrained. He didn't need to know. He shouldn't want to know.

Her honey-hued gaze met his, and her lips curved into a tentative smile. "I'm glad."

He fingered the yellow-and-white-striped fabric. "You're an accomplished cook. You sew and scrub floors. Those aren't lessons generally taught to upscale ladies like you, are they?"

"You're judging again," she said without heat. "I grew up very poor. We lived in the impoverished section of Chicago. I was only ten years old when my father died. Things were tight *with* his income, so after his death my mother had to work several jobs to support us. I started work at fourteen."

The revelation stunned him. It also explained a lot. "Doing what?"

"I was fortunate to find work with an affluent family,

the Murphys. I started out in the kitchen washing dishes. When I expressed interest in food preparation, the cook kindly took me under her wing. Later, I graduated to cleaning rooms. At seventeen, Mrs. Murphy invited me to help care for her toddler." Her expression turned dreamy. "I loved spending time with Jimmy. He was a delightful child. So curious. We spent many mornings in the parks around their neighborhood, chasing butterflies and watching toy boats in the fountains."

Her nurturing instinct must've been apparent to the mistress of the house. Otherwise, she wouldn't have trusted her child with Constance. From what he'd seen, she was a loving mother. If his life had gone differently, if fatherhood had been a possibility for him, he would choose a woman like her to be the mother of his children.

Not a woman like *her. You'd choose* her. *Constance.*

His lungs constricted with the sting of loss. Want choked him.

Her whimsical beauty, her spirit and courage, along with the loneliness in her golden-brown eyes called to him, tempting him to throw caution to the wind and take a chance. He battled the impulse to take her small hand in his and give in. To agree to Will's original plan.

With effort, he kept to his side of the bench. "Were you working at the Murphys' home when you met Mr. Miller?"

"Mr. Miller?" A light dawned in her eyes and she frowned. "Oh. Yes, well, I met Ambrose several years later. The Murphys had moved to New York, and they'd helped secure another nanny position for me with friends of theirs, the Johnsons."

"He didn't mind your employment?" Seemed to Noah that men like Miller would choose wives from among their own social circles.

"He didn't know at first. He assumed I was a member of the Johnson household. A distant relative he'd never met. I didn't give him that impression," she hurried to clarify. "I didn't lie. I thought he knew."

"Let me guess. By the time he figured it out, he was already smitten."

He glimpsed pain and regret in her expression before she ducked her head.

"I suppose."

Sensing her unease with the subject, he nodded to her project. "What are you working on?"

Pink surged in her cheeks. "Curtains for the cabin. I—I hope you don't mind. I noticed the space lacked color, and I thought to do this as a thank-you for your hospitality."

Shame washed over him at the abysmal way he'd treated her. "Where'd you get that material?"

"It used to be one of my dresses."

"I wish you hadn't sacrificed your clothes for my home."

"I don't lack for clothes." A crease appeared between her winged brows. "But if you don't like the color or design, I can purchase different fabric from the store."

"That's not it. I don't deserve your thoughtfulness. I said some things I'm not proud of." Hooking his arms on the back of the bench, his chest rose and fell on a ragged breath. "I haven't handled this situation very well." He turned his head to look at her directly. "I'm sorry, Constance."

Her throat worked. "I understand how trying this ordeal has been for you—a single man having three people foisted upon him with no warning. The timing hasn't been ideal, either, considering your recent responsibility to the town."

Noah's response was lost when a pair of approaching riders crested the ridge. He stood, his hand going to the pistol at his hip, but relaxed moments later when he recognized the mounts.

Holding a hand out to Constance, he helped her stand, the contact with her skin and the way she clung to him sending warm sensations ricocheting through him. "No cause for alarm. Those men are my friends. Suppose their impatience to meet you became too great."

Loath to release her, he forced his fingers to slide away. She busied herself fluffing her skirts, flipping her hair behind each shoulder, checking her collar. The tension in her was palpable, and he wondered at it.

Grace was about to come face-to-face with the man responsible for her trip to Kansas, the man who'd made her escape from Frank Longstreet possible. Will Canfield had no inkling of the role he'd played in her life. He believed he was meeting the real Constance Miller.

Thankfully, her cousin had written only a single letter answering his advertisement. Constance hadn't gone into specifics about her history. Instead, she'd focused on her skills, her likes and dislikes, and her hopes for the future.

As she observed the gentlemen greeting Noah with hearty handshakes and claps on the back, nervousness buzzed beneath her skin like an angry swarm of hornets. Beneath the fall of her hair, her nape was damp with sweat. She despised this subterfuge. Hated the lies. Her mother had been a devoted follower of Christ's teachings, and she'd always stressed to Grace the importance of honesty.

How disappointed she'd be. *Lord Jesus, I know asking You for help in this is wrong. But if Will Canfield was to figure out I'm not who I'm claiming to be, my chances of remaining in Cowboy Creek would disappear like a puff of smoke. I wouldn't know where to go from here.*

The West wasn't exactly known for its safety and hospitality. Traveling to Kansas had been a risk, for sure, but at least she'd had a recommendation. An invitation of sorts from one of the town founders. The prospect of starting over in a new place and not knowing a single soul was too overwhelming to entertain.

"Constance Miller, I'd like you to meet Daniel Gardner and Will Canfield."

She shook their hands in turn, praying they wouldn't notice the clamminess of her palms. "How do you do?"

Both men were tall, dark-haired and wore authority like a second skin. The tintype image sprung to mind. Like Noah, these men had lost the exuberant innocence of youth, their wartime experiences having carved character into their countenances. But unlike their friend, Will and Daniel didn't appear to have thrown up walls to keep people out. Both were married and heavily involved in town business.

The shorter, clean-shaven man, Daniel Gardner, was clad in rancher's gear. Understandable, since he owned the stockyards. His chestnut hair begged a trim—several times in the past minutes he'd pushed the strands out of his piercing green eyes. Will looked more the part of a town official. His navy suit, crisp white shirt and boots shiny enough to use as a mirror were all of the finest quality. His hair was almost military short, his beard and goatee neatly trimmed, and his eyes were a coffee brown. They were gazing at her with an inquisitive intensity that had her on the verge of confessing.

He knows. Somehow, he's guessed. Grace's fingernails bit into her skin. *He* can't *know. You've said all of one single sentence to the man!*

Turning her head, she intercepted Noah's perusal, and she experienced dread on his behalf. For the first time, she considered how her deception might affect him. As the sheriff, his judgment could be called into question. He'd be the object of gossip and ridicule. His friendships with Will and Daniel might even suffer.

Her heart knocked against her rib cage. *I don't want to hurt or humiliate him, Lord.*

Will palmed the ornate handle of his walking stick. "How did you fare during the train ride, Mrs. Miller?"

"Very well, thank you."

He looked slightly puzzled. "You weren't bothered by the close confines? You mentioned in your letter that you struggle with feelings of anxiety in those environs. I was concerned about the length of the trip."

Grace's mouth went dry. How could she have forgotten her cousin's trouble with tight spaces and crowds? What else was in the letter that might raise suspicion, and had he shown it to Noah?

"There were some taxing moments, to be sure. I tried to focus on my daughters and what we stood to gain by coming here."

Daniel broke off his study of the girls to address her. "How do you like Kansas so far? I hope Noah has been a proper host."

Noah's grunt garnered a smirk from Will.

"The prairie is breathtaking."

"My wife, Leah, would like for you and the girls to call on her tomorrow afternoon, if it's convenient for you," Daniel said.

Will thumbed his derby farther up his forehead. "Tomasina will be there, as well. Our wives are thrilled to have another lady in town and very eager to meet you."

"Thank you for the invitation. However, I'm not sure…"

Warm fingertips grazed her elbow. Noah's touch, no matter how brief or impersonal, never failed to evoke a deep, breath-stealing yearning for more. Why must he be the one to have this effect on her?

"I can come home for lunch and take you into town afterward. A change of scenery might do you and the girls good."

She managed a smile. "I'd like that."

"Wonderful," Daniel said. "I'll let Leah know to expect you."

Looking to Noah for direction, she gestured to the cabin.

"Would you like for me to make coffee? There's cinnamon butter cake to go with it."

Will uttered a sound of approval, and Daniel's smile widened. "Noah's been bragging on your cooking abilities, Mrs. Miller."

"Oh?" Flustered, she shot him a sideways glance.

His head bent, he appeared to be intrigued by something beneath his boot.

Grace excused herself to admonish the girls not to wander from the stream. The men's presence made the cabin seem fuller than usual. Self-conscious, she busied herself with her tasks. Noah surprised her by helping gather the plates and utensils.

When they were seated around the table, Will was the first to break the silence. "Mrs. Miller, I'd like to express my apologies for what's happened. Daniel and I had the best of intentions in bringing you here. As Noah has no doubt told you, we're committed to helping you make a suitable match."

Seated on her right, Noah stiffened.

Daniel set his fork down and, wiping the crumbs from his mouth, retrieved a folded piece of paper from his pocket. Unfolding it, he held it across to her.

"Will and I started on a list of potential husbands."

Will sipped his coffee. "We will tell you a little about each candidate, and you can decide which men you'd like to meet."

The tidy handwriting meant nothing to her. She cast a helpless glance at Noah, who hadn't taken a single bite of the cake, he who savored sweet treats.

He extended an open palm. "Let me see it." His scowl grew more severe as he read through the names. Grace squirmed with awkwardness. This struck her as wrong. "Surely there's another way to go about this. It's like I'm perusing a catalog advertisement."

"I understand your discomfiture." Across the table, Daniel's eyes were soft with compassion. "When my wife, Leah, arrived on the first bride train, she was an expectant widow. We were prepared to help her in a similar manner."

"Until you volunteered for the position." Chuckling, Will socked him on the shoulder.

Daniel's chuckle held no apology. Apparently, the union was a happy one.

"Mrs. Miller, most of the local bachelors are good, hardworking, God-fearing men," Will informed her. "As in any town, there are a few bad seeds. We're simply trying to steer you away from those types."

Noah's lingering stoical silence had his friends exchanging a look.

"Of course, the final decision is entirely up to you." Daniel held his hands up.

Will sampled another bite and, rubbing his middle, jabbed his fork at the list. "If any of those men get a taste of your cooking, Mrs. Miller, we'll have a problem on our hands."

Daniel polished off the remaining bites and settled against the chair back with a satisfied groan. "Noah, are you sure you want to let this one get away?"

Lowering the paper, he looked first at his friends and then at her.

Grace braced herself for one of those stinging retorts he seemed to store up for her.

"If I was in the market for a wife, then no, I wouldn't let her go."

She stifled a gasp. Grace felt as if she was drowning in the blue storm-tossed sea of his eyes and the starkness of a lost opportunity.

He seemed to collect himself and, tearing his gaze from

hers, turned it on his untouched food, his blunt fingers lining up the utensils. "But that's not the case. If you'll give me a pencil, Will, we'll get started on this list."

Chapter Eleven

Cowboy Creek had a myriad of interesting sights to see—
the dusty, chaotic stockyards, the elegant opera house, the
Cattleman hotel and many fine houses marching along the
side streets—but none of them could hold her attention like
the man at her side.

Noah had parked the wagon near the railroad station
so she and the twins could walk the span of Eden Street
and have a chance to absorb the sights and sounds of their
new home. Jane and Abigail walked ahead of them, arms
linked, expressions reflecting their wonder. While Chicago
had been grand and exciting, this prairie town had its own
unique personality.

Strolling behind them with Noah, Grace tucked her hand
in the crook of his elbow. Every few steps her shoulder
would bump into his arm, and she'd breathe another apology. He eventually ordered her to stop apologizing. He
didn't release her, however.

As he pointed out various shops and buildings, she reveled in the cadence of his Southern drawl. His voice was
becoming familiar, like treasured music to her ear, lingering in her mind long after he stopped reading to her.

"Hey, pretty lady." A pair of cowboys lounging in the
shade of the boardwalk awning leered at her. "I've got

money in my pocket to burn. What say I buy you a cup of coffee?"

Noah tucked her closer and aimed the full force of his ire at them. "The lady's not interested." At his glare, they pushed off the building and ambled in the opposite direction.

Grace didn't mind his high-handedness. He'd explained the cattle drovers were an itinerant population, here for a short time before they returned to Texas or some other far-flung part of the nation. A majority of them weren't interested in commitment or marriage. After months on the trail, they were eaten up with restlessness and the need to blow off steam.

Glancing over her shoulder, she saw Wolf following several yards behind. The cowboys gave the beast a wide berth.

"Morning, Sheriff. Any news on the Murdoch brothers?"

Grace faced ahead once more, in time to see Noah's jaw clench. Beneath her hold, his arm muscles twitched.

"Nothing recent, Mr. Jamison." He didn't slow his pace. "I'll keep the town updated on any progress I make."

The grizzled stranger in the street frowned and looked as if he would waylay Noah, but they kept walking before he could.

She angled her face toward his. "You've mentioned these men before. What did they do?"

"Zeb and Xavier Murdoch, along with their gang, have caused a lot of problems here. One of their worst crimes was interrupting a church service and robbing the congregation. They not only took money, but wedding rings and other items of great sentimental value."

"That's terrible!" she exclaimed.

"They don't care who they hurt. Right before you arrived, they robbed the bank, killing our former sheriff in the process."

"And they asked you to take his place." She hadn't

known the details before now. The danger he faced each day struck home and fear for his safety curled in her belly. "Why did you agree? Your passion is ranching. Working the land. Tending livestock."

"As cofounder of this town, I have a responsibility to its residents. I owe it to them to provide a safe place to live. To bring lawbreakers to justice."

"It's difficult for you to balance this with your ranching chores, though."

Yesterday, he'd introduced her to Timothy, a young man he'd hired to assist him with feeding and watering the animals, as well as other odd jobs.

Beneath his Stetson's brim, his gaze was steadfast as he peered down at her. "I'll make it work somehow."

Of course he would try, sacrificing his own wants and needs for the sake of Cowboy Creek. The weight of his burdens was palpable each evening when he got home. He was mentally and physically exhausted. How long before his health suffered?

"Are you happy, Noah?"

His boot caught an uneven board, and he stumbled. She lost her grip as he edged away, his features shuttering. "I've learned to be satisfied with the state of my life."

"Satisfied isn't the same as happy," she murmured. "I don't think you should do something that gives you no pleasure simply because you feel misplaced duty. Surely there are other candidates who could fill your position."

His response was cut off when a willowy, pretty young woman in head-to-toe coral pink emerged onto the boardwalk. "Hello, girls. How are you today?" Her heavily lashed gaze lifted to Noah, and her smile stretched from ear to ear. "Sheriff Burgess, good day to you." Skirting the children, she came to stand before Grace, her gray eyes lively with high emotion. "You must be Mrs. Miller. I'm Hannah Taggart. I've heard a lot about you."

"You have?"

"Of course. You're the talk of the town. Now that everyone knows you're not marrying the sheriff, they're conjecturing who you'll choose."

Her stomach flip-flopped. She had no desire to be discussed by total strangers.

Noah stepped close and placed a hand against her spine. Heat flared from the point of contact. She found herself swaying closer, eager to take shelter against his side. Fortunately, she stopped the motion before he noticed.

"Hannah arrived on the first bride train," he told Grace. "Her father is Reverend Taggart." Nodding to the window glass with scrolling gold lettering, he said, "Your dress shop is set to open tomorrow, is that right?"

Her hands fluttered like a butterfly's wings. "Yes, I'm nervous and excited at the same time. I can hardly believe my dream is about to become reality. Would you like to see it?"

"Would you, Constance?" Noah asked.

Every time he said that name, she had to remind herself to respond. "I'd like that. I'm sure Jane and Abigail would, as well."

Hannah beamed. "Your children are darling, Mrs. Miller. I'm planning to offer children's clothing in the future. I have a little girl, too. She's inside with her father."

They followed the exuberant proprietress inside the store. Custom white cabinetry lined the interior walls, the shelving awaiting fabrics and other products. Behind the counter, a ruggedly handsome man with wavy, jet-black hair was walking a fussy baby, gently bouncing her in his arms and murmuring soothing words. The fringe on his buffalo-hide vest swayed with the movement and, when he turned, the beadwork on the back became visible.

Hannah introduced him as James Johnson, her fiancé. Jane left her sister behind to beeline over to the baby.

"Look at her hands, Momma. She's the same size as my baby doll, Suzy!"

Wrapped in a thin white embroidered blanket, the baby had a smattering of dark hair and creamy skin like her mother.

"You were that size once upon a time."

"Her name is Ava." Hannah laid a loving hand upon the baby's back. "I can't imagine caring for two at once." She indicated the twins. "Did you have help?"

Noah's scrutiny was like a physical touch. He didn't ask many questions about her past. Part of her was grateful, while the other part was a trifle hurt by his lack of interest.

"I did, yes." Members of the staff who'd been paid to help her, not family members who did it out of love for her or the girls.

"James has been wonderful with her." Hannah gazed upon the young man with obvious devotion. She'd introduced him as her fiancé and the father of her child, yet there was no evidence of guilt or shame. She couldn't help wondering about their circumstances.

"I don't know about that," James murmured, dropping a quick kiss on the downy head. "I'm just doing my best."

What must it be like to have a man willing and eager to help care for a child? A man who adored his family and took pride in them? That was something Grace had never experienced. A pang shot through her chest at the thought of an unknown future. There was no guarantee she'd marry a man capable of such sentiment.

One issue she wouldn't budge on—the man she married must treat her girls right.

Hannah turned to Noah. "Are you coming to our wedding next weekend, Sheriff?"

"If my sheriff's duties don't get in the way, I'll be there."

"Wonderful!" To Grace, she said, "I'd love it if you and your daughters would come, too."

"I wouldn't want to intrude."

"You wouldn't be. Weddings are such joyous occasions. Life's tough out here. You have to seize every chance to celebrate the happy moments."

Noah shrugged as if it didn't matter to him.

Jane skipped over. "Can we please, Momma? I've never been to a wedding."

Abigail's head bobbed in agreement. "Please?"

"I suppose." Over their squeals, she said, "But only if the sheriff is free to escort us."

Hannah bounced on her toes, as excited as the girls. She struck Grace as a genuine, sweet-natured girl. "You'll make sure they come, won't you, Sheriff? The women of this town have to stick together."

"I'll do my best." Examining his pocket watch, he said gruffly, "I'm afraid we can't stay. I'm supposed to have Constance at Leah's in ten minutes."

"I'm happy to have met you," Hannah told her. "I look forward to spending time with you in the future."

Grace smiled in agreement, motioning to the shop's interior. "Congratulations on your new venture."

Expressing her thanks, she walked them to the door. Out on the boardwalk, they were greeted by a man who looked to be in his early forties. His penetrating stare made her uncomfortable.

"Sheriff Burgess, will you introduce me to this extraordinary creature?"

Noah was relieved to leave busy Eden street—and the hordes of men ogling Constance—behind. Passing Aunt Mae's boardinghouse, they walked along Third Street, where he pointed out the building with the red-shingled roof—the new schoolhouse, where the twins would attend school. Constance seemed delighted. They turned left onto Lincoln Boulevard. The only traffic here was the occasional pedestrian and stray cat, which Wolf thankfully deemed too uninteresting to chase in the dry heat.

"I'm sorry about that." He broke the silence. "Mr. McCoy can be intense."

A grimace graced her pretty mouth. "You did warn me how it would be."

For the visit with Leah, Constance had once again assumed the persona of the Chicago aristocrat. Her dark tresses had been pulled into a tight knot at the back of her head, pin curls dangling to skim her exposed neck. The ostentatious hoopskirt beneath her summery peach dress flared into a wide bell shape that flounced with each stride. If a stiff wind were to tunnel along Lincoln, it could very well sweep her away. Sunlight flickered off the jewels on her earlobes and the rings on her fingers. Her appearance emphasized the gulf between them.

Constance Miller was a member of an affluent Northern family. Noah had money but not the social connections she'd enjoyed. And he was a born and bred Southerner. The fact that he'd fought for the North didn't automatically render him without stain.

Soaking in her profile, the pert nose and lush mouth, he wished she hadn't answered the bride advertisement. He hadn't seriously considered giving marriage a chance until she invaded his world. He hadn't pictured himself as a father until Jane and Abigail came along and he found himself braiding hair and telling bedtime stories.

This trio of females was shaking the very foundation of his belief that he was better off alone, and it had him waiting for the destruction to become evident.

"There are nice houses here." Constance swept her arm to encompass the tended lawns and two-story clapboard homes. Some were simple. Others more ornate.

"You should probably consider choosing a businessman

over a rancher." He worked to maintain a carefree attitude. "You'd live in a manner in which you've been accustomed."

Annoyance crossed her lovely features so quickly, he wondered if he'd truly seen it. Combing through that list of suitable bachelors with his friends looking on had been a tortuous exercise. Imagining her with any one of them had given him a Kansas-size headache.

Daniel and Leah's house came into view. It was a large, three-story home painted gray with white trim. Trees had been planted in the yard and neat, colorful flower beds lined the front porch.

Turning up the lane, he said, "Daniel built this house before Leah arrived on the train, but he designed it with a family in mind. How does it compare to your home in Chicago?"

Jane and Abigail stopped to study a caterpillar inching along a tree branch.

"I'd say four of these houses would fit inside the Longstreet mansion."

"Longstreet?"

"Um." Her fingertips fluttered to her lips. "I, uh… Longstreet is the name my husband's family gave the estate. You know, I personally think it's silly to name a house, but that's just my opinion." Her voice was strained. "What do you think?"

Noah hadn't been a lawman for long, but he wasn't oblivious. She was nervous about something. But what?

"I don't have an opinion either way."

"Because of my humble childhood, I used to dream about living in a huge, fancy house. Working for the Murphys, I saw firsthand the privileges they were afforded, the daily luxuries they took for granted. I longed to live like they did." She blew out a soft breath. "And then I met Ambrose. His suit and subsequent proposal seemed like a fantasy. I was dazzled by the opulent parties, the clothes, the jewels. His family was connected to many influential figures. Political leaders. Military officials."

Her mouth pulled into a self-deprecating twist. "It took about six months for the novelty to wear thin, and I realized none of it fulfilled me." Falling silent until they'd passed the girls, she stared at the formal porches and flower beds. "By that time, I was already married. It was too late to change course."

Noah kept his gaze on the grassy earth beneath their feet. Her admission was a costly one. She hadn't made the right choice. Had she ever loved her husband? Or had the lure of an easier life blinded her to her real feelings?

Compassion welled up within him, and he grieved for her mistake. Of course, the marriage had blessed her with Jane and Abigail, something she would never regret. That much he knew.

"How did you cope?"

"By helping those less fortunate." He detected wistfulness in her voice. "One day when I was feeling particularly low, I was strolling in the park when I came upon a pastor and his parishioners doling out food baskets to the homeless. Taking shelter behind a tree, I stood and watched them for the longest time, fascinated by their generosity. My mother and I hadn't received assistance from anyone. After some time, I made the decision to approach them."

She cleared her throat, then went on. "Pastor Wright was very kind. He and his wife, Patricia, patiently answered my questions and invited me to attend their church. I took them up on their invitation. The people welcomed me into their fold like a long-lost sister. I learned it wasn't enough to simply know the Scriptures. I had to put God's teachings into practice."

"You helped them in their work."

Peace he hadn't witnessed in her before rose to the surface. "At long last, I discovered what truly mattered." She covered her heart. "What filled the emptiness."

Spying the sheen of moisture in her eyes, he murmured, "You miss them, don't you?"

"Very much."

If they hadn't been confronted with the wide front door, he would've put voice to the question niggling at him. Why did she leave her friends, her means of support, for the wilds of Kansas and a man she'd never laid eyes on? What had been her true reason for leaving Chicago?

"There's nothing wrong with having nice things." He and his friends had gotten rich off the railroad. They may have chosen to utilize their windfalls in different ways, but the money hadn't changed them.

"I agree," she said. "It's all about perspective and gratitude."

Valentine Ewing, a local woman Daniel had employed to assist Leah until the baby's birth, answered their summons. Speaking in her Scottish brogue, she welcomed them inside, exclaiming over the twins as she led them to the parlor.

Leah left her post at one of the numerous tall windows to meet them in the center of the room. Her middle seemed more pronounced than the last time he'd seen her. His gaze bounced away from the obvious sign of life, a product of her first marriage. Since her first two pregnancies had ended in tragedy, Daniel had insisted that his wife take every precaution this time around. He hadn't sired the baby. Still, love and pride shone in his eyes each time he placed his hand on the swell of her belly.

Noah's attention shifted to Jane and Abigail as they politely answered Valentine's questions.

I could love them, he realized with a start. *They're not of my flesh and blood, and yet, if I were to marry their mother and claim them as my own, it would be so easy to let them into my heart.*

Already he felt protective. Worried for their future.

Flexing his fingers at his sides, he shoved aside the rogue thoughts.

After the introductions were made and Leah offered refreshments, she informed him that Daniel was waiting for him in the study. Tapping his Stetson against his thigh, he navigated the hallways until he reached the masculine study with its many books. Surveying the spines, he caught himself debating which book to read to Constance once they finished the current one. Then he remembered she probably wouldn't be around long enough. A pang went through him at the mere thought.

Seated behind his desk, Daniel pushed his ledgers aside and relaxed against the chair's cushioned back. "Noah. Have a seat. There's something I wanted to discuss with you."

"Working from home today?" He sank into the plush chair and attempted to get comfortable. The gun belt and holster hindered his efforts.

"I'm going to the stockyards once we're finished here." Lacing his fingers behind his head, Daniel stretched out his long, lean legs. "I spoke with the first candidate Constance agreed to consider. Pete Lyle. He's chomping at the bit for a chance with her. He'd like to escort her to the opera house this Friday evening. Pippa's orchestrated another variety show."

His heart struggled to pump. "Pete's a rancher."

"From all accounts, a successful one."

Noah tugged on his pant legs and shifted once again, feeling trapped by the voluptuous cushions. "I don't know, Dan. Given her circumstances, I'm wondering if she'd be better off with a city man."

One dark brow lifted. "She didn't have any objections the other day. I was going to discuss this with her as soon as they're finished visiting."

Struggling to his feet, Noah paced alongside the shelves. "It's her choice."

Lowering his arms, Daniel stood and, coming around the desk, rested against the ledge. "If she agrees, would you mind watching the girls?"

He looked at his friend in consternation. So he was to be expected to send Constance off on a date while he stayed behind and played nursemaid?

"Leah and I will be happy to do it if you'd rather not."

"It's fine."

It wasn't fine. Nothing had been fine since she'd shown up.

His friend came and put a hand on his shoulder, his green eyes watchful. Serious. "Noah, if you've changed your mind and want to honor Will's original agreement with her, say something now. Before she's snatched up."

On the wall opposite, he caught his reflection in a glass-fronted cabinet and mentally recoiled. He avoided mirrors and couldn't recall the last time he'd seen his own face. If only he could grow a beard and hide the ugly scar…but it wasn't possible due to the damage to his flesh. Besides, a beard wouldn't camouflage the scars on his neck and chest. He couldn't hide such things from a wife, anyway.

Tempted though he may be, he wouldn't condemn Constance to a life with a monster.

"It would never work."

"Noah—"

"I've killed men."

"So have I. Will, too. We were at war. What choice did we have?"

"You don't understand." Fresh disgust rose up to choke him. "I didn't tell anyone at the time. There was one battle in Virginia, close to my home. I wanted nothing more than to lay down my rifle and flee, because I knew I was firing upon neighbors. Friends. Maybe even family members."

Daniel's lips parted. "I had no idea."

"But I'd pledged allegiance to the Union, to the cause of freedom for all. I refused to be a coward." Closing his eyes, he sorted through deeply buried memories, reliving that agonizing day he'd murdered a friend. "We were advancing through the field, fighting the gray coats hand to hand, when I recognized my childhood buddy. Theo Lambert. For a moment, the joy of seeing each other again eclipsed our present reality. For a split second, we weren't enemies."

"What happened?"

"He started to move away. I started to let him." Sickness roiled in his gut. "I remembered you and Will were out there on the field. I couldn't risk you or him or anyone else in our company—"

A sound of distress from the doorway had both men twisting around. Constance's honey-colored eyes pulsed with emotion, the chief one horror. She lifted a shaking hand to her lips.

"I—I was searching for the exit… The necessary… I apologize for intruding."

Her heels clicked along the polished wooden floors. Noah let her go.

"You should go to her. Explain."

"What's there to explain?" he bit out, putting space between them. "I'm going to stop by the jail for a bit. Tell her I'll be back in an hour with the wagon."

His friend wisely let him retreat. It was one of many things he appreciated about Daniel—he knew when not to push.

Wolf was waiting for him on the porch. As soon as Noah slipped outside, the big animal stood, stretched and loped over, pressing into his leg. He stroked his pet's fur, thankful for the one companion he didn't have to confess his faults to, who didn't care about his scars—the ones no one could actually see.

Chapter Twelve

It was nearly impossible to concentrate on Leah and Tomasina's conversation.

All Grace could think about was Noah's terrible confession and the agony that had twisted his features as he'd made it. Of course she'd been shocked. Embarrassed, too, that she'd stopped to listen instead of proceeding on to the exit. Only now that she'd had time to sort through those minutes did she realize how her reaction must've hit Noah…a confirmation of his warped self-image. He'd left believing she agreed with him. That, because of his actions, he was a horrible person. That he wasn't worthy of any sort of happiness.

He probably thinks he deserved to have that gun explode in his face.

Her gaze was drawn once again to the unique brooch pinned to Leah's bodice. Shaped like a dragonfly, its body was made of deep red garnets and it had two pearls for eyes.

Seated on a settee beside Tomasina, Leah noticed her distraction. She touched the brooch, her smile nostalgic. "It's different, isn't it?"

"I like it," Grace said simply.

Leah glanced over her shoulder at the twins, who were perched on a lush carpet playing with a miniature tea set and dolls. Replacing her tea cup and saucer on the coffee table, she confided, "After the Murdoch brothers busted into the church and stole our jewelry, Daniel presented me with a new wedding ring. He gave me this, as well."

Will's wife admired it. "He has great taste."

Tomasina had arrived about ten minutes after Grace. Vibrant in looks and spirit, the beautiful redhead had made her feel welcome from the first moment. Wearing a white dress with printed blue flowers, a matching blue ribbon outlining her small waist and a cameo brooch nestled in the vee of her bodice, she appeared elegant and most ladylike. So Grace was astounded when her hostess explained how Tomasina, or Texas Tom, as she was sometimes known, had come to town with a slew of cowboys and organized a rodeo show with herself as the star performer.

The fact that she and Will had bonded over an abandoned baby girl—who turned out to be Hannah and James's baby—astounded her even further. Cowboy Creek was not without drama, to be sure. The crimes perpetrated by the Murdochs were troubling. Not only did they pose a danger to the residents, but to the future of the town. If word about the violence spread, potential brides and families would look elsewhere. Noah, Daniel and Will would be crushed if that happened.

"Noah told me the other sheriff was shot during a bank robbery and later died." Grace flicked a piece of lint off her skirt. "I hope the Murdochs don't come back."

The thought of Noah being in danger, of possibly being hurt, troubled her greatly.

Tomasina and Leah exchanged a glance. "We all pray they stay away."

"Enough of this serious talk," Tomasina exclaimed. "How has it been going out on the ranch with Noah? We told our husbands it was a bad idea, delivering a bride to his doorstep without his consent, but would they listen? Oh, no." Her green eyes sparkled with genuine interest.

"We've had our moments," Grace hedged. "He's managed our intrusion into his privacy better than I would've done in his shoes."

Sunlight slanted through the window and lit on Leah's blond tresses, rendering them like glowing candlelight. Her pretty cornflower blue eyes looked at Grace with understanding.

"I'm certain it's been an adjustment for everyone. Our husbands' intentions came from a positive place. They simply wanted their friend to find happiness."

Tomasina snorted. "You have to admit it was mighty arrogant of them."

Leah's glimmer of a smile held regret. "I'm sorry things didn't work out between the two of you. I'll be praying the good Lord leads you to the right man. Someone you can trust and possibly even love."

Love…an elusive emotion she hadn't experienced with a man. She'd convinced herself she loved Ambrose, but once she'd gotten to know his true self, she'd realized it had been a convenient lie. She'd been in love with his lifestyle, a truth that brought her great shame, one she'd repented of. He'd never loved her. He hadn't even liked her, not after the newness of their marriage had worn off.

"I'm not hoping for love. My wish is to marry someone I respect and who respects me in turn. Most important, the man I marry has to be good to my girls. That's all I ask."

Unable to stomach their pitying expressions, Grace was relieved when Daniel entered the nicely decorated room. "Sorry to interrupt, ladies. Leah, sweetheart, I have to run to the office."

"All right. I'll see you at supper time."

He turned to Grace. "Before I go, I have a request to pass along to you."

Anticipation buzzed. Was it from Noah?

"Pete Lyle has extended an invitation to the opera house this coming Friday. Noah's agreed to watch the twins. What would you like me to tell him?"

No. Tell him no.

Consternation made her stumble over her response. "I suppose… I…" The women were watching her with unconcealed expectation. There was no logical reason to refuse. Noah clearly wanted her to go if he was willing to be in charge of her girls for an evening. She sucked in a slow, steadying breath. "Please tell Mr. Lyle that I accept."

Daniel nodded, his smile gentle as if he were privy to her dilemma. "He will be delighted. I'll have him come to the ranch at six o'clock sharp."

"I'll be ready." Manners dictated she express her gratitude. "Thank you for orchestrating this for me."

"We want to help in any way we can." He turned his gaze on his wife. "Leah, would you join me on the porch for a moment before I go?"

After they'd left, Tomasina adopted a mischievous expression. "I have a feeling this whole finding-you-a-husband mission isn't going to sit well with Noah."

Grace frowned. It wasn't going to sit well with her, either.

"Momma, you look pretty." Abigail trailed her fingers along Grace's bodice's intricate lace design.

"Thank you, sweetheart."

She had donned one her finest dresses for this outing, partly because it was appropriate for her destination and partly in hopes of making Noah regret casting her aside. Not that a fancy dress would likely accomplish that. Checking that not a single strand had escaped her intricate upswept style, she lifted a necklace from her jewelry box and attempted several times to clasp it. With every movement, the satiny, royal blue folds whispered in the quiet bedroom.

Abigail disappeared, returning moments later with Noah at her side. "Mr. Noah can do it, Momma."

Stiffening, she met his inscrutable blue gaze in the mirror. The mood had been stilted between them the past few days. He'd spent the bulk of his time at the jail or outside doing chores. The one time she'd attempted to bring up the overheard conversation between him and Daniel, he'd cut her off, insisting he didn't want to discuss it.

She was ready to throttle him.

Bending his blond head to address the child, he said, "What is it you want me to do, Adelaide?"

Her big brown eyes centered on his, Abigail considered him for long moments. "My name is Abigail Lorraine Lo—"

"Abigail," Grace hurriedly interrupted her, alarm exploding inside at the near slipup. She bustled past the bed's footboard to join them in the doorway. "You shouldn't have bothered the sheriff. The necklace isn't necessary."

His gaze sharpened as he scanned her from head to toe. Admiration flickered before he snuffed it out. "Abigail didn't interrupt me. I was reading the newspaper, is all." Holding out his palm, he said, "Where's the necklace?"

Jane's high-pitched chatter filtered in from the other room where she was playing.

Grace retrieved the thin gold chain with the sapphire pendant and, piling it in his waiting hand, affixed her gaze to the floor. He slowly moved to stand behind her, his solid warmth surrounding her, drawing her to him, as he bent close to lift the two sides over her head. When his fingertips skimmed her nape, tickling her, a shiver worked its way up from her toes. He faltered for the barest second.

She wished she could read his thoughts, discover if he was affected by her as she was him.

What if he hadn't fought the bridal agreement? What if it were him escorting her tonight instead of a complete stranger?

I'd be proud to be seen with him.

Noah Burgess possessed hard edges, to be sure, but his appeal couldn't be denied. His obvious strength, the vitality and intelligence that shone in his ocean-blue eyes, the fair hair, tanned skin, bold cheekbones, unyielding jawline… He was gorgeous in a rough-hewn, man-of-the-land way.

"There." His hands dropped, and he stepped away.

His distance made her ache with loneliness. Before she'd met Noah, her sadness had been a general recognition of what her life lacked. It was worse now. Now her loneliness had a name and face. Noah alone could ease the yearning inside her. A depressing thought.

Wolf's barking ricocheted through the cabin walls. Noah strode toward the nearest window overlooking the front yard. His lips thinned.

"Lyle's here."

Grace entered the main room, pressing her hands flat against her middle. Not a single part of her wanted this. She didn't exactly have a choice, though, did she? Wasn't like she could stay here in Noah's cabin forever. Even if that's exactly what she longed to do.

She kissed both girls' cheeks. "Mind the sheriff, girls."

"Yes, ma'am," they chorused, hurrying to the other window and peeking out at her gentleman caller.

Last night before bed, she'd explained the situation as best she could, careful not to place blame on Noah. They'd been confused and a little apprehensive about yet another upheaval. It said something about Noah that, even after a short time, they liked him and could envision life on the ranch with him. Asking God for fortitude, she'd tried to be upbeat about the future. She'd tried to mask her own unhappiness.

Lord Jesus, give me wisdom and discernment. I can't do this without You.

Walking through the open door, she joined Noah on the porch as Pete Lyle descended his wagon and approached with an eager gait. Whipcord lean with windswept black hair, the rancher had a blinding-white grin and gray eyes that seemed very light against his deep golden skin. She guessed him to be in his early thirties. He was an attractive man, but his coloring reminded her of her brother-in-law, and Grace knew that no matter how attentive or how kind he might prove to be, she couldn't accept his suit.

"Did you attend the opera in Chicago?"

"I was fortunate to attend many shows. I loved every minute of it."

In the opera house's opulent foyer, they waited in line for what Pete assured her were the best chicken-salad sandwiches around, supplied by the Cowboy Café's cook, Nels Patterson. Conversations hummed in the lengthy space, punctuated by spurts of hearty laughter. Anticipation and good cheer marked the predominately male crowd. Grace could feel the high interest focused on her, and she yearned for Noah's reassuring presence.

The polite smile she'd managed grew tighter. Reassuring wasn't a description she would've imagined applying to the aloof sheriff when they'd first met. But she'd seen a softer, gentler side of him that few were privy to.

The couple ahead of them moved away, and Pete put a hand low on her back to guide her forward. She gritted her teeth. *He's not Frank. He's not Frank.*

Her brother-in-law was likely in Chicago, fuming over her disappearance and taking his displeasure out on those unfortunate enough to be called his friends. Maybe he'd decide she wasn't worth the effort. Maybe he'd accept that she didn't want him.

Her spirits dipped lower. The Frank Longstreet she knew wasn't a quitter. Once his pride was wounded, he'd go to any lengths to achieve retribution.

Pete paid for their plates. The chicken-salad sandwiches were served with spears of pickled okra and half ears of roasted corn. "Would you mind carrying the lemonades?" he asked.

Taking up the ice-cold jars filled with pale yellow liquid, she followed him outside to where makeshift tables had been set up in the lot beside the building.

They located a spot at the far end of a long table, and Pete bowed his head to say grace. He peppered her with questions throughout the meal. She appreciated his interest, but discussing her former life made her nervous. She was relieved when it was time to find their seats.

The theater's main space was impressive, with high ceilings, cushioned chairs and gleaming wood finishes. Some folks chatted in groups while others picked out their seats. Intricate metal sconces lined the balcony ledge above, casting a soft glow over the attendees.

"Where would you like to sit, Constance?"

Masking her ire—the man acted as if they'd known each other for decades instead of hours—she lifted one shoulder. "You decide."

They were making their way down the left aisle when she noticed a pair of gorgeous redheads in their path, one being Tomasina Canfield. The other woman was younger, her hair a more muted shade of red and straight as a stick compared to Tomasina's corkscrew curls. The attractive woman was garbed in a flamboyant style—her white-and-pink dress possessed a bustle large enough to serve dinner on. A bold pink feather rising from her straw hat bobbed inches from her forehead.

It had to be Pippa Neely, the actress her twins hadn't stopped talking about for days. Jealous thoughts bombarded her. Did Noah think Pippa was beautiful? Had he rejected Grace because he was really interested in the younger woman? Pippa certainly didn't have the complications Grace came with…an unhappy first marriage, a deceased husband and young children in need of care and guidance. Not to mention an obsessed brother-in-law who'd stop at nothing to have her, only to then discard her like his other conquests.

Tomasina met her eye. "Constance! You look like you've stepped from the pages of a French catalog!"

"You're too kind." Asking Pete to choose seats for them, she assured him she wouldn't be but a minute. He looked reluctant to leave her side, but agreed with a nod of his head.

"I'd like for you to meet the woman responsible for tonight's entertainment. Constance, meet Pippa Neely. Pippa, Constance Miller."

The actress's hazel eyes rounded. "You're the mother of those darling twins. I'm thrilled to finally meet you." She took Grace's hand between both of hers. "I'd planned to call on you next week and discuss the possibility of the girls performing. Twins are a rarity in these parts. I can guarantee they will draw crowds. I'm sure even fussy ole D. B. Burrows would deign to write a front-page article about them. Imagine the attention such an act would draw to our humble opera house!"

Grace struggle to maintain her schooled expression. Fame and attention were the last things she wanted… It could lead Frank right to their door.

"I'm afraid that's not possible."

"Oh, no." Pippa's face fell, the pink feather swinging to the right as she cocked her head. "That's unfortunate."

"I'm extremely protective of my daughters. They are much too young for what you have in mind."

A tall, distinguished blond man jostled Pippa, forcing her

forward a step. He quickly turned to apologize, a twinkle of mischief in his gray eyes. "Please excuse me, Miss Neely."

His apology didn't mollify her. Quite the opposite. Her mouth twisted with displeasure. "You did that on purpose, Gideon."

The thin mustache about his lip twitched as he lifted his hands in a gesture of innocence. "Now, why would I do that?"

"Because." She planted her hands on her hips. "You delight in irking me, that's why."

He make a clucking noise with his tongue. "Don't be overdramatic, my dear. Save it for the stage."

She emitted a gasp that garnered the attention of passersby. Pulling herself up, she addressed Grace. "This isn't the best place to discuss the merits of your girls performing. Would you mind meeting me at the bakery one day next week? My treat."

Her mind was already made up, but she didn't want to offend the woman. Cowboy Creek was her permanent home; she had no desire to make enemies. And truly, she missed feminine companionship. "I'd like that."

"Wonderful. I'll find you after the show to iron out the details."

Ignoring the Gideon fellow, she bade Tomasina goodbye and swept toward the stage, disappearing behind a swath of thick maroon curtains.

He thrust his hand at her. "Gideon Kendricks."

She supplied her name. "Nice to meet you, Mr. Kendricks."

"Gideon works for the Union Pacific," Tomasina said. "He's here temporarily."

"My time here is short, unfortunately." His regret struck her as genuine. Did it have anything to do with Pippa?

"Will and Daniel would like it if you decided to stay." The redhead's smile included Grace. "Noah, too, I'm sure. He was impressed that you helped with the posse search."

He shrugged. "I dislike criminals as much as the next guy, I suppose, and aim to see justice prevail." Edging to the side to allow an older couple to enter the row he blocked, he said, "I'm glad I ran into you, Mrs. Miller. I heard you're from Chicago. I have a beloved aunt and uncle there who I visit at every opportunity." He named the same affluent section the Longstreets inhabited. "What part of the city are you from?"

Her mouth went dry. If she mentioned her cousin Constance's poor neighborhood, her attire and jewels would arouse suspicion and spark questions she couldn't afford. She'd banked on Will and Daniel's ignorance of the city and Constance's vagueness in her letter to avoid this exact dilemma.

What were the odds she'd meet someone familiar with Chicago all the way in Kansas?

There was no avoiding her deception. She was lying to everyone in this town…those trying to help and befriend her, like Noah, Will and Tomasina, Daniel and Leah… and those potential suitors who would offer to marry her.

Dizziness assailed her. Pete's black head swiveled round as he checked on her. *How am I to stand up in front of God and this town and pledge to honor, cherish and obey a man I'm lying to?* Another horrible thought hit home. *I'll never be known by my real name. No one will call me Grace again.*

"Actually," she forced through stiff lips, "my family lived in that same neighborhood."

His brows shot up. "Truly? What a coincidence." Scraping his chin, he shook his head. "I don't recall the Miller name. My aunt and uncle, Lydia and Terrence Lowell, are very active socially and politically. Do you know them?"

Her mind raced. Terrence Lowell was a well-known philanthropist, his fortune gleaned from multiple clothing and shoe factories he owned in the city. He and his wife often attended the same functions as the Longstreets. Grace had met him once and thought him an intelligent, gentle man.

She was saved from outright lying when the lights flickered, a signal the show was about to begin. Relief rendered her knees weak. "Excuse me, but I must rejoin Mr. Lyle."

"Of course." Gideon didn't appear to notice anything amiss. "I'm sure we'll have more opportunity to compare notes about Chicago."

Grace nodded, unable to form a response, all too aware her escape was a temporary one.

Chapter Thirteen

"And the princess lived in the castle, surrounded by her favorite animal friends, for the rest of her life. The end."

Noah closed the picture book, careful not to jar the slumbering girl. Abigail had stunned him when she'd brought him the book and, without waiting for his consent, climbed into his lap and rested her head against his chest. More shocking were the fragile, tender feelings worming into his heart. These innocent, precious girls trusted him. He suspected they even *liked* him.

Jane had bluntly told him she was not pleased they weren't going to live on the ranch forever. After he'd fed them and wiped their faces free of crumbs and jelly stains, she'd pierced him with those inquisitive eyes and asked why he wouldn't let them stay. His response—that she was too young to understand—hadn't mollified her in the slightest. Thankfully, she hadn't pursued the topic.

The question wouldn't leave him in peace, however. Why *couldn't* they stay? What would be so horrible? Truth be told, he'd grown accustomed to their enthusiastic greetings each day when he came home. They'd run up, waving and smiling, happy he'd returned…and whatever burdens he was carrying seemed lighter.

Jane yawned. "That was a nice story. Will you read another one, Mr. Noah?"

He eyed the mantel clock, irritation rising as images of Pete and Constance taunted him. They should've been home an hour ago.

"Your sister's already asleep, as you should be." Sliding the book onto the table, he gathered the sweet-smelling girl in his arms and stood up. Her head went limp, her dark hair spilling over his arm. "Come on."

He was about to enter the bedroom when Wolf, who'd been dozing near the fireplace, sat up and strained his ears. The door creaked open, and Constance entered in her regal, bell-shaped dress, her features tight and pinched. Not the expression of a love-struck woman. To Noah's shame, satisfaction slid through his chest.

Her honey-hued eyes landed on him, taking in the scene. Marching straight for him, she said, "I'll take her."

He motioned with his head. "The bed's right there. I can get her settled."

"She's my daughter. I'll do it."

Unaccustomed to finding her in this particular mood, he transferred Abigail into her arms and waited by the door until both girls were beneath the covers and the lamp turned low. Constance glanced at him as if to ask, *Why are you still here?*

She crossed her arms. "Thank you, Noah, for watching them."

She was dismissing him.

"What's wrong, Constance?" She appeared to flinch at the name. "Did something happen tonight?" Alarm flared. He pulled his hands free of his pockets. "Did Lyle do something to upset you?"

"No." Her gaze pinned to the floor, she shook her head. "Pete was the perfect gentleman."

There was a flat note in her voice denoting fatigue that

had nothing to do with physical exhaustion. A resigned air shimmered about her.

"Then what?" He took a half-step closer. "You can talk to me, Constance."

Her head snapped up, anger leaping to life. "Can I? Truly? Because I've tried to talk to you about that conversation I overheard and you refuse to open up. Why should I speak freely with you when you won't return the favor?"

"My past crimes have no bearing on what's happening tonight."

"If what you did is a crime, then you should be in jail. Half the nation should be in jail."

His upper lip curled. "You don't know what you're talking about."

Hugging herself, she presented him with her back. "I'm exhausted. I'd like to retire now."

Noah spun and stalked out, signaling for Wolf to follow and refraining from slamming the door behind him. He got little sleep that night. Rising just after dawn, he milked the cow, watered and fed the horses and, saddling Samson, rode straight for Lyle's ranch. The man answered his pounding summons half-dressed and one hundred percent confused by the visit.

"Sheriff." He blinked the sleep from his eyes, peering past Noah's shoulder at the empty yard. "Is there an emergency in town? Did the Murdoch brothers strike again?"

"What did you do to Constance?" he growled.

Pete's head reared back. "Nothing. I did nothing to her, I promise. Why? Did she accuse me of something?"

"She said you were a gentleman."

"That's the truth."

"Then why was she fit to be tied last night? I've never seen her like that."

"I don't know. I took her to the opera house, we ate and took in the show. Then I brought her straight home."

Noah twisted and looked at the horizon without really seeing it, gently probing the ridged flesh on his neck, which had gone taut and painful. Turning back, he caught Pete's quizzical expression. "Can you think of anything that might've upset her?"

"Nothing out of the ordinary occurred. I've only just met her, but she struck me as subdued. A bit uptight."

"Could be she was nervous," he snapped.

He looked sheepish. "Other than myself, she only spoke to Will Canfield's wife, Miss Neely and Gideon Kendricks."

Noah considered that information for about a minute before deciding to have a word with the train rep. "Thanks for the information."

He was hurrying for his horse when Pete called after him. "Sure you don't want her for yourself, Sheriff?"

Shooting him a quelling glare, Noah hauled himself onto Samson's back and pointed him toward town. He counted himself fortunate twenty minutes later when he spotted Gideon lounging against the livery's side exterior, his focus on the activity outside the opera house. He guided his mount alongside, blocking the man's line of sight.

Gideon thumbed his bowler hat off his forehead. "Sheriff Burgess, good morning. What can I do for you?"

"You can start by telling me what you did to upset Constance."

"Constance?" His momentary look of confusion cleared. "Oh, the widow? Mrs. Miller? I'm afraid I don't know what you're speaking of." Pushing off the wall, he came closer, gray eyes serious. "Has something happened?"

"Pete Lyle told me you and she had a conversation."

"We did." His chin at a stubborn angle, he folded his arms over his chest. "Tell me, Sheriff, what exactly are you accusing me of?"

Somewhere in his mind, Noah acknowledged he was

being unreasonable. He was overreacting. Behaving like a jealous suitor.

Beneath him, Samson shifted his weight as a wagon rolled past, stirring up clouds of dust.

"I apologize. I shouldn't have presumed you were responsible." Taking off his Stetson, he threaded his fingers through his damp locks. "Constance was clearly overwrought about something. Can you think of anything she said that might indicate what was bothering her?"

He stroked his goatee. "Not really. We didn't speak for very long. Turns out we both have family in the same neighborhood in Chicago. I didn't recognize her name, which is odd. We were interrupted midway through, so I don't know if she's acquainted with my aunt and uncle."

"Hmm." Nothing dramatic about that. "Her late husband's name was Ambrose."

"Ambrose Miller. I don't know anyone by that name." He thought a moment. "My uncle introduced me once to an Ambrose Longstreet. Now, there was a cold fish if ever I've met one."

Longstreet sounded familiar, but he couldn't pinpoint where he'd seen or heard it.

The knots of tension in his upper back started to loosen. Perhaps Constance's odd mood could be attributed to her need to choose a husband. No doubt she'd felt on display last night, out with Pete for the first time with scores of curious onlookers.

"Chicago's a big place," Noah said. "And you're not there on a full-time basis."

His brow knitted. "Still, I have a good memory for names and faces."

Raucous laughter filtered across the street. Drifting to stand at Samson's head, Gideon stared at the workers removing the makeshift tables and cleaning up leftover trash.

A trio of bulky men trudged toward the rear of the building, bringing the lively redheaded actress into view.

Gideon's interest became clear for the first time. Noah recalled seeing them dance around each other at various town functions, trading witty banter but never really talking.

"Pippa's one of the original mail-order brides, you know," Noah said. "Had a busy social calendar but hasn't settled on anyone yet. I wonder what she's looking for."

"Not me."

His resigned tone took Noah by surprise. Gideon had a secure, lucrative career. He struck him as respectful and honorable. A man who revered God's Word and lived by a strict moral code.

"Why's that?"

"She's looking to make Cowboy Creek her permanent home. I travel for my job. I like seeing new places. Meeting interesting people."

"You ever consider asking her to go with you?"

He tilted his head to indicate the opera house. "Pippa's entire existence is tied up in that building right there. I'd like nothing more than to forget the childish game we've been playing and pursue her in earnest, but we're too different. She's optimistic. Full of the kind of hope our nation needs in order to rebuild. I'm more realistic. Cynical, even."

Noah thought about Constance. Their variances in outlook and personality weren't the issue. The gulf between them had nothing to do with her—she was good, kind and nurturing—and everything to do with him. *He* was the bad apple. *He* was the defective merchandise.

Gideon didn't have that problem.

"Seems to me the obstacles you've outlined could be overcome. But you'll need to put forth a little effort, risk your pride, to find out. Ask yourself this—if you leave Cowboy Creek without exploring whatever it is between you, will you regret it for the rest of your life?"

It was as if clouds passed over the younger man's face as he continued to watch Pippa interact with the workers.

The sound of rapidly approaching riders caught their attention.

"Sheriff, come quick!" the one in the lead yelled. "A brawl broke out among the new group of cowboys that arrived last week. One's already been knifed in the gut."

"Did you send someone after Doc Fletcher?"

"Sure did."

"Need my help?" Gideon asked.

"Could use you to keep the crowd subdued."

Jogging for his horse, he called, "Right behind you!"

Noah dug his heels into Samson's flank, bits of dirt flying as the other men wheeled around to lead him to the fight.

Grace stepped back to survey her work. "What do you think, girls?"

They dutifully inspected the curtains she'd hung at the windows. The yellow added a cheery warmth to the cabin's central space. If she were staying, she'd discuss ordering a sofa with Noah. She'd purchase a patterned rug for the hearth and a few landscapes for the shaved-log walls.

"It's pretty." Jane smiled. "I think Mr. Noah will like it, too."

Abigail touched the fabric, brown eyes bright with hope. "Will you teach me to sew, Momma?"

"When we get settled in our new home, I will teach you both." In Chicago's upper levels of society, such a skill was viewed as a hobby. On the prairie, with no paid staff to tend to chores, it was vital for the family's well-being. Stroking Abigail's chin, she said, "How does that sound?"

Their response wasn't exactly eager. Jane got a disgruntled look, and sadness settled across Abigail's dainty features.

"We don't want to leave."

"We want to stay here." Abigail jabbed a tiny finger in the direction of the floor. "With Mr. Noah."

Lord, please give me the right words. I'm responsible for bringing them here. I built up the idea of living on this ranch, and now I have to help them deal with dashed hopes.

Since waking that morning, the twins had talked incessantly about their time with the sheriff. The drawings he'd helped them complete were stacked in the middle of the kitchen table, along with the picture books he'd read. Apparently, the highlight of their evening had been when Noah had shown them the chicken coop, bringing out the hens one at a time and allowing them to name them. Not a wise move on his part, considering they would soon be moving. Of course, he didn't have children. He couldn't know how easily they got attached.

The image of him holding a sleeping Abigail in his arms wasn't one she would soon forget. He looked natural, at ease and very much like a protective, caring father. He'd been kind to her daughters. Patient with them. And she was repaying him by lying about her identity and the reasons she was here in Kansas.

He would hate her if he ever found out.

A commotion outside sent alarm through her veins. Pushing the newly hung curtain aside, she relaxed when she recognized Noah's horse. But why was he here before lunchtime?

She went out on the porch. "Noah, I…"

He rounded the animal, and Grace's knees went weak. Blood was everywhere. His once-pristine shirt—the dove-gray one that deepened the hue of his eyes—was ruined. Streaked with crimson. Ripped at the shoulder seam.

"What happened?" Rushing to meet him, she seized his hand, her gaze seeking out the source of his injuries.

"I'm fine." He gave her fingers a gentle squeeze then, grimacing slightly, disengaged to tug on the fabric of his shirt. "This blood's not mine. There was a brawl at the stockyards. One cowboy's near death. Daniel and I carried him to Doc's." His eyes softened. "I hope Daniel's able to change before Leah sees him and jumps to the same conclusion as you. You look close to swooning."

"You'd swoon, too, if you saw yourself in the mirror." Picking up her skirts, she said, "Stay here."

Hustling to fetch the girls, she ushered them outside and around the side of the cabin, not giving them a chance to get a good look at Noah. She told them to entertain themselves in the yard and not to go past the stream. By the time she returned, Noah had gone inside and removed his shirt, wadding it into a ball and chucking it in the discard bucket. Turning at her soft footfall, his steady regard was inscrutable. His red undershirt of soft cotton molded to his wide, defined chest, muscular arms and flat stomach. Awareness shimmered between them, and Grace felt a soul-deep longing to be sheltered in his strong embrace.

Her gaze lifted to Noah's mouth, belatedly noticing his lower lip was bruised and busted. The skin around his right eye was turning an angry purple.

"Have a seat." Her voice came out scratchy. "I'll get your face cleaned up."

His movements unsure, stiff, he set his dusty hat on one of the chairs. "You don't have to do that."

Ignoring his protest, she poured water in a bowl and gathered a dish towel, soap cake and antiseptic paste. She arranged the items on the table and boldly placed her palm against his chest, applying pressure until he relented and sank into the chair. "Let someone take care of you for once."

One pale eyebrow arched, but he said nothing as she brushed his hair aside with unsteady fingers. As expected, his light blond hair was soft and silky. She swallowed hard, longing once again suffusing her, longing for this man alone.

Was it a trick of her senses, or did his breath catch in his chest?

Taking care not to inflict pain, she washed away the dirt and dust from his face and the bits of dried blood from his mouth and a thin cut on his cheekbone. He kept his eyes closed, allowing her the freedom to appreciate his features unhindered. His hands were balled on his thighs. Close enough to gently encircle her waist, if he wanted.

Noah Burgess doesn't want you, remember?

How would he react if she were to rest her hands on his shoulders and lean down to brush her lips against his?

He'd toss you aside and bolt, that's how.

"Are you finished?" His deep voice startled her, as did the brilliant blue of his eyes now focused on her.

She cleared her throat and hastily snatched the antiseptic cream. "Not quite."

He continued to watch her as she worked, making her antsy and self-conscious. Mere inches separated them. There was nowhere to hide. Could he guess her thoughts?

Chapter Fourteen

$\sim$

Noah craved what he couldn't have. How natural it would be to set his hands on her waist and tug her close, to cup her nape, draw her face down to his and kiss her like he'd daydreamed about on more than one occasion. He was human. Weak. Starved for affection. Constance was here, cooking his meals and cleaning his home, behaving as a wife would. Except she wasn't to be his wife, and that was his fault.

My *choice*, he corrected, frantically trying to keep his self-control in check, a task made nearly impossible due to her nearness, her vanilla scent, her tender ministrations and the concern turning her eyes a beautiful amber gold.

Her thick waves had been left loose, yet another set of sparkly pins tucked into the mass at each temple. Each time she bent to address his wounds, another shiny lock slipped free of the rest and dangled close to his chest.

Father God, help me to think straight. Help me remember what's best for her.

The cream she used was cool against his bruised cheekbone. "I'm sorry I was short with you last night... and before...about what happened at Daniel's. I wish you hadn't overheard that."

Twisting the lid on the jar closed, she returned it to the table and wiped her hands with a clean cloth. "I wish you wouldn't be so hard on yourself." Interlocking her fingers, she remained where she was, her black skirts brushing his knees. She wore an earnest expression. "War demands a high price. You were presented with a terrible choice no one should have to make."

The familiar guilt rampaged through him. "I could've let him go."

How many nights afterward had he lain in that miserable, dirty, sweltering tent with his fellow soldiers and relived the same moments, over and over again, testing different scenarios. He'd relived the good times with his friend and shed tears in the dark over the loss.

"His name was Theo Lambert," he rasped. "We called him Teddy, for short. Our parents were friends, so we'd get together for outings at the river. Teddy had a way with a fishing pole. Not sure what it was about him, but he drew fish to his line like moths to a flame." He stopped, unable to continue, wondering if Teddy had married before joining the Confederate army. He could have a widow out there. Children without a father.

"Oh, Noah," she breathed, her hands falling to her sides. "I'm sorry. I can't imagine how much you've hurt over this."

"I don't deserve your compassion."

"Have you ever asked yourself what might've happened if you'd let him go?"

He shot her an impatient look. "Of course."

"And have you considered how you'd feel if he'd killed one of your friends? What if he'd killed Will or Daniel? Leah wouldn't have a loving husband, would she? A father for her baby. Tomasina wouldn't have found love with Will. In fact, this entire town probably wouldn't exist."

Noah stared at her, the truth of her statement sinking in. "You and the girls wouldn't be here."

A jumble of emotions swirled in her eyes. "No. We'd

be in some other boomtown, without the benefit of people determined to watch out for us."

Nodding, he lowered his gaze to his lap, the burden of Teddy's death an ounce lighter. He uttered a silent prayer, asking for God's help in putting the past behind him. He'd already asked forgiveness for all he'd been forced to do during his stint in the war and according to God's holy promises, his sins had been washed away by Christ Jesus's work on the cross.

Noah didn't realize he was massaging the scarred flesh on his neck until Constance gently curved her fingers over his. He froze, drowning in her gaze.

"You do this a lot," she whispered. Her hand slipped from his and, light as a butterfly's wing, she touched the ridged flesh on his jaw. "Does it pain you?"

His throat felt full of pine needles. "At times."

Uncertain, Noah let his hand drop to his lap. She openly studied his war souvenir, her fingertips trailing beneath his ear and along his neck. No one had ever dared to do what she was doing. He felt both repulsed and elated. Mostly elated. Why was he allowing this?

"Can you feel that?" Her thick sweep of lashes blinked slowly.

"Yes. It's different, though. Not as sensitive."

"Like I'm touching you through fabric?"

Noah seized her wrist, and she gasped, her wide gaze shooting to his. "Enough, city girl," he ground out.

Her mouth parted, drawing his attention to the tiny freckle above her curved upper lip. He wanted nothing more than to kiss her. Forget Pete Lyle or any other man.

"Why do you smell like lavender and honey?"

The question startled him. "You noticed that, huh?"

She nodded, light sparkling off her hairpins.

"The doctor who treated me suggested I use the combination on my damaged skin to keep it supple. It gets tight and uncomfortable if I don't." Still holding her wrist captive, he ran his thumb back and forth over the soft skin.

"You should be proud of your scars, Noah. Your actions were those of a hero."

He dropped her arm as if it burned him. "Have you ever considered I did what I did as penance for Teddy?" he scoffed.

"I don't think that's the true reason. I think you tell yourself that in order to continue feeling guilty. Because, in your mind, you don't deserve to be hailed a hero. You don't deserve happiness or a family of your own. That's why you use your disfigurement to keep everyone away."

"No."

"Yes."

High-pitched screams pierced the air. Stark fear arrested Constance's features a second before she bolted for the door. Running a single step behind her, he registered Wolf's warning barks, the girls' obvious terror and the six-foot-long snake slithering through the grass. His heart thundered in his chest. Kansas was home to its fair share of poisonous snakes. He couldn't see its pattern from his vantage point.

Noah shouted a warning, but Constance ignored him. Running full-out for the girls, she put herself in between them and the reptile, yelling for them to go to the cabin. Time slowed as the snake, as thick as his calf muscle, coiled into a strike position.

Constance was minutes away from injury and possible death, and he experienced fear unlike the kind he'd known on the battlefields staring down cannon fire and Confederate bayonets. Then, he'd dreaded the unknown...pain and suffering...doing the wrong thing and letting his men down. The terror fizzing through his veins now was different. It weighed down his feet, slowed his thoughts, drove home just how important this woman had become to him. He couldn't bear to see her suffer.

"Constance, stop!"

It was as if the sound of her name didn't faze her.

Catching up, he snagged her arm and jerked her back against him. She struggled. "The girls—"

He kept his gaze trained on the snake, whose tongue was testing the air, weighing the threat. "They're out of harm's way." He pressed his mouth close to her ear. "Please, be still."

The girls were crying on the porch, the sounds tugging at his heartstrings. Wolf continued to bark, unhappy about the intruder and about to pounce.

"Wolf, stay." He threw out his hand.

The giant animal seemed to roll his golden eyes in frustration. His barking ceased, but his lips were curled back to reveal sharp canines.

"Constance? Are you listening to me?"

She'd gone quiet in his hold, her whole body trembling, her breaths coming in short bursts. She nodded.

"This snake is as unhappy as we are. What I want you to do is back away slowly. Go stand with the girls on the porch. Stay there."

"What about you? And Wolf?" The concern for his well-being throbbing in her voice warmed the part of him that had gone cold.

"We'll be fine. I've got my gun."

While she retreated, Noah studied the snake's pattern. He eased closer. The shape of his head and the slits in his eyes indicated it was poisonous. He had to kill it in order to keep the girls and Constance safe.

"Go inside," he called.

When the main door slammed shut, he removed his weapon and fired, wishing it had been harmless and he could've let it go.

Constance's earlier words about war scrolled through his mind. Life was full of hard choices. Regrettable choices.

Every action had consequences. He was pretty sure not one man who'd served, either for the North or South, had emerged from the war unscathed. They'd all been changed. Altered forever. Physically. Mentally. Emotionally.

For the first time since his discharge, he had hope God would heal his broken places, would help him shed the guilt he carried.

That hope did not extend to his relationship with Constance. He wasn't good enough for a woman like her— brave, sincere, compassionate, pure. She deserved someone better than him. Someone who could be what she needed.

"Some of us aren't convinced you're giving enough attention to our problem."

Wade Claxton, the owner of the saddle shop, stared down his long nose at Noah, who was seated behind his desk.

Noah's chair creaked as he shifted and pulled a sheaf of papers from the top-right drawer. "These are mine and Sheriff Davis's notes on the fake deeds. You're welcome to pore over the information if you think you can come up with a lead we overlooked."

Frustration fired through him. Claxton was right. Between dealing with matters on the ranch, breaking up brawls and navigating townsfolk's petty grievances, he had his hands full. And he didn't know how to proceed in this case. He'd interviewed the man at the land office again, as well as the affected business owners. They lacked a suspect and motive. To what end would someone replace the authentic deeds with false ones? What did that person stand to gain?

Every crime in Cowboy Creek couldn't be pinned on the Murdochs.

The man's weathered face reflected impatience. "That's not my job. I've a shop to run."

His hinted accusation didn't go unnoticed. For probably the hundredth time, Noah questioned why he'd ever agreed to be sheriff. He was a rancher, not a lawman. The folks of this town were counting on him to solve their problems, and he was afraid he was bound to let them down.

Constance was the only one who'd looked past the badge and asked him if what he was doing made him happy.

"I'll post a meeting for tonight. Six o'clock at the Cattleman. We'll put our heads together and try to come up with answers. Could be it's the same person responsible for burning that first shipment of lumber and tossing Will's rooms."

The shop owner's lips thinned, but he jerked a nod. "I'll spread the word."

After Wade had gone, Noah stationed himself at one of the wide windows facing Eden Street. A young lad left the newspaper office next door lugging a stack of the *Herald*'s latest edition. Prudence Haywood crossed the street and, ignoring the men doffing their hats and grinning like fools, ducked into Hannah's dress shop. Odd that she'd come to Cowboy Creek in search of a husband but hadn't deigned to spend time with any potential suitors. Hannah hadn't been interested in anyone because of a hidden pregnancy. What was Prudence's excuse?

Across the way, the hotel bustled with activity. Milk and food deliveries were made every day at this time. Simon, the young hotel porter, was speaking to a worker washing the windows while another man swept the boardwalk. Daniel's father, Oliver Gardner, who'd decided to settle here after Leah arranged for a surprise visit, escorted Valentine Ewing through the main entrance and set his bowler atop his head, no doubt having treated her to a sumptuous breakfast. Romance had been brewing between the two since the moment they'd met.

He was about to return to his desk when Daniel and Will

turned onto the boardwalk and approached, deep in conversation. Excitement marked Will's definitive gestures.

"We have news, my friend." He waved a paper in front of Noah's nose. "The Webster County representative is coming next week for a final inspection of our town. His name's Gregory McAllister. Depending on what he finds here, he could decide to make Cowboy Creek the official county seat."

Daniel closed the door behind him and checked that the cells were empty. "If Mr. McAllister finds out about our growing list of unsolved crimes, I'm not convinced he'll choose us."

Noah went and sat on the desk's ledge, crossing his arms as he glanced at both men. "I'm meeting with the property owners tonight in hopes that, between the lot of us, we'll come up with a solid theory concerning the deeds. Maybe we'll solve at least one of these mysteries before this man arrives."

Will stuffed the paper in his coat's pocket. "That still leaves the poisoned cattle, sabotaged lumber shipments and the attempt to steal railroad funds from my room."

"We're not required to present him with a list of every single issue we're dealing with here." Daniel looked thoughtful. "No town is crime-free."

Will ran his fingers along his trim goatee. "Good point."

"We could be Mr. McAllister's personal guides," Noah said.

"Tomasina and I will host him in our home," Will offered. "What if we have a grand party to welcome him to town? He can be introduced to some of the business leaders and permanent residents."

Daniel nodded slowly. "I think that's the best plan."

"And what if one of the partygoers mentions our recent troubles?"

Noah despised this aspect of town leadership. He longed

to be on his land—tending his cattle, mending fences, tinkering in his vegetable garden or carving something out of wood.

Pacing, his cane thwacking the floor, Will shook his head. "It's not right to order them to keep quiet. However, if we stress how important it is that we cast our town in the best possible light, they'll understand the need for restraint."

Daniel slapped his knees and stood. "Now that that's settled, we can turn to the next order of business. Is Constance willing to see Pete Lyle again?"

Noah's mood soured. "You'll have to ask her. From what little I gleaned, she's not interested in him."

"Okay." Removing a folded paper from his pocket, he borrowed a pencil from the desk and marked a line through Pete's name.

"You carry that everywhere you go?"

Noah scowled at the list of men who had a chance of winning the one woman who'd breached his defenses and made him care about more than himself.

"I have to," he exclaimed. "You wouldn't believe how many times a day I'm approached by fellows wanting to know who's next in line. It's exhausting." He pointed the pencil at him. "Unless you'd care to take over the task?"

"No thanks." Standing, he edged away. This was difficult enough without having to orchestrate her outings.

"Looks like Colton Bailey's day is about to get better." Refolding the paper, he headed for the door. "I'm going to deliver the happy news. Tell Constance to expect a visit from him."

Noah was quiet as his friends let themselves out. For the sake of his sanity, he hoped she fell for Bailey on the first try. They could have a quick wedding. He'd be free of her then, both her and the girls. They'd be Bailey's responsibility, not his.

Goodbye, trouble. Hello, solitude.

Chapter Fifteen

Weddings weren't supposed to be sad. This one wasn't. The bride and groom were ecstatic, almost giddy with joy as they repeated their vows. When Hannah's father, Reverend Taggart, proclaimed them husband and wife, James Johnson swooped in to claim a kiss. Hannah blushed scarlet, her sweet smile poignant and tear-inducing.

Hannah Taggart Johnson had a healthy baby, an adoring husband and a new business venture. Grace hoped she recognized and cherished those blessings. Not everyone was so fortunate.

She hated feeling sorry for herself on a day like today, but Grace couldn't help the sorrow rendering her heart sore and heavy. Not so long ago, she'd boarded a train, uncaring who was waiting at her journey's end. The name Noah Burgess had meant nothing to her. The prospect of a loveless marriage hadn't bothered her, so intent had she been on escaping the city and her brother-in-law, and procuring a husband who could provide protection.

She risked a glance at the handsome, stoic man seated beside her. Noah in his cowboy gear was enough to make her breathless, but gazing upon him now, in a tailored navy suit that hugged his muscular build and complemented his fair hair and sun-bronzed skin, had her struggling with foolish yearnings.

Spending time with the man described in Will's letter had skewed her outlook. He'd gone from being a vague concept to a flesh-and-blood human being. Noah had turned out to be a man of contrasts...strong and implacable on the outside, hurting and lonely on the inside...a tough, hardworking, honorable lawman who held her hair while she was sick, read to her beneath the moonlight, tended to two little girls' needs without complaint. She wasn't thinking practical thoughts anymore. Time and distance had dimmed her worry about Frank, making way for more fanciful ideals. A marriage for protection's sake wasn't enough anymore.

As Hannah and James walked the grassy aisle hand in hand, eager to embark on their life together, Grace acknowledged she wanted love. She wanted affection. And she wanted it with Noah.

Bowing her head, she closed her eyes for a brief moment as the truth suffused her with the wonder of first love. Here she was, a twenty-six-year-old widow with children, discovering authentic love for the first time in her life. What she was feeling wasn't grounded in false reality. Unlike Ambrose, Noah hadn't tried to impress her or woo her with flashy gifts. Quite the opposite. He'd repeatedly warned her away, listing his weaknesses. Told her point-blank he didn't want her.

"Constance? Time for refreshments and cake."

His low, rich baritone washed over her, and she relived those moments in his cabin when she'd dared explore his scars.

It's Grace. Not Constance.

Opening her eyes, she saw that the guests were leaving the chairs set up in Daniel and Leah's garden and meandering to the multiple tables on loan from the hotel, all of them covered in white tablecloths and set with rose-emblazoned china dishes. Three tables beneath the trees held trays of sumptuous meats and vegetables. The newlyweds were already stationed behind the three-tiered cake festooned with fresh berries, seemingly lost in a world all their own. Nearby, Tomasina held a sleeping Ava in her arms, swaying slightly while Will leaned in to caress the infant's cheek.

The aspiring politician and rodeo star made a striking picture, his dark hair and debonair good looks combined with her lush figure and flame-red curls. Grace wondered if Will and Tomasina would start a family soon like Daniel and Leah.

Both of Noah's friends had found true, abiding love with their spouses. Did that make him feel left out?

As he escorted her without speaking to the food tables, she sensed tension in him, like a bowstring drawn tight and primed to fire. Was it the wedding having this effect on him? His sheriff's duties troubling him? Or something else entirely?

He led her to his friends, and she missed the reassuring heat of his hand on her back as soon as he removed it.

Tomasina smiled and winked. "You look exceptional today, Constance. That shade of ice blue is lovely on you. Don't you agree, Noah?"

Will hid a smile by dipping his head. Noah gave a clipped nod, his gaze scanning the milling wedding guests. "Constance always looks beautiful."

Grace's tummy did a somersault. Sure, he'd been forced into complimenting her, but there was an inflection in his voice that hinted at sincerity.

Daniel and Leah strolled up and, after a few words of greeting, the men separated themselves and went to speak to Gideon Kendricks, who was standing close to Pippa on the house's rear porch. Pippa went up on tiptoes to inspect a bruise on his cheek, one he must've garnered in the same brawl Noah had gotten injured in. He'd related how, once again, the train rep had pitched in to help without prompting. She could tell Noah highly respected the man.

"Jane and Abigail look as pretty as a picture today in their matching pink dresses," Leah said.

Grace automatically scanned the property for them, finding them beside the cake table, where they watched the newlywed couple and chatted with another little girl their age from an outlying ranch.

"Would you believe Noah fixed their hair?"

Tomasina gaped. "I can't picture that!"

Leah's fine eyebrows lifted an inch. "I didn't realize he knew how."

"He has three younger sisters," Grace explained. "I'd intended to do their customary curls, but they insisted they wanted braids, and they wanted Noah to do it."

"The three of you have been good for him." Still cradling the baby close to her body, the redhead gazed at the men with furrowed brow. "I wish he'd cease being stubborn and admit Will did the right thing bringing you here."

Leah nodded and fiddled with her dragonfly brooch. "He barely spoke to me when I first arrived. Gradually, he relaxed his guard." She touched Grace's sleeve. "Do you have a moment? I'd love to show you what Noah made for the baby."

Grace agreed, her curiosity piqued. On their way to the house, the reverend waylaid them and took his granddaughter from Tomasina, a proud grin on his face. Inside the quiet home, their footfalls seemed loud as they climbed the grand staircase and followed Leah along the hall and into the sunny nursery.

"Isn't it delightful?" Leah went straight for the dresser and a hand-carved ark complete with painted animal pairs. She picked up an elephant and lifted it for them to inspect.

"He's incredibly talented. I can't imagine how long it took for him to do all this."

Grace ran her fingers along the ark's top, amazed at his workmanship, which rivaled the toys she'd seen in Chicago shops.

"He certainly is," she murmured, a dart of wistfulness burrowing into her heart.

It wasn't difficult to picture him bent over a tiny animal sculpture, paintbrush in hand, his eyes squinting at the corners as he worked. She would very much like to see his process from start to finish. Did he sketch drawings first or create from mental images? If only he'd felt comfortable enough to share this private part of himself.

He doesn't love you, Grace. Even if he did have feelings for you, they'd be based on a lie.

Overwhelming sadness pressed in on her, dark and oppressive, out of place on this happy occasion and in this room lovingly decorated by excited parents awaiting their new family member. Carefully replacing a carved lion, she averted her face.

"I, ah, should go and check on the girls. Thank you for showing me."

The other women murmured soft goodbyes, lagging behind as she hurried down the stairs and out the front door in an effort to avoid seeing Noah. He'd guess something was wrong and question her. She wasn't sure she wouldn't blurt out everything. Her fake identity. Her fear of Frank. Her love for Noah.

She couldn't do that. Couldn't bear to see the disgust in his eyes. Her lies aside, he'd likely feel sorry for her if she confessed her true feelings. Just the other day, he'd informed her of another suitor who'd be coming around, his manner offhand. Like it didn't gut him to think of her with another man.

Circling the house, she kept to the edge of the crowd and headed for the secluded wooded area, in search of refuge.

Where was she?

Noah had been on edge since before the wedding ceremony had commenced. The single men in attendance, particularly James Johnson's cowboy buddies, had been ogling Constance in a way that made his blood boil.

He'd kept his attention on the house's back door, expecting her to emerge any minute. When Leah and Tomasina finally rejoined the party, and she wasn't with them, he stalked over.

"Where's Constance?"

Tomasina arched a brow at his abrupt manner.

Leah looked confused. "She should be out here. She came out about fifteen minutes ago."

Pivoting, he searched the grounds for a glimpse of her ice-blue dress and dark hair, frustrated when he couldn't see her. "She's not here."

"Maybe she's off on a secret rendezvous with a dashing cowboy," Tomasina suggested with a mischievous grin.

"That's not funny," he fumed.

"You do realize you're acting like a jealous husband, right?" she responded.

Clenching his fists, his gaze left hers to scour the woods. "I'm going to look for her. Will you keep an eye on the twins?"

Leah and Tomasina shared knowing smiles. "Of course, Noah."

Uncaring what they thought or wrongly assumed, he told himself it wasn't jealousy spurring his behavior. It was simple concern.

Stalking through the thicket like an angry bear, the noise of the celebration lessened and crickets' chirping filled his ears. He caught a flash of color off to his right the same instant he became aware of male laughter.

Fire ignited his blood. Constance stood with her back to a large oak, surrounded by three spit-shined cowboys. The foursome jerked their heads up at his abrupt arrival in the flower-dotted meadow. The surprise on Constance's face disappeared, her features shuttering as her gaze lowered to the grass. Annoyance flushed his system. He couldn't tell what she was thinking, whether she welcomed his intrusion or resented it.

"Sheriff Burgess, are you lost?" one particularly stupid cowboy drawled.

The second one laughed and actually stepped closer to Constance.

Bad decision.

His movements deliberate, he made a show of resting his hand on his weapon. Because of the no-gun policy within the town's limits, he and his deputies were the only ones armed. The men lost their sense of humor really quick.

"I'm not lost." He matched their lazy drawl, easy to do for someone who hailed from Virginia. "But you three are. Party's that way." He jerked a thumb over his shoulder.

Looking exasperated, they reluctantly trudged off, grumbling among themselves.

Only when he was certain they were gone did he approach Constance, who at long last lifted her gaze to his. Her beauty socked him in the gut, though her impish features were twisted in confusion.

You're mine. The words nearly left his lips.

"What were you thinking?" he demanded instead. "Coming out here with those three?"

Pressing into the trunk, she raised her chin. "I didn't come out here with them. I was seeking a moment of privacy. They happened upon me and stopped to chat. Why are you so angry?"

Noah rested his palm on the rough bark beside her head and leaned in so that very little air remained between them. Her lips parted, and a puff of breath fanned his nose. Unchecked longing turned her eyes dark amber. Longing. For *him*.

Shock pounded at his temples. Constance hadn't ever been disgusted by his scars, but the knowledge that she was attracted to him made his world go sideways.

Unable to stop himself, he skimmed his fingertips along her cheekbone and the curve of her cheek, glorying in the creamy texture.

"You don't want a cowboy, city girl," he managed in a gruff voice.

Her eyes were huge, the pupils tiny black points. "Why not?"

"Because they're not looking for commitment. They're here for fun. The temporary kind."

Her slender neck worked as she swallowed. He wrapped a stray lock of her hair around his finger, wishing things were different, wishing she truly could be his.

This is madness, Burgess.

Constance's hands fluttered up to bury in his suit's lapels. "Noah?"

His elbow bent as he rested even more weight against the tree, bringing their faces together, their lips almost touching. "What is it, city girl?"

"Kiss me?"

Noah didn't wait for her to ask a second time. He brushed his mouth across hers, emotion drowning him as she responded with breathless enthusiasm, holding nothing back. He cradled her face. She shifted so that his weight supported her, transferring her hands from his suit jacket to his hair, her fingers exploring the short strands.

Noah lost himself in the sensations her caresses wrought, this connection with Constance making him think crazy thoughts, filling him with reckless dreams that featured her as his wife. She would be his. He would be hers. They could spend a lifetime getting to know each other, loving each other.

His mind recoiled at the word *love*. No way did he love Constance.

Hateful logic rushed in, and he savored one last kiss of her sweet mouth before lifting his head and gently putting her from him.

"Noah?" Her face crumpled, her hands reaching for him, the gaudy rings flashing. "What's wrong?"

"I don't think Colton Bailey would approve of me kissing you." His voice was thick and raspy. He turned his back.

"I don't understand." She laid a hand on his arm. "He has nothing to do with us."

He sidestepped, forcing her hand to fall away, his lungs constricted with regret. "There is no us."

Her sharp inhale punctuated the silence.

"Forgive me," he murmured, desperate to get away before he took her in his arms again.

"Oh, here you are…" Pippa appeared in the clearing, stopping short when she took in their expressions. "I didn't mean to intrude. Tomasina and Leah were looking for you, Constance, so I volunteered to help. The girls wanted cake and weren't sure if they were allowed to have any."

He schooled his features. "Pippa, would you mind returning to the party with her? I've got an errand I forgot to tend to."

She nodded uncertainly. "Sure."

Half turning to address Constance, he didn't lift his gaze above her shoulder. "If I don't return before you're ready to leave, either Will or Daniel will take you home."

Without waiting for her response, he strode on ahead, skirting the house and heading for town.

Chapter Sixteen

When the refreshment tables became visible through the leafy branches, Pippa paused midstride and, turning toward Grace, placed a beseeching hand on her arm. "Are you okay?"

Unwilling to add another lie on the pile she'd already constructed, she met the other woman's gaze and opted for the truth. "No, Pippa. I'm not."

The actress studied her with those lively hazel eyes, a pleat between her ginger-hued brows. Grace knew she wouldn't have to wait long for her opinion. They'd spent a pleasant afternoon together earlier in the week, enjoying pastries and tea at the bakery while the girls ate and played quietly at another table, after which she'd given them a tour of the opera house. Pippa had respected Grace's decision not to let the girls perform. Nor had she pressed her for information about her life in Chicago. While she felt they were on the way to being friends, she couldn't ever be her true self, not when she had to keep up this deception.

"There's something between you and the sheriff, isn't there?"

"I care for him." It felt wonderful to admit her private feelings to someone. "The problem is he doesn't feel the same."

Pippa heaved a deep sigh, the purple feather dangling from her hat sweeping low. "Why must some men insist on making our lives difficult? For what it's worth, I don't get the impression he doesn't care. He's not an easy man to read, however. Still waters run deep, and all that." She fluttered her fingers.

Grace twisted the heavy ruby ring on her first finger, hating what these jewels represented—not tokens of affection from a husband who adored her but meaningless objects intended to flaunt the Longstreet wealth—and wished she could forget them in a drawer somewhere to collect dust. But they'd provide instant funds if she and the girls ever had to leave town in a rush.

"You came here on the first bride train. Have you not met anyone you can see yourself marrying?"

"There are plenty of nice gentlemen in Cowboy Creek," Pippa said. "Of course I'd fancy the one who isn't planning on sticking around."

"Gideon."

"Yes."

Grace gave her a commiserating look. "Is there a chance he'll change his mind?"

"He loves his job. All he talks about is how grand his life is, the adventures he gets to experience traveling the nation. There's no possibility of him staying in a boring Kansas boomtown."

"I wouldn't call Cowboy Creek boring. Perhaps he's testing you, gauging your reaction, before working up the courage to ask you to join him."

"I don't know." Her usual confidence slipped, allowing Grace a glimpse of vulnerability. Pippa truly cared for Gideon, that much was obvious.

Hitching up her purple-and-black-striped skirts, Pippa squared her shoulders. "Come. Let's forget about our irksome gentlemen and take advantage of the celebration."

Grace's smile was halfhearted, her mind consumed with Noah's kiss, the joy his embrace had evoked and the sorrow following his heartbreaking rejection.

As soon as they left the tree line, a man with a stocky build, wavy brown hair and kind brown eyes approached with his hat in his hands. He possessed boyish good looks and a hesitant manner.

"Mrs. Miller?"

Her stomach tightened. "Yes?"

"I'm Colton Bailey. Sheriff Burgess was supposed to introduce us today. Guess he forgot." Sticking out his hand, he shook hers as if sealing a deal with a fellow rancher. "Would you like to accompany me on a picnic tomorrow after services?"

Grace considered postponing before Noah's parting words reminded her the kiss didn't mean anything to him. She had an obligation to find a replacement husband as soon as possible. Because he'd rebuffed her. Over and over again. Pain arrowed through her.

"Why don't you join us for Sunday lunch out at the ranch?" she offered on the spur of the moment, savoring the thought of Noah's reaction.

Colton's expression faltered. "You don't think the sheriff will mind?"

Oh, he'll mind, all right. "He doesn't have to join us."

He nodded. "Then I accept. Thank you kindly, Mrs. Miller."

"Please, call me Constance."

Pippa, who'd been silent during the exchange, shot her a surprised sideways glance.

Colton smiled. He had a nice smile. He struck her as young, but apparently he was old enough to have his own spread and old enough to be searching for a wife.

"Good day, Constance."

After he'd swaggered away, Pippa's laugh was low. "I'd like to be a fly on the wall of the sheriff's cabin tomorrow."

Grace shrugged, striving for a nonchalance she didn't feel. "Noah doesn't want to marry me. In fact, he's helping Will and Daniel in this scheme to marry me off to someone else. Courting potential suitors is what I'm expected to do. If he doesn't like it, he shouldn't have insisted I stay at the ranch."

Pippa grinned. "I'll expect a full report on Monday."

Noah pondered his options with careful consideration. He could throw Colton Bailey out of his house and order him off his property over threat of bodily harm. He could toss Constance over his shoulder, cart her outside and demand to know why she thought inviting another man to eat at his table—a man clearly besotted with her—was a good idea. Especially considering Noah had held her in his arms *just yesterday*.

Less than twenty-four hours ago, he'd made a naive mistake, one he somehow couldn't regret. He'd take those precious moments with him to the grave.

Grinding his back teeth together, he sliced into the roast on his plate with too much force, the resulting screech causing everyone at the table to cease their conversation and stare. Meeting Constance's inscrutable gaze, he set his utensils aside and focused on getting his coffee down without choking.

She'd done this to goad him. If her notable unease was anything to go by, she regretted it as much as Noah. Her laughter in response to Bailey's jokes was forced, her speech stilted as she answered his questions.

Jane had been telling him about the fun things she liked to do in Chicago. Unaware of the adults' tension, she gushed, "My second cousin played dolls with me. She sewed dresses and bonnets for them out of scrap material."

Bailey's smile was authentic. He didn't seem to mind the girls' chatter. *Good for him*, Noah thought sourly.

"That was thoughtful of her. What's her name?"

"Oh, um…" What could only be described as a guilty air came over her. From beneath lowered lashes, she shot her mother a questioning glance. "I—"

"The girls really miss their family." Constance rushed to intervene, her color heightened. "Do you have family close by, Colton?"

Something wasn't right. Noah studied the three females. Jane kept her gaze downcast, as if she'd blundered. Abigail gaped at her sister. Constance was clearly flustered. But why? Was there some secret family scandal involving her cousin?

The moment passed, and eventually the topic of favorite hobbies came up. When Bailey mentioned he liked to fish, Jane brightened. "Would you teach me how?"

"Me, too!" Abigail bounced in her seat.

Noah scowled. If anyone was going to teach the twins how to fish, it was going to be him. Why they'd asked a man they'd just met instead of him he couldn't figure. He was pretty sure Colton Bailey had never fixed little girls' hair before.

"I'll show you, girls." Scraping his chair back, he carried his half-full plate to the counter. "In fact, why don't we head out to the stream now and give your ma and Mr. Bailey a few moments alone?"

The suggestion delighted the twins. Bailey dipped his head, his attention on his plate, while Constance's lips pressed into a line of displeasure.

"That's not necessary," she said, starting to get up.

Noah aimed a false smile at her. "I don't mind. You and your beau take your time over coffee and dessert. No need to rush."

His mouth felt full of nails at Bailey's obvious approval of that idea.

Angry as a hornet whose nest had been disturbed, he

stalked toward the door. "Jane. Abigail. I'll be in the barn fetching the poles. Meet me at the stream."

"Yes, sir!"

Resting on the porch, Wolf hopped up and followed him across the yard and into the barn. Rummaging through his tool room, he said over his shoulder, "This is a disaster, Wolf. A nightmare."

The wolf dog stood watching him, his tail wagging, looking almost as if he was smiling.

"There's nothing funny about this, you know."

If only he could wake up and find this messy situation was just a dream. That he'd returned from the fruitless search for the Murdoch gang to an empty cabin. That his friends had actually listened and heeded his objections.

He pinched the bridge of his nose trying to ward off a headache.

But then, he wouldn't have met Constance. Or the girls. He wouldn't have had anyone to read to. Or share delicious meals with. He wouldn't have pictures drawn specifically for him. He wouldn't feel connected or wanted or needed. And he had to be honest, it felt amazing to be those things to the widow and her daughters. Sure, the town needed him to do a job, but that was different. This thing with Constance, Jane and Abigail, it was *personal*.

He was beginning to dread the day they would leave.

Emerging into the steady sunshine, he joined the girls on the bank and showed them how to dig for worms. Abigail surprised him. The worms didn't seem to bother her. Jane was more squeamish, her freckled nose wrinkling as she held one away from her body.

He found himself fighting a grin. Which was shocking, considering his brain persisted in conjuring images of Constance and Bailey together inside.

When they at long last had their lines in the water, Noah sank against the tree and rested his pole against his bent leg. Wasn't difficult to picture endless lazy Sundays just like this one, the mint-scented breeze lifting his hair and cooling his skin, the kids' giggles of delight mixing with the birds' song above their heads. He could picture more children. His and Constance's. Maybe a little boy to tease his older sisters, one with dark hair and honey-colored eyes and impish features like his ma. Or would he have blond hair and blue eyes like him?

Longing for the impossible lodged in his chest as sorrow weighed his heart.

He'd made his decision. Pushed her away repeatedly. She deserved a man like Colton Bailey. A man whose soul hadn't been darkened by past horrors.

Jane lifted her gaze from the water. "Where's your ma and pa, Mr. Noah?"

"And your sisters?" Abigail added. "The ones whose hair you said you fixed."

Noah didn't like discussing his family because it brought him grief and remorse. He couldn't, however, snub their innocent curiosity.

"They're in Virginia."

At least, he thought they were. He couldn't say for sure. Constance's rebuke fresh in his mind, he decided then and there to write to his parents. He owed them that much.

"I ain't no thief!"

Noah kept a firm hold on the cowboy's arm, propelling him away from Drover's Place, where the drovers who didn't camp on the town's outskirts paid for a real bed and a solid roof over their heads.

"I have proof that says otherwise."

"I don't know how those wallets wound up in my room, honest. You've got the wrong man, Sheriff."

"Well, you see, your trail boss told me you've been accused of stealing before. Said he warned you to keep your hands clean this trip or you'd be finished. Should've listened."

At the corner of Second and Eden, mere steps from the jail, Deputy Hanley rushed up, hat waving in the air. "Sheriff, I've been lookin' all over for you," he panted. "Mr. Canfield wants you to come to his house right away. The county seat rep arrived on the one-o'clock train."

He was a day early. Noah thrust the thief toward Hanley. "Lock him up. I'll be round to do a report later today."

Hanley looked the man up and down. "Yes, sir."

After waiting until the two men were inside the jail, Noah continued up the street and turned left on Third. Will's house was almost complete. There weren't as many workers milling on the property today because the brick facade was nearly done. The couple was surely impatient for peace and quiet.

Tomasina answered his summons, grinning like a cat with a big bowl of cream. "Well, good afternoon, Noah. How was your Sunday? I heard you had a gentleman caller."

He glared at her, knowing she wouldn't be cowed. "*I* didn't have a caller. Where'd you hear that, anyway?"

"Will told me." Stepping back in a sweep of green skirts, she waved him inside the grand entryway.

He slapped his Stetson on the side table, careful not to disturb the vase of fresh-picked flowers. "And who told him?"

"I believe Pippa told Leah, who in turn told Daniel. And you know Will and Daniel share most everything."

Boldly linking her arm with his, she led him in the direction of the parlor. "Know what I think?"

"You're going to tell me whether I want to know or not."

Her grin grew even wider, if that were possible. "I think you should give in to your friends' wishes and marry the woman. You'll have meals on your table, holes in your socks mended and, best of all, you won't have to come home to a silent house."

Noah had no trite response for her because he'd already considered these things. Fortunately, she took pity on him, letting him stew over her comments. In the parlor's wide entry, she slipped free to go to her husband's side. Will stood to welcome him, as did Daniel and Gideon Kendricks. A distinguished gentleman with wiry gray hair and a beard occupying one of two wingback chairs gained his feet while Will made the introductions.

"Gregory McAllister, this is the man we told you about, Noah Burgess. He's one of the main reasons we're here today. Without him, Cowboy Creek wouldn't have earned a place on the map."

Noah shook the man's smooth, age-spotted hand. "Pleasure to meet you, sir. And I can't take all the credit. These two are the ones with the big dreams. I just happened to be here from the outset."

"A pleasure."

When they were seated again, Gideon relaxed into the sofa cushions, one long leg propped over the other. "My employer, the Union Pacific, is very pleased with how the town has grown and prospered. We chose Cowboy Creek because we believed it to be the best spot for a railroad terminus in this part of Kansas. We haven't been disappointed."

Mr. McAllister wore a stern expression. Gideon's recommendation didn't appear to impress him. "That's good to hear, Mr. Kendricks." To Daniel, he said, "On my way from the station, I saw that the stockyards were full of longhorn cattle. How are your local ranchers handling their presence?"

"A couple of issues have arisen, occasional disputes and such, but we resolved them to all parties' satisfaction. It's to be expected when you've got a fluctuating population."

Noah could see the sudden tension in his friend's shoulders. Did McAllister? Daniel didn't plan on mentioning the rancher's poisoned cattle unless asked directly. That they didn't know who was responsible or why they'd done it wouldn't reflect well on their leadership abilities.

"I see." Adjusting the rims of his spectacles, he peered at Will. "I'd like to see the town proper and speak to some of the residents. I'd also like to confer with the trail boss of this cattle drive and a couple of his drovers to discover their point of view."

"Certainly." Will nodded, his demeanor more relaxed than Daniel's. "As soon as we have coffee and refreshments, we'll take you on a tour. We've planned a gathering for tomorrow evening so that you can mingle with the locals."

"I'll make sure the drovers are represented," Daniel added.

"I look forward to it."

Noah, who'd remained standing by an unoccupied cushioned chair, took the opportunity to welcome the man again and make his escape.

"I'll see you at the gathering tomorrow," he said. "I've got to get back to the jail."

Tomasina brought a tray of tea cakes. "Don't you want to stay for coffee?"

He lifted a hand. "No, thanks. Another time."

Mr. McAllister's gaze sharpened. "You have pressing business, Sheriff Burgess?"

"Just some papers to fill out."

Not willing to linger, he bid everyone goodbye and left before the man could question him further. He was uncomfortable with this entire situation. While they weren't required to divulge every single tidbit of information about the town, deliberately hiding the recent troubles—unsolved, serious troubles that included a bank robbery and the murder of the previous sheriff—struck him as deceptive. He had plenty of faults, but deceit wasn't one of them. His parents had insisted on honesty, had taught him and his sisters to tell the truth from the time they were old enough to understand.

He knew Will and Daniel shared his sentiments.

Passing the saddle shop, he encountered Colton Bailey, who lit up like a bonfire when their gazes met.

"Just the man I wanted to see," he said, grinning. "I wanted to thank you for allowing me to call on Constance. It was a pleasant afternoon."

For you maybe. "No problem." He started to walk on, but Bailey continued speaking.

"I was wondering if you'd mind watching the girls tomorrow night so Constance and I can go out alone. I'd like to treat her to dinner at the hotel."

"She's busy tomorrow night." He seized on the excuse, only just now deciding to ask if she'd accompany him to the gathering at Will and Tomasina's. "Besides, you'll have to ask her if she's inclined to go first."

"Oh, I already have." His dark eyes danced merrily. "She accepted my invitation."

Noah's nails bit into his palms. She must fancy Bailey then. Especially seeing as how she had declined to see Pete Lyle a second time.

"Unless something comes up, I'm free Thursday evening."

Colton slapped his hat against his leg. "Wonderful! Thursday it is. I have a feeling, Sheriff, that I may be taking her off your hands really soon."

The familiar dread weighed down his feet. "Not just her, Bailey. Are you prepared to be a father to those girls?"

He kicked up a shoulder. "I like the girls. They're sweet. Cute as a button, too."

"Raising kids is hard work," he snapped.

He wasn't a father, but in the brief time he'd spent with Jane and Abigail, he'd seen it was a daunting task. Frustrating at times. Yet the rewards couldn't be underestimated.

Smiles. Hugs. That feeling of wonder and accomplishment when a child mastered a new challenge.

"I'm a quick learner." His positive manner didn't falter. "Look, I have an order to pick up and a sick cow to get back to. See you Thursday, Sheriff."

Noah watched him leave with the knowledge that, in his eyes, no one would ever be good enough for Constance.

Chapter Seventeen

Some problems couldn't be improved or forgotten by indulging in sugary confections. Grace sank the fork's prongs into the glossy white glaze and springy carrot cake, her emotions a whirlwind of discontent. She hoped Pippa, who'd invited her and the girls to the bakery once again, wouldn't probe. As an actress and apt observer of human behavior, the other woman would notice her mood. Whether or not she'd comment on it remained to be seen.

Decked out in a resplendent white dress with tiny pink polka dots and an ostentatious hat angled atop her upswept hair, she could've stepped from the pages of a storybook. For this reason alone, Jane and Abigail were awed by Pippa Neely.

Her own outfit of head-to-toe charcoal and black was made more stark in comparison. After yesterday's disaster of juggling Colton and Noah, the depressing colors suited her.

"Perhaps we should meet here every week," Pippa said now, savoring her dessert one slow bite at a time. "The girls would like that, wouldn't they?"

Grace watched them at their table beside the window, their dolls in their laps as they nibbled on saucer-size cookies. They looked like summertime in their matching yellow dresses with white smocks.

"I'm not sure my future husband will allow that."

The prospect of being at the mercy the whims of another man like Ambrose stirred up fresh worries. What if she made the wrong choice a second time? What if she was blinded by first impressions again?

Pippa's pretty face scrunched dramatically. "I hadn't thought of that. I'm so accustomed to doing what I want, when I want."

"Not all men are dictatorial," she felt obliged to point out. "If there's love and respect between spouses, they can find a balance between each person's needs and that of the household."

Grace hadn't experienced it for herself, but she'd seen it in others' marriages. Even here in Cowboy Creek. Noah's friends had unions built on those foundations.

The thought of him and her newfound feelings made it difficult to eat. Putting her fork down, she cradled the warm china cup and inhaled the tea's fruity aroma.

He hadn't been the least bit pleased to have to put up with Colton's presence. Every time he'd looked at her across the table, the accusation in his eyes had burned a cold tundra blue, along with questions she wasn't sure he realized were there. Like her, had he relived their embrace countless times? Yearned to repeat it?

She'd tried to put it from her mind and give Colton a fair shot. But she kept wishing his eyes were pale, not dark, and that his hair was lighter and his mouth fuller, more sculpted.

"How did Mr. Bailey's visit go?" Pippa asked in quiet tones since several of the bakery's tables were occupied. Grace appreciated her discretion.

"My acting abilities were an abysmal failure, I'm afraid. However, Colton didn't let on that he noticed. He was eager to please. Kind. Patient with the girls. He strikes me as a genuinely nice man."

"What you're saying is that he's a safe choice."

"I don't have the luxury of time, Pippa. Once I've decided, there'll be no going back."

Pippa's gaze slid to the girls. "I understand your concern." Leaning forward, she dropped her voice. "What about the sheriff? Why not tell him how you feel? Maybe you're wrong about him."

"No." Her grip on the cup tightened. "I'm not wrong."

The entrance door opened. Pippa was seated with a clear view, and her eyes flared and lips parted a second before she adopted a careless expression. Steady footsteps carried Gideon Kendricks to their table.

"Good afternoon, ladies." He lowered his tall frame into the seat beside Pippa without waiting for an invitation. Leaning so that their shoulders touched, he swiped a finger through her cake's frosting and tasted it. "Mmm. That is delicious. Do I detect a hint of cinnamon?"

Pippa's glare could've melted the icing off all the cakes in the display. "What do you think you're doing?"

The other patrons had ceased their conversations and were gazing at their table with interest. The train rep and the actress had been engaging in flirtatious behavior for weeks, according to overheard snippets from Hannah and James's wedding.

"Don't be angry, Pippa. I was simply testing your dessert to see if I might like one for myself."

Twin flags of color bloomed in Pippa's cheeks. Grace found she couldn't look away. The spark of attraction was undeniable between the two.

"You didn't try Constance's."

Gideon's gray gaze seemed reluctant to leave Pippa. He benefitted Grace with a lazy smile before returning his attention to the woman at his side. "I'm not about to tease Sheriff Burgess's lady."

Two tables over, Dora Edison and her mother gasped in unison. Whispers from other patrons followed. Grace fought the urge to slink under the table.

"Go away, Gideon," Pippa ordered coolly, very real distress gripping her features. "Your games have lost their appeal."

Looking properly chastised, Gideon said, "I apologize, Mrs. Miller. I didn't intend to involve you. Or offend you."

Grace nodded, busying herself with sipping her tea.

Clasping Pippa's hand in between his, he lost all humor. "No more teasing. Say you'll come with me tonight to Will and Tomasina's gathering."

She gazed deep into his eyes, seemingly weighing his sincerity. "I don't know if I should. You do recall the town bought my passage on the bride train. You're just passing through. To what end would I spend any more time with you?"

"Say yes and find out," he urged, caressing her hand.

Her ginger lashes swept down and, after long moments, she nodded. "Fine. I'll go."

His broad shoulders lost their tension. Grinning like a schoolboy, he said, "I'll pick you up at the boardinghouse at a quarter of six."

"You'll be on your best behavior?" She arched a brow.

"The best. You have my word." Then, landing a quick kiss on her cheek that left her gaping, he left the bakery.

Grace couldn't help but smile. Resident or no, the man was clearly besotted. "You do realize he didn't purchase anything."

Still gaping, Pippa recovered and, with a furtive glance around, shot her a questioning look.

"He didn't come in here for dessert, Pippa. He came in to see *you*."

Sinking against the chair back, she stared out the window. "Oh."

For the next half hour, they spoke of Pippa's true reasons for coming to Cowboy Creek, and it wasn't to snag a husband. Having grown up with overbearing, protective older brothers, she'd seen the journey West as an opportunity to be independent for the first time in her life. Sure, marriage was something she aspired to, someday. Just not right away. She wanted time to pursue her interests in theater and acting and, coming from an affluent family, she could afford to put off choosing a husband.

She hadn't counted on crossing paths with Gideon Kendricks. And certainly hadn't expected to develop feelings for someone so quickly. She worried how the town leaders would react if she did allow him to court her, considering they brought her here to marry a local.

Grace tried to give her sound counsel, all the while feeling like the fraud she was. She'd promised to pray about the matter when Noah entered the bakery. Pippa had already bid the girls goodbye and was on her way out.

"Afternoon, Sheriff."

"Pippa." His intent gaze took stock of their half-eaten confections before centering on Grace.

"See you around, Constance."

Grace lifted her hand in a halfhearted wave, conscious of the fact that their every move was being watched.

Noah gestured to the door. "Can I speak to you outside?"

His mood was as somber as hers, as it had been since the wedding and their forbidden kiss. How would she face him once she was wed to another man? How could she stomach seeing him, knowing her heart belonged to him, while pledged to respect, honor and obey another?

I can't do this, Lord Jesus. I have to tell him the truth. About Frank. About everything.

Leaving the girls to finish their tea, Grace preceded

Noah outside onto the crowded boardwalk. Sandwiched between the bank and the laundry, the street was full of customers.

With a light hand on her elbow, he steered her closer to the bakery's exterior. "Did you enjoy your time with Pippa?"

Her and Pippa's conversation fresh in her mind, she challenged him. "Why do you ask? Would you rather I be home tending your garden or preparing your supper?"

Noah stared at her, brows coming together in confusion. "You know I don't expect you to do those things. I've never asked you to, have I?"

"Tell me something. If I were your wife, would you mind my occasionally meeting friends?"

His expression went flat. "That's an irrelevant question."

"Just answer it, Noah."

Breathing deeply so that his chest visibly expanded, he probed the scars beneath his ear with his hand. "*If* you were my wife," he said gruffly, "I wouldn't mind you spending time with your friends, as long as it didn't interfere with Jane and Abigail's needs, and the household chores. Just as I wouldn't shirk my duties, I wouldn't want my wife to do so, either."

"I see." Of course he'd give a satisfying answer.

"What's this about, Constance?" He spread his hands wide.

"I was curious, that's all." Waiting until a trio of cowboys passed by, she said, "Why did you seek me out? Is there something you need?"

Considering her for several heartbeats, he then scanned the wagons and pedestrians instead of meeting her gaze. "Will's hosting a party to welcome the county seat representative tonight. I was wondering if you'd like to come."

Shocked, Grace wasn't sure she'd heard right. "You want me to go with you? To a party? Tonight?"

Fiddling with his shirt collar and smoothing his hair, he

shrugged. "I thought you might like to see Will and Tomasina's new house. I spoke to Hannah. If it's okay with you, she's agreed to care for Jane and Abigail."

She was tempted to ask him why, after repeatedly pushing her away, he'd request her company. But questions might lead to him rescinding his offer, and she desperately wanted one evening out with him. One night to pretend they could be together, that Noah cared about her enough to ignore his fears.

Smoothing her hands along her skirts, she said softly, "I'd like that."

"Good." He nodded, his face yet unsmiling. "Oh, I almost forgot..." Pulling an envelope from his pocket, he handed it to her. "You received a letter from someone in Chicago. The postmaster asked me to give it to you."

The letter wasn't addressed to her, of course. The name Constance Miller was scrawled in familiar script. She and her cousin had agreed contacting each other would be risky. Something must've happened.

Fingers trembling, she stuffed the letter into the reticule swinging from her wrist.

"From your family?" he prodded.

"Yes. My cousin."

"The one Jane always talks about?"

Grace's mouth was as dry as cotton. He'd clearly caught their blunder at the dinner table yesterday. So far, he hadn't questioned her. A blessing, because she wasn't convinced she'd be able to maintain her secrecy in the face of his interrogation. Any confession would have to wait until she'd heard Constance's message.

"That's the one."

"Want me to read it to you?"

"N-no," she rushed to reject his offer. "Jane will do it." At his doubtful expression, she tacked on, "She enjoys reading to me."

A breeze ruffled her hem. Above them, gray clouds stretched across the sky, threatening rain. "Noah, I should get the girls home. We do have a few chores to tend to before tonight."

"I'll get the wagon and take you home."

Home. Too bad it wasn't really. Not hers, anyway.

"Thank you, Noah. Soon I'll have to learn how to manage a wagon myself."

"Maybe I'll have time to teach you. If not, Bailey would be thrilled to have the honor."

Pivoting on his heel, he stalked toward the livery where he'd left the wagon earlier. She was too distracted by the unexpected letter to give much thought to the hint of jealousy in his voice. Going back inside the bakery, she told the girls to prepare to leave, dreading her one recourse. No one in this town could be allowed to see the contents of Constance's missive. Outside, she found a deserted bench and, drawing Jane and Abigail down beside her, unsealed the envelope. Handing the paper to Jane, she explained what she needed.

Constance,
Please be careful. The snake found me not long after you left, demanding answers. He was so very angry. I managed to put him off, but he's hired men to discover your whereabouts.

Stumbling over some of the words, Jane shot Grace a fearful look. Grace hated that she'd had to place this burden on her daughters. She gave Jane's hand a reassuring squeeze and indicated for her to continue.

I saw one of them in my neighborhood today seeking information and offering a reward. I'm afraid for you, cousin...

Her heart thudded against her ribs in a frightened cadence. Constance went on to say she'd agreed to a match in a Western town and would make contact again once she was settled. She didn't mention specifics.

"What will Uncle Frank do if he finds us?" Abigail whispered, her eyes huge.

"He's not going to, sweetheart."

But what if he did?

The letter was dated two weeks ago. Frank could have already ferreted out her location. Constance's neighbors didn't owe Grace their loyalty. They needed money. The sight of her and a pair of twin girls wouldn't have gone unnoticed. What if he was already on his way to Cowboy Creek?

Nausea welling up, Grace set her bonnet in place but had trouble tying the ribbons beneath her chin. She couldn't tell Noah now. She had to marry, and marry soon. Frank couldn't have her if she were already taken. Colton may be a few years younger, but he was a rancher accustomed to fending off varmints—animal or human. He'd fight to protect what was his.

Her brother-in-law was a horrible, selfish man. But he wasn't a murderer.

You can't be sure though, can you? You never dreamed he'd force his attentions on you, and yet look what happened.

By the time Noah arrived with the wagon, she'd managed to soothe the girls' fears. Her own weren't so easily contained, however, and all she could think was that she had better enjoy this one evening with Noah. Because it was all she'd ever have. After tonight, she had to cut him from her heart and accept the reality of a future with Colton Bailey.

Chapter Eighteen

Noah couldn't take his eyes off Constance.

The big city in her was on display, and he couldn't find it in him to complain. Her dress was a floaty creation of soft coral fabric, a hue that made her bare upper shoulders and slender arms gleam like alabaster. Candlelight from the chandelier and wall sconces created mahogany streaks in her lustrous brown hair. She'd arranged her heavy mane into an elegant twist and tucked tiny white blossoms into the mass. She was summer kissed with mystery, sophistication mixed with an earnestness that had him fighting to subdue his wayward heart.

Asking her to accompany him had been a rash decision, one spurred by immature jealousy. He didn't regret it. What he regretted was the way his heart leaped in his chest every time he looked at her. This was out of control. He never should've agreed to let her stay. Even temporarily.

A commotion at the living room entrance—a space that could easily house two of his cabins—finally drew his attention away from her. Tomasina guided Gideon and Pippa over to Mr. McAllister. As Gideon introduced Pippa, he said something that made her pinch his arm. He threw back his head and laughed.

Good for him, Noah thought. Gideon had decided she was worth pursuing, after all.

He hoped it ended well for them. Noah wouldn't wish the grief he was experiencing on anyone else. And just like that, he was back to watching Constance again.

Surrounded by ladies, she nodded and commented in all the right places, but he detected a rigidity in her, unease that had dogged her since that afternoon. On the ride out to the ranch, she'd been jumpy, constantly searching their surroundings. For what, he hadn't a clue.

She looked up from the untouched glass of lemonade in her hands, misery marking her features before being masked, hidden from everyone but him.

Pushing off the mantel, he set his own drink on the coffee table as he rounded one of several couches arranged in the narrow, high-ceilinged space.

The ladies' conversation trailed away at his approach. He touched a spot above her elbow. "May I speak to you for a minute?"

Startled, she affected a strained smile. "Certainly. Excuse me."

Keeping a light hand against her lower back, he ushered her through the dining room and busy kitchen, earning them surprised glances from the hired workers preparing refreshments. The heat and intriguing scents of spices gave way to moisture-heavy air on the rear veranda and the distinct hint of roses.

Stopping at the railing, she turned to him, her hands folded primly at her waist. "This is the second time you've done this today. Tongues are bound to wag."

"Let them."

"You don't mind if people speculate about us?"

"I'm used to it." The tightness of his jaw, neck and chest reminded him he'd skipped his usual application of honey and lavender.

Frowning, she let her gaze wander to the manicured flower beds along the grand house's foundation and the wooded grounds extending toward the church building, its steeple visible above the trees. The sun hung low on the horizon, pink and orange streaks mixing with blue sky. Fireflies blinked on and off in the shadows.

"I didn't have a chance to tell you how beautiful you are tonight. Not that you aren't beautiful every day, but that dress—" he made a circling motion "—and your hair…" The tips of his ears burned. He wasn't used to handing out compliments.

Inhaling sharply, she scrutinized his black suit and crisp white shirt. "And I didn't say how handsome you are all cleaned up and looking like a proper gentleman."

He stifled a disbelieving snort. The admiration warming her eyes couldn't be argued with.

"Constance…" Noah edged closer, lifted a hand as if to cup her face, only to drop it again. The ache to hold her in his arms was excruciating. "The real reason I asked you out here is because I know there's something bothering you, and I'd like to know what it is."

Her lips parted. "I don't know what you're talking about."

Gently taking her chin between his thumb and forefinger, he murmured, "You're lying, city girl."

"Noah—"

"Yesterday at lunch, you didn't want the girls to talk about your cousin. Your reaction when I gave you the letter and the fact you refused to read it in front of me tells me you're keeping secrets. What is it? Maybe I can help."

The color leached from her face, and she swayed. Alarm worked its way from the base of his spine. Supporting her arm, he led her to a wrought-iron bench. He sat beside her, close enough that her skirts spilled over his leg. "Tell me, Constance. You can trust me." Threading their fingers together, he held tight to her hand, attempting to infuse her cold skin with his own warmth.

"Y-you're right. I have been keeping a secret."

She stared straight ahead. Noah studied her profile, waiting for her to continue.

"My cousin has a problem." Her voice was higher than normal, threaded with fear. "There's a man who's obsessed with her. He's ruthless. He will stop at nothing to possess her, and I don't know what to do." Her fingers flexed in his. "What I mean is, I don't know how to advise her."

Disgust filled him. No man had the right to impose his will and desires on a woman. "Has she made her feelings clear?"

"Many times. He refused to listen. He went so far as to corner her alone and force himself on her several times..." A shudder racked her body. "Thankfully, she managed to fight him off."

"That's unacceptable, Constance. If this man has accosted her, he's bound to continue. He has no conscience. Has she gone to the authorities?"

Her laugh was harsh. Humorless. "That won't help."

Disengaging her hand, she rose and walked to the banister, gripping the newly painted wooden ledge with both hands. Her knuckles shone white. Noah followed and, standing facing her, rested a hip against it and folded his arms.

"Why not?"

"He's a powerful individual with influential friends. Even if someone believed her account, they wouldn't act."

Noah shook his head, frustrated he couldn't ease her worries. With hundreds of miles between the cousins, Constance must indeed feel helpless. No wonder she'd been on edge. They stood in silence for many minutes before he got an idea.

"Gideon Kendricks's aunt and uncle live in Chicago. I wonder if they'd be willing to reach out to her."

She stiffened. "How do you know that?"

"He mentioned it once. Why?"

"No reason." Touching her fingertips to her nape, she said, "Look, Noah, I shouldn't have involved you in my problems. I appreciate you listening, but there's nothing you can do."

He caught her arm as she turned to go. "Together we can think of something. Will and Daniel have connections. Gideon, too. We can—"

"No. Please." Her fingers dug into his biceps. "I don't want anyone else to know."

Confused, he said, "This man has acted abominably already. You admitted he's obsessed with her. Someone has to intervene before she gets hurt."

Footsteps punctuated by the click of a cane against the floor announced Will's arrival. "I apologize for intruding. Noah, we have a problem. D.B. showed up uninvited."

"That is a problem," he agreed.

Constance put distance between them. "Why?"

"As the newspaper editor, D.B. thinks everyone else's business is his business." Will's brows drew together. "He has a habit of prodding people. Stirring them up."

"Not what we want with the county seat representative here sizing up our town," Noah said.

"I can help."

Both men stared at her. "How?"

"Since I'm new here, I can distract the editor and use his tactics on him. Pester him with questions while you two occupy Mr. McAllister."

Will nodded, a slow grin lifting his lips. "Good idea. I'll ask Tomasina to take over when you're through with him."

She'd been terribly reckless. Foolish. Rash. Most of all, she'd been so very frightened and alone, her cousin's warning repeating itself in her head. Telling Noah, even in a roundabout way, had helped her regain a smidgen of equilibrium.

And what if he finds out you were talking about yourself, not your cousin? He won't thank you for deceiving him.

The newspaper editor shifted on the cushion, his impatient gaze once again seeking out Mr. McAllister. She wouldn't be able to hold him much longer. Waylaying him in the hallway a half hour ago, she'd guilted him into fetching her a lemonade and maneuvered him onto this out-of-the-way settee, far from the main activity.

"You mean you're not originally from Cowboy Creek?" She seized on this tidbit. "I had no idea. Where is Harper exactly?"

"Eighty miles east of here," he said absently, completely focused on the group by the door, which included Daniel, Leah, Will, Tomasina, Gideon and Noah. He plunked his empty glass on the carved walnut side table and made ready to stand.

"What brought you here?"

"If you'll excuse me, Mrs. Miller, I must cut our exchange short. I haven't yet had a chance to meet our newcomer."

He popped to his feet without awaiting her reply. Rudely leaving her there, he strode straight for his quarry. Pippa's path intersected his. Appearing to trip, she fell into D.B., the contents of her glass and plate upending on his front.

"Oh my!" she exclaimed, quickly righting herself. "I am so sorry, Mr. Burrows. Look at what my clumsiness has done!"

The trail boss and his drovers elbowed each other, snickering behind their hands as the editor scowled down at his soiled suit. Gideon watched her performance with appreciation. Noah looked ill at ease.

Someone supplied Pippa with a napkin. She dabbed at the blobs of meringue sticking to his suit jacket. Scowling deeply, D.B. swatted at her attempts, which were only making it worse.

"Stop. That's not necessary."

Will and Tomasina joined them.

"Come upstairs, D.B.," Will urged. "I've got a change of clothes you can borrow."

Tomasina smiled and nodded in agreement. "Yes, come with us. I'm sure that wet shirt can't be comfortable."

When the three had disappeared upstairs, conversation resumed and Noah made his way to her side. She admired his confident stride, the soldier-like efficiency of his movements. He looked especially handsome in his three-piece suit, the midnight-black material a striking contrast to his fair hair and eyes.

"Would you mind if we cut our evening short?"

She would've minded if they'd been alone, perhaps strolling in the twilight and chatting about inconsequential matters. Instead, they'd spent much of their time apart, he with his friends and she occupying a troublesome editor.

"Not at all."

Her spirits were low as they bid everyone goodbye and started on their way to pick up the girls. She'd hoped—foolishly—to experience one more kiss from Noah before she had to become serious about Colton. A few more priceless moments in his arms to treasure for a little while.

Once she committed to Colton, she wouldn't be able to think about Noah. She must be faithful not only in deed but in her thoughts as well, no matter how difficult it proved to be.

Hannah and James had a small house on the other side of town. As the weather had been pleasant, they'd parked the wagon and walked to Will's. While she'd been chatting up D.B., fat clouds had rolled in, their broad undersides a deep gray hue. The wind had kicked up as well, tugging at her skirts and hairpins.

Noah studied the low skies that blocked the remaining light. His black hat, the one he reserved for Sunday services, flew off behind him. Waiting as he dashed to retrieve it, she peeled strands of hair from her lips.

"Didn't see this coming," he remarked, his hand on her middle back, urging her onward.

Just as I didn't see my feelings for you until it was too late, she thought, relishing his protective touch.

"We may have to wait a little while at Hannah's before heading out to the ranch," he said. "Don't wanna get caught in a storm with the girls."

"They'd be terrified. But I'm sure you'd be able to reassure them."

"I don't know about that."

Their route took them along Grant Street, which ran parallel to Eden. It was comprised mostly of humble clapboard houses and a handful of vacant lots. They were alone due to the lateness of the hour and the impending downpour.

"I do. You're good with them, Noah. You'd make a fine father."

His pace faltered as he stared over at her in surprise. "You mean that?"

"I wouldn't have said it otherwise."

Focusing straight ahead, he looked grim as they passed Irving's furniture store and turned left onto First Street. They walked east in complete silence.

On the corner of Eden and First, yellow light shone through the Cowboy Café's many windows. Straggling customers sipped steaming mugs of coffee and conversed over bowls of pinto beans and ham. They had just passed the closed bakery when the first raindrops hit the dirt. Seconds later, the skies released their bounty in earnest. Grace gasped as cool drops pelted her hair and exposed skin.

Noah clasped her hand and pulled her into a tight alley between the laundry's main building and its storage shed.

The overhang was barely wide enough to shelter them from the onslaught. Noah situated her against the exterior wall, her back against the boards while he faced her, his broad body a barrier between her and the weather. Rain splashed onto her boots and hem, as well as his pant legs.

"You're going to get drenched," she scolded, tugging on his sleeves to urge him closer.

He took a hesitant step forward, his hat's brim shading his eyes. "A little water won't hurt me," he drawled.

Feeling cocooned in a private world with him, Grace's nerve endings tingled as she dashed water from her cheeks. Her hair was wet and heavy against her neck. She shivered in the damp air.

Noah noticed, his gaze darkening as he set his hands on her upper arms and ran them down the length, displacing the excess droplets. The scrape and slide of his roughened palms didn't help settle her.

"I'd give you my suit jacket, but it's wet."

Nodding, she hugged her middle and stared past his shoulder to the gray curtain of rain.

"Thanks for what you did back there," he said, drawing her attention to him. "With Burrows."

"I did my best."

He released a soft, husky laugh. "You always do. I have yet to see you give less than your all." His features warmed with tenderness. "I never thought—"

A screeching animal landed at Grace's feet. Frightened, she latched on to Noah, her arms going round his neck as she let loose a screech of her own and tried to escape.

"Relax. It's only a cat." His lips brushed her earlobe as he encircled her waist, anchoring her against him. While he was scanning the alley, she buried her face in his lapel, inhaling his distinct scent.

"You're sure?" Her words were muffled.

"Positive."

Time to let go now, Grace.

A shaky sigh escaped. She started to pull away, smoothing the black suit front. "I'm sorry."

His hold tightened a fraction, preventing her. "No need to be."

Raising her chin, she looked deep into his eyes, searching for a glimpse of what was in his heart. While there were no answers to that mystery, there was longing.

"You never finished your sentence," she said.

Noah's gaze was roaming her face, snagging on her mouth. "Hmm?"

"You said, 'I never thought.' You never thought what?"

"I never thought a city girl would take to boomtown life so effortlessly." He gave his head a little shake, beads of moisture flying from his Stetson. "I had you pegged wrong from the beginning. Not much surprises me these days." His palm splayed against her back, warming her skin through the thin material. "You surprised me, Constance."

He curved his big hand over her cheek, and she squeezed her eyes shut. That name didn't belong to her, and she was beginning to hate hearing him say it.

This is wrong.

Before she could move, speak, act, she felt the coolness of his firm lips settle against hers. She clung to him. Bittersweet and tortuous, Noah's kiss gave her no peace. Only unfulfilled dreams and the promise of a joyless future. This didn't change anything. His actions were fueled by a loneliness he refused to acknowledge. He didn't love her. Didn't wish to mesh his life with hers.

And how could he?

He knew her as Constance Miller, not Grace Longstreet. He didn't know her deepest, darkest secrets.

Neither of them heard the riders at first. By the time the male voices registered, it was too late. A pair of young men clad in dusters, their hats pulled low against the rain, had spotted them and slowed to stare. They didn't look amused.

Noah's demeanor changed in an instant. His features hardened, any softness in him gone. Slowly disengaging from her hold, he met the riders' perusal with a glare until they kicked in their heels and rode off. The horses' hooves kicked up mud.

Cold leached into her. "Noah, what's wrong? Who were those men?"

"Colton Bailey's ranch hands."

Lifting trembling fingers to cover her mouth, she tried to sort through her jumbled emotions. Colton was a nice man. She didn't want to hurt him.

Noah's expression was grim. "Looks like he's off the potential-husband list."

Chapter Nineteen

"Oh! What a sight you two are! Come in out of the rain."

Hannah ushered Noah and Constance inside her cozy house, peering past them to what was now a drizzle, while James brought them each a towel.

His infant daughter was tucked against his chest, wrapped in blankets and sleeping without a care in the world. James doted on Ava. Noah thought the young cowboy was making up for lost time, as he hadn't been around for the baby's birth or the first few weeks of her life. He hadn't even known she existed. Hannah had hidden her pregnancy and the birth of their baby because she'd been scared of her father's reaction. While Noah understood her concerns, he wasn't sure he'd have been able to forgive her so quickly if he'd been in James's shoes. There was never a good enough reason for dishonesty.

What about what you and the others are doing to hide recent crimes from Mr. McAllister? a voice persisted. *Isn't that dishonesty by omission?*

"We're getting your floor all wet," Constance murmured, her voice low and strained.

She'd gone pale beneath that awning and hadn't yet regained her color.

He'd messed up in a major way. By casting reason aside,

he'd unintentionally ruined her chances with Colton, a good man who would've treated her right.

He hadn't wanted to mention it, but depending on how far word spread, he might've damaged her reputation. There was no way to make up for that.

"Don't worry about it." Hannah nodded to the bedroom. "We were reading books, and Abigail drifted off to sleep. Jane is still awake, I think. If you want to go on in, Constance, I'll heat some warm milk." Her somber gray eyes met his. "Sheriff, may I speak to you in the kitchen?"

For a wild moment, he thought she knew about the kiss and was about to scold him. But she couldn't know. Yet.

Inside the small but efficient kitchen just off the main living area, Noah took a seat at the table and waited, uncomfortable in his wet clothes, as she tossed kindling in the firebox and filled a pan with milk.

James stood in the opening, quiet and watchful, the doorjamb supporting his weight.

"How was the party?" she asked, taking a pair of enamel mugs from the shelf.

"Not bad. We had a close call with D.B., but we managed to keep him away from Mr. McAllister."

Resting her hands against the counter, Hannah said, "Was Prudence there?"

"No. Come to think of it, I haven't seen her around lately. Why do you ask?"

"From the moment we met on the train, something about her struck me as familiar. I've pondered it off and on in the weeks since and yesterday it came to me. When I was in Harper, I met a man there named Isaac Burrows. He founded Harper and built it into a prosperous town."

Harper had since gone bust—all because the Union Pacific chose Cowboy Creek for their terminus. Unfortunate for Burrows and the residents.

"Burrows. Any relation to D. B. Burrows?"

"I don't know. Here's the strange part—Prudence and Isaac look enough alike that they could be brother and sister."

"D.B. hails from Missouri. Prudence Haywood is from Chicago." He furrowed his brow in confusion. "I don't see a connection. Perhaps it's coincidence."

"Maybe. The other girls and I think it odd how Prudence treats D.B. He's her boss at the paper, yet she acts as if he's her fellow employee. She bosses him around, and he lets her." Releasing a breath, she hesitated a moment before going on. "At first, we wondered if there was a romance brewing between them. We haven't seen any evidence of that, however."

He ran a hand through his hair, which was wet at the ends. "The widow Haywood hasn't shown any inclination toward romance."

"I don't know what this means, if anything. Telling you seemed the right thing to do."

"Thanks, Hannah. I'll look into it."

Sorting this puzzle would at least help get his mind off Constance for a little while.

Noah left the train station the following morning, feeling relieved and a whole lot less guilty. Confession was good for the soul. He could attest to that. After a lengthy discussion with his friends, they'd decided to come clean to Mr. McAllister. Standing on that train platform, he'd considered all that Noah had told him and thanked him for his forthrightness. He'd let them know his decision in the coming weeks.

Whatever the outcome, at least he, Will and Daniel could move forward with clear consciences.

The thick envelope in his pocket represented another effort to attain peace. Long before Constance confronted him, his silence toward his family had bothered him. He couldn't continue to let them wonder what had happened to him. Last night, he'd taken pen and paper out to the barn and written page after page, apologizing for waiting so long and explaining where his life had taken him. Making his way to the post office, he encountered Gus and Old Horace rocking in front of Booker's store.

"Here comes the sheriff," Gus drawled, stroking his straggly gray beard. "I heard you've been a naughty boy. You hear that, Horace?"

"Sure did."

Noah stopped, hoping against hope they weren't talking about what he thought they were. "I haven't been called a boy in a long time, fellas."

Gus pinned him with a pair of bloodshot eyes. "Maybe that's 'cause you ain't acted like a boy in a long time."

"Until now." Horace kept rocking.

"Until now," Gus parroted. "Never figured you for a man who'd take advantage of a defenseless widow, Noah Burgess."

Noah's day was about to get worse. If these two knew about it, the entire town would soon.

At the post office, the clerk acted as if he was a notorious criminal. On his walk back to the jail, a pair of older ladies whispered furiously at the sight of him, and it wasn't because of his scars or Wolf trotting beside him.

He shouldn't have been surprised to find Colton Bailey waiting for him.

Noah wondered if he'd be nursing a black eye. Not that he didn't deserve one. The rancher looked more resigned than angry, however.

Shooting up from the bench situated between the newspaper office and the jail, Colton fisted and unfisted his hands. "Sheriff Burgess, I'd like a word."

"Of course." He unlocked the door. "Let's talk inside."

He didn't need a spectacle right here on Eden Street adding to the scandal.

His key ring landed on the desk with a thunk. Rounding it, he sat down and gestured for Colton to do the same. He refused.

Noah spoke first. "I owe you an apology, Bailey."

He held up a hand. "I don't want an apology. Constance and I...we didn't have a commitment." Sadness turned down the corners of his mouth. "Not yet, anyway. I thought we were on our way to having something good." Slapping his hat against his thigh, anger blazed in his dark eyes. "What I want from you, Burgess, is an explanation. If you wanted her for yourself, why pawn her off on another man?"

Guilt burned in his gut. He'd resolved the county rep problem with one conversation. However, this situation he'd created wouldn't go away so easily.

"I'm not in the market for a wife. That's common knowledge around here, I believe."

The excuse sounded inept, even to his ears.

Red tinged Colton's cheekbones. "Do you dislike Constance that much?"

"What are you talking about? Of course I like her."

Be honest. Your feelings for her go beyond mere friendship. How far beyond he was afraid to think about.

Hands on his hips, the younger man glared down at Noah. "Her good standing in this town is in jeopardy because you couldn't keep your hands to yourself. You refuse to marry her. What man in his right mind would offer for her now?"

Standing abruptly, Noah stalked to the nearest cell and curved his hands around the cold metal bars. What had he done? He belonged in one of these for his selfish, reckless actions. Clearly he hadn't been thinking rationally. Not last night in the alley. Not at Hannah and James's wedding. If someone besides Pippa had discovered them that day in the woods, someone inclined to gossip, they would've been dealing with this before now.

Colton wasn't finished. "If she's not good enough for Cowboy Creek's sheriff, who is she good enough for?"

Noah whipped around. "My not wanting to marry has zero to do with Constance!"

A single raised brow mocked him. "Try telling that to the local bachelors."

The door creaked open. Will, his silver-handled cane striking the planks with more force than usual, entered seconds before Daniel, whose chestnut hair was slightly mussed and one suspender twisted at the shoulder. They'd obviously heard.

Colton mashed his hat on his head. "Think about what I said."

Ignoring the other men's greetings, Colton brushed past them, slamming the door behind him.

Daniel folded his arms across his chest and looked more irate than Noah could ever recall seeing him. "Please tell me the gossips have it wrong. I know you, Noah. You aren't this dumb."

"Or careless," Will added.

He scraped a weary hand over his face. "I can't."

Will threw up a hand. "You realize how bad this looks, don't you?"

"I do."

Daniel smirked. "Practice those two words, my friend. You'll be repeating them soon."

Noah stared at the pair of them, speechless.

"He's right," Will said. "You have no choice but to marry her."

Marry Constance. The part of him that leaped with anticipation, even hope, was overwhelmed by the shadows of his past and the insecurities wrought by his disfigurement.

"She deserves better than a bitter ex-soldier."

"Should've thought about that before you kissed her," Daniel retorted. Then, softening, he put up a hand. "Look, I have full faith that you and Constance will make a great match. She's a fine woman and caring mother."

"And she apparently likes you."

She was attracted to him, strangely enough. But as for how she felt about him? That was a mystery. She'd seemed willing to give Colton Bailey a chance. *After you rejected her*, a voice reminded him.

His head began to ache behind his temples. "I can't think about this right now."

Striding to the desk, he snatched up the keys.

"Where are you going?" Will's brows crashed together.

"I hope it's to talk to Constance."

"No. Not yet." When Daniel opened his mouth, he said, "I need time to organize my thoughts before I see her. First, I'm going to have a chat with our friendly newspaper editor."

They blocked his exit. "What about?"

He relayed Hannah's observations. Since he was so curious, they accompanied him next door. D.B. looked harried when he saw them.

Sorting papers, he spoke with his gaze on his desk. "Whatever brings you here, gentlemen, it will have to wait."

Noah sat on the desk corner, earning him a frown from the older man. Daniel sank into one of two hard-backed chairs and made himself comfortable, his long legs stretched straight and crossed at the ankles. Will meandered about the office, studying articles pasted along the walls.

"We just have a few questions," Noah said, studying him closely. "Ever heard of a man named Isaac Burrows?"

D.B.'s fingers stilled on the upmost paper. Lips tightening a fraction, he lifted his distinctly unfriendly gaze. "Isaac was my brother. Why do you care?"

"Was?"

A vein throbbed at his temple. "Isaac died a couple of months ago."

"My condolences."

D.B. nodded stiffly. "Is that all, Sheriff?"

"Tell me, D.B., do you have any other siblings? A sister, perhaps?"

While his expression didn't alter, his gaze shifted to the left. "It was only me and Isaac."

"So no more family?"

"Our parents passed before the war. Why the interest in my family tree?"

"Because a little bird told us that your assistant bears a striking resemblance to your late brother."

D.B. didn't visibly react. His forehead appeared damp, however.

Will turned from the posting he'd been perusing. "Where is Prudence today? I rarely see her without you."

"Mrs. Haywood left town on yesterday's train." He looked perturbed. "Before you ask, she told me it was because Cowboy Creek lacked suitable husband material."

Was the editor annoyed because he'd lost a valuable assistant? Or because their questions were making him uncomfortable?

"She didn't seem inclined to give any of our bachelors a fair chance." This from Daniel. "Not what I expected from a mail-order bride."

"Don't ask me to explain the workings of a woman's mind," D.B. responded drily.

The mention of mail-order brides pushed Noah's thoughts right back to Constance.

"So you deny any family connection to Prudence Haywood?" He put his final question out there.

"That's not information I would hide." Shuffling his papers, he said, "You gentlemen obviously have too much time on your hands if you're digging around in my past. I'd think you'd put that time to better use." His beady gaze arrowed through Noah. "Like seeing to your own muddled affairs."

Noah stiffened. He was referring to Constance.

Tamping down the urge to throttle him, he slipped off the desk. "Thanks for your cooperation. Good day, Burrows."

"You, too, Sheriff." He smirked.

Outside on the boardwalk, Will wore a thoughtful frown. "Do you believe his story?"

"He struck me as uneasy." Noah wiped a handkerchief over his brow. Only midmorning, but the humidity was thick, making his clothes stick to his skin. "I'm going to speak to Aunt Mae over at the boardinghouse. Prudence was a guest there. She might can tell me something useful."

"I've got to return to the stockyards," Daniel said. "Promise me you'll fix things with Constance."

Sighing, Noah jerked a nod. "I'll handle it."

How he was going to do that, he had no idea. *I've landed myself in a heap of trouble, God. Constance, too. What am I supposed to do?*

It was a request for direction he probably should've prayed for a long time ago.

Chapter Twenty

"What's this horse's name, Momma?" Jane held her hand flat so the mare could take the carrot.

Abigail clasped the stall slats, happy to observe.

"Cherry." Grace stayed close to supervise. As soon as they'd finished with lunch, they had begged to visit the barn.

The girls giggled. "That's a funny name."

"Are you making fun of my friend here?"

At the sound of Noah's deep, rumbling voice, Grace reluctantly turned toward the entrance. She hadn't spoken to him since before their stop at Hannah's. The ride home had been completed in silence, and he'd headed straight for the barn and stayed there. She'd missed their nightly reading sessions. They were getting close to the story's end, and she was eager to hear the rest. Eager for his companionship, too.

With his sheriff's badge pinned firmly to his vest and a gun on each hip, he looked like the lawman she knew him to be, not the fancy gentleman who'd escorted her to the party and kissed her in the rain.

Abigail ran over to him, her braid swishing to and fro, and tilted her head way back to smile up at him. "Mr. Noah! What do you have in the box?"

Grace's heart squeezed with wistfulness. The formidable

sheriff had won Abigail's trust without trying. Jane joined them. Grace remained by the stall while he crouched down and let them look inside. The hat on his bent head blocked his face from view.

A loud gasp lifted to the rafters. "Momma, come see!" Abigail bounced up and down. "Mr. Noah brought us a rabbit!"

"Can you take him out?" Jane asked.

"May we pet him?" Abigail added.

"You sure can." Noah scooped out the brown ball of fur with floppy ears and long feet. Holding it against his chest, he gave them a chance to make friends.

"It looks like Pepper," Abigail murmured to Jane. Her big brown eyes fastened onto Noah. "Are we allowed to keep him?"

For the first time since he'd walked in, he looked at Grace, his eyes shining like the blue Kansas sky in the barn's dimmer light.

"That's up to your ma," he drawled, a bit of his Southern accent creeping in.

They ran over, tugging on her skirts, trembling with excitement. "Please, Momma?"

Jane clapped her hands. "Say yes!"

Smoothing Jane's silky hair, Grace smiled. "Yes."

Watching them dance about in happiness, she noticed Noah was smiling, as well. A rare sight. His smile lit up his face.

Placing the rabbit into the box, he stood. "You girls entertain him while your ma and I talk outside, all right?"

"We have to think of a name," Jane told her sister as they knelt on either side of the box.

Outside, Grace squinted in the too-bright sunshine. She cupped a hand over her eyes.

Without a word, Noah dropped his Stetson on her head and moved to stand against the barn wall near the corner closest to the corral. The hat was too big for her. Adjusting it, she trailed behind him, her nerves as jumpy as the grasshoppers in the fields.

When he faced her, all lightheartedness was gone. She missed his smile immediately.

"You're not gonna like what I have to say."

Unable to stay still, she adjusted the folds of her brown skirt, then righted her sleeves and collar. Checked the pins in her hair. "That's not unusual. You've had plenty to say since I arrived."

He sighed. "The entire town knows about us. Bailey paid me a visit this morning."

This wasn't a surprise. "Was he terribly upset?"

"At me." He scuffed the ground with his boot. "He's right. I wasn't thinking about your reputation. Mine either, for that matter." Leveling his gaze at her, he fisted his hands at his sides. "There's only one solution, Constance. We have to get married. The sooner, the better."

She couldn't help it. She laughed. Couldn't stop laughing.

It bubbled up inside, frantic and bordering on hysterical.

A scowl carved grooves on either side of his mouth. "I fail to see the humor in this situation."

Before she knew it, tears streaked down her cheeks. Not happy ones. "Oh, Noah." Bracing her hands on her knees, she shook her head at the sparse grass stalks beneath her boots. "You've lost your mind if you think I'd marry you."

"You don't have a choice," he gritted out, exasperated. "Tell me. What man is going to want to court you now that everyone knows about our little rendezvous?"

Sadness welled up inside her. Her head whipping up, she demanded, "Is that all it was to you? A convenient opportunity to *not* be lonely for a few minutes? Kissing me had nothing to do with *me*. You would've kissed any one of Cowboy Creek's available women!"

His jaw hardened to marble. "That's not true, Constance."

My name is not *Constance*, she longed to scream. Her cousin's recent letter prevented her. All of a sudden, her options narrowed to one. "I have a better solution—the girls and I will leave."

His pale brows lowered. "And live where? At the hotel? I doubt even you have that much money. Not for long-term lodging."

"Not the ranch." Straightening, she spread her arms wide. "Cowboy Creek."

"Leave town?" he murmured slowly. "Where would you go? Chicago?"

"No. I'm not going back there." Not willingly. Scanning the rolling plains and the horizon where they met blue sky, she shrugged. "We can head further west. I'll speak to the train station manager. I'm sure he'll have useful information that would help me choose a suitable location."

Approaching her as he would a nervous filly, he erased the distance between them with measured steps. He didn't touch her, thankfully. She couldn't have withstood that.

"You would really rather pick up and move to another town, uproot Jane and Abigail again, than join your life with mine?"

He was close enough that his warm breath fanned her cheek, and she could see the waves of cerulean blue in his irises. His lashes were light blond and spiky.

"You don't want to share your life with me, Noah." Her voice caught on a sob. "You've made that plain from the first day. You've endured our presence simply because you're too honorable to force us to leave."

His throat worked. Emotions ravaged his face. His fingers tangled with hers.

"City girl, I—"

She'd never know what he'd been about to say, because his deputy came barreling into the yard.

Pulling away, she hugged her arms about herself as Noah intercepted him.

"Hanley, what's happened?"

The horse came to a staggering stop. The deputy panted as if he'd run here on his own two legs. "The Murdochs. Out at Pete Lyle's ranch. One of the hired hands was out checking a well and spotted them."

Noah was already moving to his own mount. Hauling himself into the saddle, he looked at Grace. "I don't know what time I'll get home. Don't make any rash decisions while I'm gone."

What did he expect? That she'd pack up and leave before he returned?

As much as that idea appealed, she couldn't do that to the girls or him. They deserved a chance to say goodbye.

Aware of the deputy's gaze, she swallowed hard and nodded. "Be careful."

"Always."

She watched the pair until they were dots on the horizon.

Noah paced alongside the cell. "Tell me where your brother and the rest of your outlaw buddies are, and I'll make sure the authorities grant you leniency."

Xavier Murdoch let loose a string of foul words. He was sprawled on the lone cot, one arm thrown over his face. His wrinkled, stained clothes hung loosely on his thin frame.

"Doesn't look like a life of crime has paid off," Noah observed. "At least in prison you'll have three square meals a day. Plenty of rest in your very own cell. Medical attention for any injuries."

At that, Xavier flung his arm down and sat up, his eyes narrowing to slits. "You're responsible for my injuries. Just like the former sheriff almost succeeded in killing my brother."

Noah flicked a gaze at the outlaw's upper arm where a

white bandage peeked out from the tear in his sleeve. He and Hanley had ridden straight to Lyle's spread and, with the help of Pete and his hired boys, cornered Xavier.

"I wouldn't have had to shoot you if you'd surrendered peacefully." Still pacing, he said, "How did Zeb get clipped?" He snapped his fingers. "Oh yeah, making off with the congregation's belongings."

Weeks after the Murdochs had brazenly interrupted a church service and stole everything from wedding rings to the offering money, Noah had come across a very ill Zeb behind the laundry. His wound had turned septic and, desperate, the gang had left him in town to be discovered and treated by a doctor. Although Sheriff Davis and the others had expected his cohorts to try to bust him out, they'd failed to prevent it from happening.

Xavier scratched his scraggly beard and glared. "I ain't helping no lawman."

"Fine." Nodding, Noah ambled to his desk and removed a sheaf of papers. Lifting the top one, he said, "You'll be shipped off to Lawrence in the morning. And when I find Zeb and the others, I'll make a point of sending him the opposite direction. You'll never see your brother again."

Xavier's upper lip curled. "You ain't gonna find him."

Noah made a point of reading the paper. "You recognize the name Sarah Paulson?"

"Nope."

"Hmm. Hang on a minute. Her maiden name might ring a bell." Twisting slightly, he studied Xavier's reaction. "Sarah Murdoch Paulson. That sound familiar?"

Alarm followed by rage had the outlaw up and at the bars in an instant. "How do you know about her? Leave my little sister alone, you hear? I'll make your life miserable, Sheriff. I'll—"

"You'll what, exactly?" The paper drifted to the desk.

Noah propped his hands on his hips, waiting, letting the man imagine the possibilities.

"She's done nothing wrong." He rattled the bars. "She ain't seen me or Zeb in years!"

"Why would I take your word for it? I don't have a choice but to have her investigated. You know, once word gets out that she's related to the infamous Murdoch gang, I wonder how her new husband and in-laws will react? I'm sure the locals in her town wouldn't take kindly to having a Murdoch relation in their midst." Strolling over to the cell, he added, "Your gang has left a lot of irate folks in your wake. I wonder how many of them might aim for a bit of revenge. If they can't get to you or Zeb, a man might go after Sarah. She has a six-month-old baby boy. Did you know?"

Xavier blinked fast, his dirt-stained fingers flexing on the metal bars before dropping away. He presented Noah with his back, shoulders slumped.

"He's not named after his uncles, rest assured," he tacked on.

Silence reigned in the jail, except for the sounds of supper-time traffic filtering in. Through the glass, he could see the innocent citizens traversing the streets, unaware of the dangerous criminal mere yards away. They wouldn't be truly safe until the rest of the outlaws were captured and made to face justice.

"I'll tell you which hideout they're in, but you have to swear to leave Sarah alone." Turning, he stared at Noah, defeat aging him.

"I'll put it in writing."

Major details and a crudely drawn map later, Noah met his deputy on the boardwalk outside.

"I need for you to round up a half dozen able-bodied men. Gideon Kendricks might be interested in riding along." He waved the paper. At last, they had key information that could help them put away the Murdochs. "We're going after Zeb."

"How'd you get Xavier to cooperate?"

"As soon as I was appointed sheriff, I hired an investigator to do some digging. Fortunately for us, Xavier Murdoch has a weak spot."

Hanley looked at him with admiration. "Nice work, boss." Going to the hitching post, he climbed into the saddle. "Oh, I forgot to mention, earlier today there was a man in the office searching for a woman by the name of Grace Longstreet. I'm not familiar with all the recent mail-order brides. Told him I'd ask you."

His mind on the coming search, Noah dismissed the query. "I'm not aware of anyone here by that name. Right now, capturing the gang is the priority. I'll see what I can do to help this man out later."

"Got it."

"Hanley, I've got to see to something out on the ranch. We're riding that direction anyway. You and the men meet me out there as soon as you can."

"Yes, sir."

Leaving his other deputy, James Johnson and another sentry to guard Xavier, Noah headed out to the ranch, working out in his mind exactly what he should say to Constance.

When he spotted her in his vegetable garden pulling weeds, his prepared speech vanished. This thing he was about to do carried inherent risks. Zeb was holed up with six other outlaws that they knew of, and not one of them was about to be captured without a fight. He couldn't leave without knowing her future was settled.

Glancing up in surprise, Constance stood and wiped the bits of grass and dirt from the apron over her navy skirt. She walked to the end of the row.

"Noah—"

"We've got five minutes. Let's make them count."

Her brows knitted together in bewilderment as he took her elbow and steered her toward the cabin. Inside, the girls looked up from where they sat practicing their letters at the table.

"Stay there, girls," he told them. Ascending the steps to the loft, he turned and extended his hand to help her up.

"What's this about?" she said, taking in the desk and bookshelves. "Did you find the outlaw?"

"One of them is sitting in the jail." Hastily writing out his declaration, he handed the paper to her. "We're going after the rest. I've no idea how long we'll be gone. Or who'll make it back."

Fear registered where before there'd only been concern. Going to her, he tapped the paper. "This will ensure your future, Constance."

"I can't read this."

His voice grew thick. "It says that, in the event of my death, this ranch transfers to you and the girls."

She went white, shaking away his words. "You can't do this, Noah."

"I can and did."

"You're coming back safe and sound," she said forcefully, as if she could make it so simply by stating it.

"I certainly plan to." Tenderly brushing away a single tear sliding along her cheek, he murmured, "I can't go unless I know you'll be okay."

Then, because he couldn't stop himself, he kissed her cheek. Before he could haul her into his arms for a reassuring hug, he descended the steps and went to say goodbye to Jane and Abigail.

Patting their heads, he said, "Mind your ma, you hear? And take care of your bunny."

"We named him Sheriff." Jane grinned.

"After you," Abigail piped up, the adoration on her face making his eyes wet.

He left before he could make a fool of himself.

A thump outside the door an hour later made Grace's heart stutter. Noah's rifle hung in its spot above the fireplace. She should've asked him to teach her how to use it, but she hadn't felt this sense of impending danger before.

Be honest. You relied on him to protect you when you should've been relying on yourself. You'll have no one else around once you leave Cowboy Creek.

"Girls, go into the bedroom and stay there until I tell you."

"Yes, ma'am."

Moments later, a succinct rap rattled the wood. Grace snatched the largest knife and, hiding it in the folds of her skirt, prayed for protection.

Through the curtains, she could make out a wagon. She didn't recognize the man on the seat. With blood rushing in her ears, she pressed her cheek against the door. "Who's there?"

"It's me." The feminine voice filtered through. "Pippa."

Sagging with relief, she replaced the knife and rushed to let her in. "I'm so glad it's you," she cried, embracing the other woman.

After a moment's hesitation, Pippa returned the hug. "Are you all right?"

Embarrassed, Grace released her. "Sorry to ambush you like that. It's just…" Pressing her hands against her cold cheeks, she continued, "With the men hunting down this gang, I suppose I'm more sensitive than usual."

Pippa instructed the driver to wait for her, and that she'd pay him for his time. He nodded his acquiescence. Closing the door behind her, she walked to the fireplace, her aquamarine dress swishing as she moved. Unpinning her hat, she laid it on the mantel.

"Gideon is with them. I'm as worried as you are." Her hazel gaze roamed Grace's face. "I suppose you have added burdens on your mind, what with the current rumors swirling around town."

Grace sank into the nearest chair, relieved the bedroom door was closed. Shielding the girls from the tales about her and Noah was another reason to start over elsewhere. The prospect of leaving Cowboy Creek was a daunting one, especially as they'd be heading into the unknown to live among utter strangers. The prospect of staying here, however, was even more unsettling.

Pippa joined her, taking the seat opposite and folding her gloved hands atop the surface of the table. "I, for one, happen to think kissing in the midst of a rain shower is quite romantic." She gave her a half smile full of sympathy. "Are you still convinced he doesn't care about you?"

"He doesn't love me, I know that much." It grieved her to admit it aloud. "He said our only recourse now is to get married. You should've heard him, Pippa. He sounded as thrilled about marrying me as he would about putting down his favorite horse."

"I'm sure he's simply weighing the gravity of the situation." She cocked her head to one side. "You were willing to marry for other reasons besides love. Why is it different with Noah?"

"Because I can't stand the idea of living with him, day after day, knowing he never wanted me. Oh, he'd be polite. Solicitous. He's too good of a man to be anything less. But it would slowly destroy me...knowing I was the cause of his unhappiness."

And living a lie. Don't forget that.

Pippa covered Grace's hand with hers. "I understand. I do." Sagging against the chair rungs, she frowned. "I've come to realize I have feelings for Gideon. As he hasn't declared himself or given me the slightest hint about his intentions, I'm in the dark, the same as you."

"Gideon's different," Grace argued. "He's clearly besotted with you. I think perhaps he's holding part of himself back because he sees how much you love this town."

"I'll be honest. I do love Cowboy Creek and all the wonderful friends I've made. But I'd leave it behind for him." Sadness dimmed the sparkle in her eyes. "I don't think he's going to even ask."

"Maybe you should tell him. Take a risk."

"Maybe we should both take a risk," she murmured. "See what happens."

Standing and crossing to the kitchen window with a memorable view of the prairie, Grace blinked away tears. "I'm leaving Cowboy Creek, Pippa. I won't submit Noah to a lifetime of misery and regret."

"Are you certain that's the best course?"

"It's the only course." Moving to the counter, Grace drummed up a smile. "Thank you for your friendship, Pippa. It's meant a lot to me."

"Aw, don't do that," she exclaimed, swiping beneath her eyes. "Don't make me cry!"

"When we get settled in our new home, I'll write to you. Who knows, you may not be here by then. You may be traveling the country with your dashing young man, experiencing grand adventures you can tell your grandchildren someday."

"Here's my prayer, Constance Miller—I pray that, despite the prairie-size obstacles standing in our way, you and I both get our happy-ever-afters. And that our friendship will continue until we're old and gray."

"That sounds like a lovely prayer."

While Pippa deserved her happy ending with Gideon, Grace didn't have faith that she'd get one with Noah.

Chapter Twenty-One

Three miles outside town, Noah and the others discovered a hideout—just not the one Xavier had described. Tucked amid a small copse, a ragged canvas tent had provided someone shelter. And recently, too, if the pile of chicken bones with hunks of roasted meat still clinging to them was anything to go by.

He, Gideon and Deputy Hanley dismounted to survey the site while the remaining men scouted out the land around it on horseback.

"You think Xavier lied?" Hanley crouched to pick up a chipped coffee mug.

"No." Noah's investigation into the Murdochs' past had yielded valuable information that worked for his purposes. Everyone had roots. A family. Fortunately for him, Xavier actually cared about their younger sibling enough to want to protect her. "Zeb has at least half a dozen men with him. Looks to me like one, maybe two people have been hiding out here."

Gideon emerged from the tent with a plain wool blanket wrapped about a leather satchel. "Noah, you'll want to see this."

Letting the blanket slip to the ground, Noah set the satchel at his feet and opened it. The title on the topmost document had him setting back on his haunches. "These are the missing deeds. The authentic ones."

Gideon and Hanley crowded around. Noah lifted the stack out. "Amos Goodwin's deed to the boot-maker shop." He handed it up for them to inspect. "Wade Claxton's claim to the saddle shop." Rifling through the paperwork, he found all ten deeds.

"I don't understand." Gideon looked around. "What do these deeds have to do with a gang of outlaws? Doesn't make sense."

After carefully replacing the satchel's contents, Noah stored it in his saddlebags. "We've assumed for some time that the Murdochs weren't involved with the attempts to sabotage our town. What would they stand to gain by poisoning cattle, burning lumber and replacing real deeds with forgeries?"

Gideon stroked his goatee. "You're saying that whoever's behind all that isn't affiliated with the gang?"

"Could be someone's out to stir up trouble simply for kicks. Or there's a more sinister motive." Nudging the smoldering ash with his boot, Noah blinked as a small gold piece slipped free. With his gloves protecting his hands, he picked it up and brushed the soot away.

Hanley peeked over his shoulder. "Now, why does that look familiar, boss?"

"Because." Turning it this way and that, he said, "It belongs to Prudence Haywood."

Everyone had thought her brooch had been stolen during the church service along with the other jewelry. Turned out, she'd hidden it, risking the Murdochs' ire and retaliation. According to D.B., the piece held sentimental value for her.

He looked over to find Gideon pulling a scrap of burned material from the ash. Dusting it off he held it out to Noah. "Recognize this?"

"Looks like the fabric of a woman's dress."

"You think the widow was staying out here?" Hanley sounded incredulous.

The tree limbs swayed as a light breeze tumbled across the prairie. Fat, misshapen clouds created large shadows on the fields. The men rode in ever-expanding circles, examining the tall grass for clues.

"According to Aunt Mae, Mrs. Haywood hasn't stayed in her room at the boardinghouse in over a week. D.B. told us she left yesterday on the train. So either the editor is lying to cover for his assistant, or she led him to believe she left."

"The bank was robbed by two people," Hanley said slowly. "We assumed Zeb and Xavier were responsible. What if we were wrong?"

Frustration fired through him. When the brothers had robbed the church parishioners, they hadn't acted alone. Didn't make sense that they'd change their pattern for a bank heist. Quincy Davis had been shot during the bank robbery. If Prudence was involved, she was a corrupt individual. And she had a partner working with her. Someone equally as dangerous.

Was it D. B. Burrows? If so, what did he have to gain by wreaking havoc on the town?

"We need to get this evidence to Will," he said.

Gideon spoke up. "I'll take it. Deputy Hanley can ride with me if the rest of you want to go ahead to the Murdoch hideout."

The pair rode for town while Noah and the others continued on. According to the map, the gang was holed up in an abandoned cabin a mile and a half farther west. His concentration wasn't on the coming confrontation, however. Constance's tearful face dominated his thoughts. If he made it back to her, he had to somehow convince her to marry him. For the sake of their reputations. For the sake of the girls' best interests.

While marriage hadn't been a part of his plan, he wasn't

one to shirk his duty. He'd let his attraction to her mar his good sense and now they'd both have to pay the price. If she left with the girls, he'd worry himself to death. Better they stay here where he could watch over them and see to their needs.

Lost in thought, the echo of gunshots caught him unawares. He jerked in the saddle.

Pete Lyle was riding closest to him. He pointed to the northwest, where the outline of a shelter was visible beneath a lone tree. "See that?"

Withdrawing his weapon, Noah spurred his horse into a gallop. Closer to the cabin, chaos reigned. Other men, strangers to Noah, were firing upon the structure. One of them spun and aimed in their direction before holding up a hand and yelling at his group not to fire.

A gold sheriff's badge glinted on the man's chest. "I'm Trenton Jameson," he yelled, "sheriff of Morgan's Creek."

"Noah Burgess. Cowboy Creek." Beneath him, Samson pranced sideways. "We're after Zeb Murdoch and his boys."

"Same."

Movement out of the corner of his eye registered, and he recognized Zeb's lanky figure sprinting away. Before he could react, one of Jameson's men chased after him on horseback. Noah joined the pursuit, dodging Zeb's poorly aimed shots.

The distance between the man and Zeb narrowed. Swinging out, he slammed the butt of his gun on the outlaw's head. Zeb went down and sprawled facedown in the grass. A groan escaped him as Jameson's man leaped from the saddle and, seizing the man's arms, locked a pair of cuffs on him.

Jumping down from Samson, Noah helped the other man rouse Zeb. Together, they marched him back to the cabin. By that time, Sheriff Jameson and his group, along with Noah's men, had the rest rounded up. With their leader deserting them, the others had surrendered.

"Good work, gentlemen." Jameson eyed Noah. "Glad you came along. How'd you know about this place?"

"Xavier's sitting in my jail. He had the information. All we needed was the right incentive to get it out of him."

Zeb spit at his feet. "My brother ain't no snitch."

"He is when his sister's well-being is at stake."

Beneath the unkempt beard, the man blanched.

"Brotherly love is a powerful motivator, I found out," Noah drawled. He looked to Jameson. "What about you?"

The outlaw nearest Morgan Creek's lawman held out his wrists. Jameson proceeded to release him.

Pete Lyle made a sound of protest. "What are you doing?"

"This here's no outlaw. He's one of mine. Been playing pretend in order to catch the Murdochs."

Someone let loose a low whistle. The real criminals spouted threats of retaliation.

Ready to get home to Constance and figure out how to convince her to stay, Noah jerked a thumb over his shoulder. "I don't have enough cells to house everyone. How about you take Zeb and those two. I'll take the rest."

"Agreed. We'll coordinate their transfer to Lawrence in preparation for their court proceedings."

Noah turned to his posse. "Good work today, gentlemen. Let's go home."

The thought of seeing Constance kept his exhaustion at bay. Despite the major events of the day—discovering the deeds and capturing Zeb and his cohorts—Noah's biggest hurdle had yet to be scaled. She wasn't going to be easy to convince. Not after his repeated attempts to push her away. While he couldn't offer her love, he could offer her respect and affection. He'd be good to her daughters. Surely that would be enough.

Quickly settling Samson in the barn, he strode to the

house and let himself in. Constance emerged from the bedroom, her hand pressed against her bare throat. She was alluring in a blue-and-white housecoat. Her dark waves cascaded about her shoulders, framing her face and making her look like a young girl of eighteen.

"You're all right."

Noah hung his hat on a peg and tried to right his mussed hair. Maybe now wasn't the right time. He was dirty and sweaty from spending all day in the saddle. He probably smelled like horse and leather and who knew what else while she smelled like a fresh summer flower.

"How did it go today?" she asked. He noticed the picture book she held.

Going to the table, he ran a hand along the top wood slat of a chair, wishing he had the freedom to luxuriate in the softness of her long, beautiful hair.

"The outlaws are locked up. They won't be troubling our citizens anymore."

"That's a relief." Her gaze scanned him from head to toe. "Did anyone get hurt?"

"None of our men sustained injuries. God protected us."

"Momma." Jane's voice carried through the doorway. "Can Mr. Noah read to us?"

Constance fiddled with her high collar and lifted the book. "We were looking at the pictures." Turning to the side, she addressed the girls, who were already in bed. "He's had a long day, girls. I'm sure he's tired. Maybe tomorrow, okay?"

Noah glanced at the book's cover and moved to the doorway. "*Hansel and Gretel* is one of my favorites. If you don't mind my stench, I'll read it to you."

Abigail wiggled with glee. "Yes, please!"

Standing at his shoulder, Constance's cheeks pinked. "You smell like a normal, hardworking male to me."

He tweaked a lock of her hair. "How about I read to the girls while you fix us some warm milk?"

"Oh, you liked that, did you?" She winked. "Hannah has no idea what she's started."

Noah got distracted watching her as she moved about the kitchen. How easy it was to envision her here permanently...as his wife. He'd be free to take her in his arms anytime. Free to kiss her. Hold her. Console her when she was feeling sad. Laugh with her over the twins' antics. His chest seized up. Maybe she'd even be willing to have babies with him.

"Mr. Noah, aren't you coming?" Jane and Abigail got tired of waiting.

Feeling as if maybe his reasons for wanting this marriage weren't as cut-and-dried as he'd thought, he went to the bed and motioned for them to scoot over. By the time he finished the story, Abigail was asleep, her gamine features relaxed. Jane's lids were heavy as he tucked the covers about her.

"We can't go home again, either," she said drowsily. "Just like Hansel and Gretel."

He smoothed a stray lock of hair from her forehead, smiling at her ramblings.

"Momma said we can't go to cousin Constance's house again, either." Her blue eyes were sad as she blinked up at him. "I miss cousin Constance."

Frowning, he straightened to his full height. "Your ma's name is Constance."

"Shh." Her lids drifted closed. "Not supposed to tell her name is Grace."

Uneasiness lodging in his gut, Noah joined Constance in the kitchen, the Sunday dinner with Colton Bailey surging in his mind. She'd cut Jane off without provocation the moment she started talking about their Chicago relation. Unusual behavior for a mother who was typically patient in instruction. He thought about the letter she'd received. Her jumpiness and overall refusal to discuss her cousin should've roused his suspicions.

Stopping at the counter, he studied her profile and wondered if she'd been hiding secrets more insidious than mere family drama.

"Did they enjoy the story?" she asked, pouring the milk into mugs.

"They did." He waited until she stood on the opposite side of the counter facing him. "Jane said something peculiar just now."

Her knuckles whitened as she gripped the mug. "You know children can be unpredictable," she murmured, her gaze skittering away. "They have vast imaginations."

The unease inside him grew into certainty that something was off. His pulse raced and his temples throbbed. He recalled thinking in those first days that the name Constance didn't quite suit her. At least twice that he could remember, she hadn't immediately responded when he'd called for her.

He left his milk untouched. "Your name isn't Constance, is it?"

Her head whipped up, horror dawning in her eyes. "Wh-what?"

"You heard me," he bit out. "What is your real name? Is it Grace?"

Her mug hit the counter with a thunk, sloshing milk over the rim. Trembling hands pressed against her chest. He knew without her having to say a word that he'd been duped. Deceived. And so had his friends.

"You came here under false pretenses, didn't you?" Noah began to back away. He felt sick to his stomach. "What's your actual name?"

"Grace. Grace Longstreet." She extended a hand. "Please, Noah, I can explain—"

"Longstreet. You said that name once. You messed up and, instead of saying the Miller estate, you said Longstreet. You lied and said that was what the family had named the mansion." She'd shared so little about her past. He should've seen through her charade. A massive headache began to form behind his eyes. His skin felt hot. "You lied about a lot of things."

He felt as if he'd soared to the clouds on the prospect of building a life with her, only to be dropped unmercifully to deep, jagged caverns below.

"I'm so sorry," she gasped. Coming around to his side, she reached for him. "I know you're angry and hurt, but if you'll just hear me out—"

Unable to look at her, he spun and headed for the door. "I don't want to hear any more of your lies."

His chest a gaping hole of emptiness, he stormed out of the house, saddled a horse and let the darkness swallow him whole.

Chapter Twenty-Two

Grace raced outside, her voice trapped in her throat, frozen like the rest of her as Noah disappeared into the night. She collapsed onto her knees, unmindful of the dirt or the ants crawling about in the dark. Her heart ached with loss and self-recrimination.

She'd made a terrible, unforgiveable mistake. The girls weren't to blame. Asking them to protect her lie had been born of desperation, fear of the lengths Frank might go to foil her scheme.

Noah's disgust seared her soul. What must he think of her? Whatever feelings he might've had for her were gone now, erased by her willful decision to deceive him.

Somewhere near the water, a frog's bellow joined the grasshoppers' buzzing. A cow lowed a ways off. Closer to the cabin, a twig snapped. Grace grabbed hold of the post and yanked herself up. Without the moon or stars, the prairie held innumerable mysteries.

Feeling more alone than when her father died and her mother spent a majority of her time working, more alone than the day she'd discovered her pregnancy and Ambrose hadn't met the news with joy, she turned and reentered the house that wasn't hers. Lowering the slat into place, she leaned against the smooth wood and stared at the room through gathering tears.

She'd never forget her temporary home on this vast Kansas prairie. Nor would she ever forget the lonesome rancher sheriff who owned it.

First thing tomorrow morning, she would pay the stationmaster a visit and figure out where to go next.

Someone intruded on his privacy long before he was ready. Laying aside the razor and wiping the last bits of shaving soap from his skin, Noah tugged on his shirt and hurriedly worked the buttons.

The person on the other side of the door knocked a second time.

"Hold your horses, why don't you?" he muttered.

His sock-covered feet sank into the plush carpet, a far cry from the splinter-infested barn floor. He wrenched the door open.

"How come I'm the last one to learn of your presence in *my* hotel?" Not waiting for an invitation, Will pushed past him, stopping before the grand marble fireplace. Dressed in his typical outfit of a well-cut suit and crisp shirt, he rested his weight on the cane handle. "I brought Tomasina in for breakfast and before I could have my first sip of coffee, Simon and Mrs. Foster were bearing down on me with the news." His gaze raked him. "What happened? You get tired of sleeping with the livestock?"

He wished it was as simple as that. Closing the door, he sank into the leather desk chair and tugged on his boots one at a time. "Maybe."

"Did you and Constance have an argument?" Threading his fingers through his hair, Will frowned. "If I left home every time Tom and I tussled over some minor detail, I might as well move back in here."

"Her name's not Constance."

"I'm sorry?"

Wandering over to one of the room's pair of windows, he took in the steady drizzle turning Eden Street into a muddy river. At least the weather was cooperating with his mood. "We've been hoodwinked. Duped. Taken for a ride." He'd lain in the too-soft bed last night calling himself all sorts of a fool. "I found out last night that Constance Miller is, in fact, Grace Longstreet. The real Constance is still in Chicago, I suppose. The woman who arrived here is her cousin."

His friend's soft tread grew closer. "I don't understand. Why? How?"

Noah let the thick curtain fall into place. Confusion was reflected in Will's countenance, along with pity that made him want to cast up his accounts.

"I didn't stick around for her explanation." Not that he would've believed anything she might have said.

Will scrubbed a hand down his face. "I'm sorry, old friend. I never should have sent for a bride for you. Leah and Tomasina tried to warn me, but I refused to listen. I didn't think one impulsive act could wreak such unexpected consequences."

"Forget it. I plan to. She's leaving Cowboy Creek. Pretty soon, we'll look back on this and laugh."

"You care for her." Will studied him. "Of course you do. You wouldn't have kissed her in the middle of town if you didn't."

"I'll get over it." Snagging his vest from the bed, he shrugged it on. "With everything that's happening around here, I'll have plenty to keep me busy."

"Constance—" He halted at Noah's quick look. "I mean, Grace—strikes me as a genuine lady. You know how I get hunches about things. I can't help thinking she has to have had an awfully good reason to pull the wool over the eyes of an entire town."

"I don't care what her reasons are, Will. I'm through talking about her." On the dresser sat his badge. He pinned it on, thankful for the first time since Will had presented it to him in the days following Quincy Davis's death. Without this duty, he'd have no chance of avoiding Constance.

He ground his back teeth together. *Grace, remember? Her name is Grace.*

The fact he really liked the name and thought it fit her didn't mean a thing.

"What did you do with the deeds?" he asked, strapping on his gun belt.

His friend looked reluctant to leave the original subject, but he caught sight of Noah's expression and gave a small nod. "Daniel, Gideon and I went to the land office to show the clerk. We agreed that, with all the recent troubles, the safest place to store them was the bank. They're in a lockbox in the vault for the time being."

"Good. What about Prudence's brooch and dress remnants?"

"I put those in the hotel safe." His brows drew together. "I never could bring myself to like that woman."

"I'm going to go the *Herald*'s offices first thing and have a chat with D.B. You coming?"

"Tomasina's probably halfway through her eggs and pancakes by now." Grimacing, he opened the door and stepped into the hallway. "I should at least try to join her before she gives up on me. You have to eat, too. Have breakfast with us and then we'll go interview the good editor."

He didn't want to agree, but he couldn't skip meals. The last thing he wanted was for Will to feel even guiltier for his role in bringing Grace Longstreet here.

"Fine."

Putting a hand on Will's arm at the landing, he said, "What's your opinion on D.B.? You think he's innocent or Prudence's partner in crime?"

"D.B. innocent? Not likely. Those two acted as if they were long-lost companions from the beginning. They knew each other before Cowboy Creek, I'd stake my livelihood on it. What we have to figure out is how."

"And what kind of grudge they hold against the town."

He clapped Noah on the shoulder. "We'll get to the bottom of this, buddy. I promise. Pretty soon your biggest headache will be rowdy cowboys."

He didn't tell Will he dreaded calmer days. More time to wallow in his humiliation was not something he looked forward to.

"A slice of apple pie always cheers me up." Tomasina slid three plates onto their corner table. Taking her seat, she doled out the forks, saving Grace's for last. "You're not going to cry again, are you? Because salty tears don't mix with nutmeg and cinnamon."

Beside Tom and opposite Grace, Leah's sharp inhale was barely audible above the clatter of dishes and hearty male-dominated conversation in the Cowboy Café. "Tomasina."

"Crying ain't gonna solve anything." The vibrant red-head looked every inch the sophisticated lady. Sometimes, though, the drover and rodeo star in her slipped out. "It sure ain't gonna get Noah to cease being stubborn and forgive her already."

Grace poked at the spice-coated apple slivers and flaky crust, eating but not really tasting the dessert.

Not once had Noah been out to the ranch. The twins were sad and confused, and she hadn't known how to answer their questions. He'd sent his hired boy, Timothy, each day to do the chores and offer her a ride to town if she needed it. Mired in misery, she'd thanked him for the offer and declined. She wasn't ready to see Noah. She wasn't sure she'd ever be, despite how much she missed him. Just being in town had her nerves on edge.

She'd been perusing the list of suitable towns the stationmaster had given her this morning when Tomasina and Leah had paid her a surprise visit. Ashamed of her behavior, she'd immediately begged their forgiveness. The women had been surprisingly understanding and concerned for her. While she didn't deserve their friendship, she was thankful for their support. They'd insisted on treating her to lunch. The girls were happily playing at Hannah's house so the adults could talk.

"Everyone's talking about him staying at the hotel." Tomasina speared another bite. "After the steamy kiss you two shared, they're saying he refused to offer for you, so you kicked him off his own ranch."

Her cheeks flushed and she darted a glance about the café. Most customers were minding their own business. The few diners eating alone seemed more inclined to stare at her because they had no one to talk to.

"You're not helping," Leah intoned. "Grace, dear, not everyone thinks that."

"I hate that my actions have caused him so much trouble." Her voice wobbled with emotion. She willed it away. This wasn't the time or place. "His life was fine before I came. I've ruined everything."

Leah put her fork down and rested her hand atop her swollen belly. "His life was sad and lonely before you and the girls came to stay with him. He would never admit it, but it was obvious to those who care about him."

"I still think you should tell him about this Frank person." Tomasina's eyes burned green fire. "He'll understand why you kept everyone in the dark. If I see that man, I'll hogtie him like I did that nasty old Mr. Harding."

Grace gifted her with a sad smile. She'd heard the story of Tomasina's stint as a cleaning girl—among other things—in Will's hotel and the fate of the guest who'd attempted to accost her. The image of Frank trussed up like an animal was a satisfying one.

"You didn't see his reaction. Besides, he probably won't agree to see me again." Looking down, she was surprised to see the plate empty. She picked up her reticule. "I'll go and see to the bill."

"Oh no," Leah protested, dabbing at her mouth. "We're the ones who insisted you come. I'm paying."

"You've both showed me such grace and kindness." Her throat grew thick. She'd thought she'd lost not only Noah, but her new friends, as well. Perhaps they'd welcome her letters from her new home. "It's my treat."

While she settled the bill, they gathered their belongings and met her at the entrance. Grace avoided meeting folks' gazes as they traversed the boardwalk. The closer they got to the jail, the slower her steps. Her rescue came by the way of Pippa, who emerged from the bank just as they were passing by.

"Well, if it isn't Grace Longstreet," she greeted, a merry twinkle in her eye. "Who knew there was a finer actress than myself in Cowboy Creek?"

Grace stiffened, unsure of Pippa's intentions. But the younger woman linked arms with her and eyed her curiously. "Apparently I have more to learn than I thought. How were you able to carry off your ruse for that length of time without slipping out of character?"

"I'm sorry for deceiving you, Pippa. I understand if you're angry."

Words she'd be repeating until she booked their train ride farther west. They weren't meaningless words, however. The last thing she wanted was to hurt anyone or ruin friendships.

Pippa arched a brow. "You're not one of those notorious female bandits, are you?"

"Of course not!"

"So you're not hiding out from the law?"

"I haven't committed any crime." Was lying to a lawman a crime?

"You're hiding from something, though." The actress's gaze was assessing.

"Not something. *Someone*." Tomasina inserted herself into the conversation. "Her loathsome brother-in-law is determined to make her his. Tell her, Grace."

Pippa listened to Grace's brief explanation, her expression growing alarmed. "You have to tell Noah."

"I tried." She paused as an older couple emerged from the bank and ogled their group. "He's not interested in hearing my story."

Leah patted Grace's hand. "I have to go. Valentine has taken the day off to spend with Daniel's father, which means I'm in charge of supper. I'll be praying for you, Grace. It'll all work out, you'll see."

Giving her a quick hug, Grace thanked her. Tomasina had business to tend to, as well, which left Grace and Pippa.

"I'm not angry with you. Disappointed, maybe, because you didn't feel comfortable enough to confide in me." Linking arms, Pippa guided her away from Eden Street. "I understand how someone in your situation would feel like there are scant options, especially considering a powerful, controlling man is involved. I suppose Noah is feeling disappointed, too."

"If that's true, it's the least of his emotions. He despises me for making a fool of him, Pippa." Guilt pummeled her. "I don't wish to talk about him, okay?"

Frowning, she nodded, the flowers on her flamboyant hat bobbing.

As they strolled along Second Street, Grace glanced at the shops and houses. "Where are we going?"

"To the opera house. The long way around."

So she wouldn't have to risk seeing Noah. "Why are we going there?"

"You are due some cheering up. In order to do that, I'm going to do your hair and stage makeup. You are going to try on any costume that catches your fancy."

Grace allowed her friend to take the lead, even though dressing in outlandish costumes wasn't going to lift her spirits. Nothing could accomplish that.

"I have an hour or two before I have to pick the girls up from Hannah's."

Pippa waved her hand in dismissal. "Plenty of time."

When they were inside the opulent space, Grace breathed a sigh of relief that they hadn't encountered Noah or his friends. Behind the stage where the dressing rooms were, she watched in awe as the other woman paraded brilliant costumes before her. Because she was unable to choose, Pippa selected one for her, a heavy, ornate gown fit for a queen.

An hour later, Grace stared at her reflection, amazed at the transformation.

"You're too lovely for words."

She fingered the string of pearls threaded in her upswept hair. With the thick makeup, bright red lips and rouged cheeks, she didn't look like herself. "I'm unrecognizable."

"That's the beauty of being an actress. You can pretend to be anyone you like."

Lowering her hand to her lap, she shook her head. "I'm tired of pretending."

Sensing her change in mood, Pippa joined her on the cushioned bench and gently clasped her hands in hers. Excitement bubbled out of her. "Want to hear a secret?"

"What kind of secret?" She was done pretending, and didn't want anything more to do with subterfuge.

"I know you don't wish to discuss Noah, but he's privy to my scheme. And he approves." She bit her lower lip. "Well, *approve* may be too strong a word. He agrees. Mainly because there's no other way."

"No other way for what?" she said, confused. "What scheme, Pippa?"

The story spilled out how Noah, Will and Daniel suspected D.B. had been Prudence Haywood's coconspirator in the attempts to cause havoc in Cowboy Creek. The men's efforts to garner evidence had proved fruitless. While the editor admitted to being Isaac Burrows's brother, he denied any familial relationship to the widow.

"Why would D.B. and Prudence do any of that?"

"Revenge. Isaac built Harper into a thriving city. When the railroad came through, he lobbied for them to choose Harper." Pippa shrugged. "They chose Cowboy Creek, and Harper went bust. Isaac died a broken, disillusioned man."

"So you're saying that D.B. came here to foil Noah, Will and Daniel's success?"

"Yes, that's right." Her hazel eyes took on a speculative gleam. "I guess printing unflattering articles wasn't getting the job done, so he sent for Prudence to aid him in more drastic measures. I'm not sure what their connection is, but I'm going to find out."

"How are you planning to do that?"

Bolting to her feet, Pippa threw out her arms and bowed. "Pretending to be other people is my profession. I'm going to transform myself into Prudence Haywood and trick D.B. into confessing."

Disbelief stole her breath. "You're taller than her. Less curvy. Your hair's the wrong shade." Getting up took some effort as her queen's costume weighed a ton. Maneuvering the voluminous skirts, Grace went to her friend. "If D.B. is the culprit, he's a dangerous man, Pippa. And cunning. How will you convince him?"

"We're going to do it at night. I'll be wearing a hat with a decorative veil. Prudence wouldn't want anyone to recognize her, so he won't be suspicious about my attire. I'll disguise my voice. Don't worry. I have the training and skills to pull this off."

"I can't believe Noah agreed to this."

"He didn't want to. I'd gone to the office in search of Gideon. He wasn't there, but I overhead Will and Daniel sharing their frustrations. I offered my services and, as they were out of ideas, they reluctantly accepted."

"Does Gideon know what you're planning?" Grace asked.

Her first hint of disquiet became visible. "Not yet. I'll tell him this evening. He's taking me to the Cattleman for dinner."

"He won't like it."

Instead of her standard flippant reply, she said, "This will be a chance for him to show whether he trusts my judgment or not."

"Promise me you'll be careful."

"I promise." Her expression brightened. "Grace, will you be here with me while I prepare? It would be much more fun if you were here."

"I'll have to arrange for someone to watch Jane and Abigail." While she wanted no part of this daring scheme, she had a duty to support her friend. "When?"

"Tomorrow night."

"I'll be here."

As she changed into her regular clothes, Grace prayed and asked God to keep His hand on her friend. She hoped this wouldn't prove to be a costly mistake.

Chapter Twenty-Three

Where was Grace? How was she doing?

Surely the twins were wondering where he'd been these past few days. Did they miss him as much as he missed their happy smiles and unconditional love?

Stop thinking about her, he ordered himself for the hundredth time. *Nothing good can come from dwelling on your biggest mistake.*

"Sheriff Burgess."

Noah halted outside the hotel's entrance. Old Horace and Gus were waving him over to their usual spot in front of Booker & Son. He sighed. Now that he'd seen them, he couldn't very well ignore their summons.

Traversing the light morning traffic, he stepped onto the boardwalk and welcomed the awning's shade. It was going to be a scorcher.

"Morning, gentlemen. What can I do for you?"

"How ya like living at the Cattleman?" Gus peered up at him.

Old Horace snickered. "Never thought I'd see the day a man allowed himself to get run off his own land by a female."

Noah's disagreeable mood soured further. "What do you need, gentlemen? I've got work to do."

He still couldn't believe he was allowing Pippa Neely to do his job for him. But he, Will and Daniel had had zero success ferreting out D.B.'s secrets. Her plan had struck them as sensible at the time. She'd been so convincing. But the more he thought about her scheme, the less he liked it.

Gideon's late-night visit to his room had underscored his unease. The normally easygoing train rep had been irate and visibly disturbed by the thought of Pippa exposing herself to danger. He'd blamed Noah for ruining what was supposed to have been a romantic evening culminating in a marriage proposal. Instead, he and Pippa had engaged in a stunning row. She'd accused Gideon of not trusting her. He'd accused her of being reckless. The lovebirds had parted on bad terms.

Gus pushed his boot off the planks and set his rocker moving. "We saw a suspicious individual last night, Sheriff."

Old Horace spit a stream of tobacco juice. "He was lurking around. Peering in windows. Asking questions. Suspicious, I say."

Impatience gripped him. "Did he do anything unlawful?"

"Nope."

"Not that I saw."

He kicked up a shoulder. "Then my hands are tied." He made to leave.

"He weren't no drover," Gus called after him. "This feller was a highfalutin businessman. Tall. Dark hair slicked back off his face."

"Fancy suit," Horace chimed in.

"Had a gun on him. I saw the pearl handle when his jacket gaped open."

Noah tipped his hat up. "Now, that I can do something about. Firearms aren't permitted within town limits. I'll keep my eye out for him."

"You're a right good lawman. I don't care what anyone else says." Old Horace spit again.

Grimacing, he bid them good day. He didn't need the old codgers to remind him that his reputation wasn't quite as sterling as it had been. *You have only yourself to blame. You should've marched Grace Longstreet straight to the hotel that very first day.* Muttering under his breath, he headed for the jail, not at all in the mood to deal with Xavier's needling and sarcastic remarks.

The day should've dragged. But one minor catastrophe after another kept him hopping from one place to the next, and before he knew it, the clock chimed six. He left Daniel's office at the stockyards and was passing beneath the opera house marquee when he came face-to-face with Grace.

As lovely as usual in a sunflower-yellow dress, she stopped short when she noticed him, her gloved hands knotting at her waist.

"Noah." Her forehead creased. "I didn't expect to see you. I, ah—"

The ice encasing his heart had begun to melt the moment he saw her. He couldn't let himself soften. Couldn't give in to the voice insisting he forgive her. Or at least give her a chance to defend her actions.

"What are you doing here, Constance?" He deliberately used the false name. "Oh, I forgot. *Grace.*"

She paled. "I came to see Pippa."

"She's busy," he said brusquely. "You'll have to see her another time."

"She's expecting me." Her chin lifted a fraction. "I know about your plan."

Noah glanced about to make sure no one was listening. This far end of Eden Street was deserted at the moment.

"You shouldn't be here." He fisted his hands at his sides. "You'll only distract her."

Her lower lip trembled. Lifting a hand to him, she whispered, "Noah, please. Won't you let me at least try to explain?"

He nodded. "I would like for you to tell me something."

"Anything." Surprise brightened her eyes, along with hope. Wasted hope.

Schooling his features into an unyielding mask, he said, "When exactly are you planning on leaving? 'Cause I'd like to have my house back."

Blinking rapidly, she dipped her head, hiding from his hard stare. He felt like an ogre, but the anger and humiliation were like a raging inferno inside.

"I'll let you know tomorrow," she said in a small voice. "I'm going to purchase my tickets first thing."

He would not ask where she was going.

He didn't care where she was going, Grace acknowledged with a pang. He just wanted her gone.

She shouldn't be surprised. She'd tricked him about her past and her identity. No way would he believe she'd tumbled in love with him.

Being this close to him was agony. His bright blue eyes were as cold as Lake Michigan in the middle of winter. It was as if he were staring down one of his captured outlaws, someone despicable, someone without honor. For a soldier who'd risked his life for his convictions, a rancher-turned-lawman who brought the lawless to justice, her deception must be particularly difficult to comprehend, much less forgive.

"Will you ever accept that I'm sorry for what I did?"

His mouth flattened into an unforgiving line. "I accept that you're sorry for getting caught."

Grace nodded, unable to speak past the emotions crowding her chest. She left him standing on the boardwalk and was almost to the set of double doors when he spoke.

"Grace?"

Her glove slipped from the brass knob. "Yes?"

"Don't stay long. Go back to the ranch and stay there until this is over."

Escaping into the darkened opera house, she sucked in deep breaths in an effort to subdue the crying fit threatening to overtake her. She couldn't let Pippa see her distress. Noah was right about one thing—she couldn't afford to distract her tonight.

When she was confident she had herself in hand, she made her way along the aisle and behind the stage to the dressing rooms. An impassioned male voice drifted to her.

"It's not that I don't trust your acting abilities. I've seen your performances, and you're a fine actress. I'm worried, that's all. I can't lose you, Pippa."

Grace hesitated on the threshold. Gideon and Pippa were sharing a private moment.

"I overreacted," Pippa admitted, affection evident in her voice. "I don't want you to worry. The men will be close by, listening for the confession. They'll leap to my rescue if need be."

"I'll be there, as well."

Knocking on the door frame, Grace took a few halting steps into the room, the smells of velvet, perfume and musty air blending together. "I'm sorry to interrupt. I can come back if you'd like…"

Gideon put distance between himself and Pippa, clasping his hands behind him. With his blond hair brushed off his forehead and dressed in his dove-gray suit, he looked ready to whisk his lady away to a romantic spot.

Seated at her dressing table, Pippa turned a half circle on the cushioned bench. "Grace, hello. I'm so glad you came."

Concern eclipsed her reluctance to intrude. Pippa was stunning, as always, but a closer look revealed beads of perspiration on her brow and a tightness to her jaw.

"Are you nervous?"

"I'm never nervous," she denied, only to grimace.

Gideon put a hand on her shoulder. "What's the matter?"

"I—" She gulped and clutched her stomach. "I don't feel…" Bolting to her feet, she lurched through a door. The sound of her retching was undeniable.

Gideon started pacing. Grace kept her gaze on the door. When Pippa came out minutes later, she was weak and trembling.

Assisting her to the bench, Gideon brushed a stray lock behind her ear, tenderness in the touch. "Is this normal before a performance?"

"No. I'm afraid it's something worse," she moaned.

"What?" he grew alarmed.

"I've felt nauseous since I woke. I think the coleslaw I ate last night made me sick."

"I didn't eat the coleslaw," he said.

Burying her face in her hands, her words were muffled. "Be glad. I thought it tasted sour but ate it, anyway."

Grace went and crouched before her. "You can't go through with the masquerade."

"She's right." Gideon rubbed Pippa's back. "I'll let Noah know what's happening. We can reschedule."

When she raised her head, the black liner around her eyes had smudged and half her lipstick had rubbed off. She looked like a bedraggled doll. Poor Pippa.

"D.B. knows he's being investigated," she said. "What if he bolts?"

"That's not your priority right now."

"What if this is our only chance?"

Grace glanced at the pots of makeup littering the table. "I'll do it."

Both of them stared at her like she was insane Pippa was the first to recover her voice. "You're not an actress. You lack professional training."

She crossed her arms. "You said I could give you pointers."

"Why would you offer to take her place?" Gideon's eyebrows met over his nose. "It's not without great risk."

"If D.B. is guilty, he deserves to be punished." When the train rep continued to regard her, she revealed the true reason. "This town is everything to Noah. It's his home. His sanctuary. I've spoiled that. Doing this for him is a small way for me to make up for my actions."

Pippa looked pained, whether due to the conversation or her illness, Grace wasn't sure. "I don't know, Grace. It's a noble offer, but—"

"Please? Let me do this for you. For Noah. For Cowboy Creek."

After an interminable silence, Pippa slowly nodded. "I'll help you get into character."

"This is going to work." Daniel's whispered reassurance as he crouched beside him in the dark testified to Noah's nerves.

He couldn't shake the feeling of dread lodged in the pit of his stomach. Putting an innocent female's life in jeopardy went against his Southern upbringing.

"This was our only recourse," Daniel spoke again, nothing more than a hulking shadow. "Relax, old friend. I can hear your bones rattling from here."

Noah nodded, the cold weight of his rifle a comfort. He and Daniel were the closest to the newspaper office's rear porch. They were using the storage shed for cover, close enough to hear what was being said and to intervene if necessary. He prayed it wouldn't be.

Will was hunkered down several yards away, his own weapon at the ready.

There was no way of knowing exactly who they were dealing with. Gideon had used his connection to the railroad to get a hasty reply on his query—turned out Prudence hadn't bought a ticket. She hadn't been on the train.

D.B. was either covering for her, or he honestly believed the lies she told him.

Please let it be the latter.

His instincts told him D.B. was guilty. The man's attitude toward them, his unflattering articles about the town, didn't indicate a satisfied citizen.

"Five minutes to go," Daniel warned.

"I'm ready for this to be over with," Noah muttered, more nervous in this moment than when he'd faced down a couple hundred gray uniforms.

Running footsteps behind them had his finger going to the trigger. Flattening against the shed's exterior, he and Daniel did their best to blend into the darkness and gloom.

The person approaching headed straight for them. Daniel sucked in a harsh breath.

"Don't shoot" came a fierce whisper. "It's Gideon."

Noah's muscles relaxed a fraction. Irritation sharpened his voice. "You shouldn't be here."

He understood why Gideon had come. If the woman Noah loved was in imminent danger, no one would be able to keep him away. Thankfully Grace was at the ranch, safe and sound.

As that last thought fully registered, he nearly dropped his rifle. Love Grace? Everything in him rebelled. He didn't *know* Grace. He'd thought he'd known the woman called Constance. He'd admired her. He'd even admit that he'd cared for her. But these past weeks had been a mirage.

An alluring, tempting mirage that he'd come close to buying as truth.

Gideon's uneven breathing sounded loud. Too loud. Any minute, Pippa was going to come walking along the street to knock on D.B.'s door, as planned. The man was risking the plan.

"Pippa's ill," he panted, seeking shelter on the other side of Daniel.

Disappointment crashed through him. He lowered his rifle. "So this was all for nothing."

"You don't understand. Grace was at the opera house. She volunteered to take Pippa's place."

Noah worked to make sense of what he was saying. "That's ridiculous. She has nothing to do with this."

"You told her no, right?" Situated between Noah and Gideon, Daniel shifted in the dirt.

Gideon's pause spoke volumes. Noah's heart hung suspended in his chest for long, excruciating seconds before exploding against his rib cage in a defiant rhythm. He eyed the vacant street. Denial ricocheted through his mind.

"She insisted. We agreed it was the best alternative," he finally admitted.

"No." He gritted his teeth. "I can't believe she'd go through with something so dangerous." The weathered boards bit into his back. His hands grew slick with sweat.

All he could see was her face earlier that day outside the opera house. He'd willfully spoken with the aim to inflict pain. To hurt her as deeply as she'd hurt him. Judging from the misery and regret that had been present in her beautiful eyes, he'd succeeded.

Daniel placed a hand on his arm. "We don't know for sure that we have anything to worry about."

"You believe that as much as I do," he retorted. "If the man was innocent, he would've come to us about the missive he received from Prudence." The fake one they'd planted in his office late last night. "I've got to stop her."

"Too late," Gideon murmured.

The three of them froze as a black-clad figure came into view. Grace. A veil concealed much of her face. The pale hair peeking out must be a wig. Grace was shorter than Pippa, which put her closer in height to Prudence.

Everything in him commanded him to move. To stand

up and intercept her. To stop her from doing this mad thing because he couldn't survive if any harm befell her.

Daniel must've read his mind, because he clamped a hand on Noah's shoulder to hold him in place.

Her boots scuffed across the porch's planks. She rapped lightly on the door. Four short bursts. Silence. Two more. As they couldn't know what sort of code the two had between them, they'd made one up and informed D.B. in the fake missive.

Noah squinted, hoping to see more of Grace's features, to measure her state of mind. The shadows prevented him from doing so. As he had countless times on the battlefield and in the years since, he turned to his heavenly Father for help. *Dear God, I know I've been harsh with her. I'm still angrier than I've ever been at anyone, but please...please keep her safe.*

Repeating the prayer in his mind, he saw the door open halfway, the editor's body outlined by the faint light inside the office. He quickly shut it as he moved to join her.

"What are you doing here?" D.B. was irate. That much was obvious by the fury in his tone. "You're supposed to be on your way to Illinois! If they find you here, it's all over."

Daniel's fingers gripped Noah's shoulder tighter. Their hunches had been right. D.B. had lied.

Grace coughed. "I couldn't leave until I knew we'd succeeded in destroying Cowboy Creek."

She was trying to disguise her voice. Would D.B. buy it? And if he didn't, what would be his next move?

D.B. ran a hand over his hair and gripped his neck, a gesture of frustration. "Are you sick?"

Noah hated that he couldn't make out their expressions. It put him at a disadvantage.

"My throat's sore from too many hours over a campfire," she snapped, planting her hands on her hips and tapping her boot, just as the real Prudence would have.

Good girl, Grace. Keep it up.

"They found your brooch, linking you to the missing deeds. What were you thinking, sister? Now you've put that irritating lawman's suspicion on me."

So Prudence Haywood *was* D.B.'s sister after all? The puzzle pieces started to fit together. Isaac Burrows, brother to Prudence and D.B., had started Cowboy Creek's rival town. When the Union Pacific chose Cowboy Creek, it had meant the end for Harper.

Coughing again, she said, "I left the camp to take care of private business. On my way back, I heard the riders approaching. I had no alternative but to hide until they'd gone."

Noah's admiration for Grace's skills was steeped in anger. She really was an excellent actress.

"I thought poisoning those cattle would achieve our goals, but of course Gardner had to bring in that veterinarian. The burned lumber hardly set them back at all on construction. Those three think they're so smart." His bitterness was undeniable. "They won't win. We won't let them. Not when our brother died at their hands."

Grace's gasp echoed through the night. "Noah's not at fault. You can't blame him!"

D.B. went rigid. Noah sprung to his feet. In defending him, she'd forgotten to disguise her voice. And now she might pay with her very life.

Chapter Twenty-Four

Moving faster than anyone could have predicted, the older man's hand shot out and ripped the hat and wig from Grace's head. She cried out in pain. In an instant, D.B. slammed her face-first against the door, a gun barrel to her temple.

"I know you're out there, Burgess!" He gestured wildly with his free hand. "You and whoever you've conned into skulking in the shadows can drop your weapons. If you don't, she's a dead woman."

Noah's hold on his rifle, aimed at the porch, faltered. D.B. would make good on his threat. He'd already killed Sheriff Davis. If he felt cornered, he might act out of desperation.

Will emerged slowly from his hiding spot. "You don't have to involve her, Burrows. She's not even a resident here. Your issue is with me and my friends. Not her."

"Because of you, my brother took his own life. By destroying his home, you ruined him. Left him with nothing but broken dreams. Just like how I'm going to ruin you." He seethed with hatred. "Drop your weapons *now*, I said!" His gun hand moved, and Grace whimpered in response.

Rage clouded Noah's vision. Burning-hot rage and ice-cold fear.

"Let her go." He crept forward. "You're not angry with her. Take me. Use me as insurance to get yourself out of Cowboy Creek."

Grace was crying. "Noah, don't. I'm sorry. Please—"

Her words were cut off by a sudden downward motion of D.B.'s hand. She slumped to the floor.

With a roar, Noah sprinted forward. Daniel protested. Will muttered an oath.

Dim light startled him. Shadows blended together. Shooting at them without aiming, D.B. dragged Grace inside the building and slammed the door.

Noah reached it, frantic to get to Grace, his mind focused solely on her rescue.

"Open this door!" He pounded on the wood. Inside, glass shattered. Crashed. What was he doing to her?

Moving back, he rammed it with his shoulder. It didn't budge. He kicked it repeatedly. "Grace!"

"I'll go around the front," Will yelled.

Daniel and Gideon ran onto the porch.

"I smell smoke," Gideon gasped.

Noah stopped what he was doing. Pressing his face against the seam between the door and frame, he detected the same stench. A heavy curtain obscured the window beside the door. "He's going to burn down this town."

The image of Grace in there, unconscious and alone, made rational thought impossible.

"Stand back." Hefting his rifle above his head, he slammed it through the window, scattering shards of glass. Dull pain radiated up his arm.

"Noah!" Daniel's voice rang with alarm. "If you go in there alone, you'll get yourself shot. Or burned worse than before. Let us help get this door open. We'll go in together."

"No time." Using the butt of his rifle, he punched out as much of the window glass as he could. Then he climbed through.

The place was in ruins. Papers littered the floor. Chairs overturned. Flames licked the floorboards along the far interior wall, climbing up the walls and eating up the curtains at the front windows. Thick smoke churned near the rafters.

Covering his nose with one arm, he braced himself for a shot from D.B.

But there was no sign of him. Through the open front door, he saw Will and the older man scuffling in the street.

He called for Grace. Prayed for mercy.

Spotting her boots behind the far side of the hulking desk, he breathed a silent thank-you and dashed to her side. The smoke was thicker here. The heat seared his skin. His scars burned as if flames kissed them, his past pain rearing up to paralyze him.

Focus. Grace needs you.

His lungs clamoring for oxygen, he went on his knees and, scooping her limp body against his chest, surged upward and lumbered to the rear entrance. Gideon had managed to get it open. Then, following Noah into the sparse grass, he lit a match.

Still cradling her in his arms, he studied the wound at her temple. The delicate skin was bruised, but not broken. Every single moment with her—from the first time he'd laid eyes on her to now—marched through his mind. He was wrong. He *did* know her. Constance. Grace. Whatever her name, he knew her heart, and it was good. He should've listened to her instead of letting his wounded pride dictate his reaction.

Love for this woman rushed into the starved, lonely crevices of his heart and, instead of resisting, he welcomed it. The newfound feelings zipped and zinged inside, bright and magnificent like a rare display of aurora borealis against the Kansas sky, beautiful and surprising like a rain shower on a sunny day, complete with a rainbow. Grace was everything he hadn't allowed himself to want in a wife. When she looked at him, she didn't see the bitter, scarred ex-soldier. She saw him as better…more…a conqueror of past horrors.

She made him believe good things were possible. She'd restored his ability to hope.

And in return, he'd repaid her with anger and accusations. He couldn't be sure she'd trust in his love or even if she'd welcome his feelings.

"Noah." Gideon's voice startled him out of his musings. "You shouldn't stay here. In case Burrows escapes."

"You're right," he rasped. "I'll take her to Doc Fletcher's house."

"I'll go help the others."

Heading away from town, Noah carried her to the doctor's home since the hour was late. Fletcher answered his impatient summons wearing only pants and a shirt with the top buttons undone.

"I was on my way to bed, young man." His gaze fell on Grace's limp form, and he stood back to give them entrance. "Take her into the parlor. Use the brown sofa. What happened to her?"

Giving the older man a brief rundown of events, Noah gingerly laid her on the indicated furniture. She moaned. Her eyelids fluttered.

"Grace?" He squeezed her hand. "Can you hear me?"

Fletcher brought a lit lamp and placed it on the side table. He bent to examine the wound. "Any other injuries besides this one?"

"Not that I know of."

Her dark tresses had been tamed into a tight bun. Pippa had applied her stage makeup. Grace's eyebrows were auburn slashes and a bold rose hue clung to her lips.

Another groan escaped her and, forehead creasing, she opened her eyes. The first thing she focused on was him.

"Noah." Her smile was more of a grimace. "You're all right."

Still holding her hand, he caressed her cheek. "The important thing is that *you're* all right. How's your head? Does anything else hurt?"

"I believe those are questions I should be asking, young man." The doctor nudged him. "Go to the kitchen and fix us some coffee, will you?"

He considered arguing. His worry was still a palpable thing. Reluctantly, he released her and got to his feet. "I'll be close by," he reassured her.

Inside the kitchen, he went through the motions of heating water and gathering mugs and milk, reliving in his mind the moment he had spotted her boots peeking past the desk. Limp and unmoving. He could've lost her forever.

Will arrived then, saving him from further depressing thoughts.

"How's Grace?"

Noah joined his friend on the veranda. "Doc's still doing his examination. I think she's going to be fine. She woke up shortly after we got here."

"Good to hear." Will's gaze was sympathetic. "We subdued Burrows. Because of the commotion, several townsfolk came out and helped us put out the fire. Neither the jail nor the boardinghouse sustained damages. I came to fetch your keys. Burrows will be joining Xavier in the jail tonight."

Handing over the keys, he growled, "He deserves to be hung."

"We'll let the courts decide that." Will clapped him on the back. "You're going to mend things between you and Grace, right? Don't let pride keep you from being with the woman you love."

He didn't bother denying his feelings. "I'm going to give it my best shot."

"You can always try kissing her in the middle of town again." With a wink, he descended the stairs. Noah went inside, grateful Burrows was in custody and that no one else had gotten hurt. Doc met him at the parlor entrance.

"She's going to need rest in the coming days. However, I don't foresee any problems. Maybe aches and tenderness from the blow to her head." Shuffling along the hall, he said over his shoulder, "I'll be in my office with my coffee. Give you young folks some privacy."

"Thanks, Doc."

Grace was sitting on the far end of the sofa, her eyes large and a bit wary as she watched him enter. Crushing the need to go to her, he veered toward the fireplace and rested an arm along the mantel. Little scrapes and bruises were only now making themselves known. He'd deal with them later.

"Should you be sitting up?"

"I'm a little shaky, that's all." She touched the spot where D.B. had struck her. "My head's sore, but Doctor Fletcher assured me it would ease with time." Clasping her hands in her lap, she regarded him with unguarded longing.

An answering longing erupted inside him. He wanted nothing more than to hold her.

He couldn't afford to be distracted, though.

"You were very brave," he said. "Because of you, Burrows will get the justice he deserves."

"Doc explained what happened. You saved my life."

"Why did you do it, Grace?"

"Pippa needed someone to fill in, and I was there." She visibly swallowed. "And I thought maybe, by doing this for you, I could make up for some of the pain I've caused you."

Tears pooled in her eyes as she braced for his rejection.

"You could've gotten yourself killed," he said hoarsely. "And I couldn't have lived with that."

Her lips parted. "What are you saying?"

"You offered to explain your actions." Pushing off the mantel, he couldn't resist joining her on the sofa. With the span of a cushion between them, Noah shifted to face her. "I was too stubborn before. I'm ready to listen now."

Grace hadn't expected to be given this opportunity. She wasn't prepared. Her head throbbed, and the stench of smoke clinging to her and Noah's clothes was making her nauseous. Her throat was raw and dry, and the tears refused to be stemmed.

She'd come so close to dying, to orphaning her precious daughters.

"I don't know where to start," she blurted. Right this second, her chief desire was to scoot across the cushion and sink into his embrace, to rest her head against his shoulder and feel his strong arms come around her. She craved his reassurance and, ultimately, his forgiveness.

His hair was spiky from him running his hands through it. Soot streaked beneath his right eye. "How about you start with why you switched places with your cousin?"

Grace didn't like to talk about Frank. She hadn't shared many details with her own cousin, so it was hard to put the right words together.

Noah's fingertips skimmed her knuckles. "I'm being insensitive. You've had a shock. We can wait until tomorrow to talk. Or whenever you're ready."

Once again, someone she cared deeply about was showing her grace. It made her love him even more than she did already.

"I appreciate your understanding, Noah, but I'd like to get this out."

He sank back against the cushions and gave a slow nod. "All right."

"I assumed Constance's identity in order to leave Chicago without my brother-in-law finding out." There was a slight change in his expression, an expectation in his blue eyes that made her think he knew what was coming. She toyed with the ribbon entwined with lace on the costume's bodice. "Ambrose's brother, Frank, is the type of man who has a high opinion of himself. Because of his affluent upbringing and position in society, his sense of entitlement knows no bounds. What Frank wants, he pursues. No obstacle is too great."

One particularly crushed young bride he'd debauched rose in Grace's memory, and she shuddered. The girl had believed herself in love with Frank. Even after her public ruin and divorce, she'd come to the Longstreet mansion and begged him to take her back. His cold reception and utter disregard for her feelings had left Grace in shock.

"In the early months of my marriage, Frank took me aside and admitted he wished he'd met me first. I rebuffed him, of course. I naively thought that would be the end of it. From that day forward, I became a game to him. A challenge he couldn't ignore."

Noah leaned forward to rest his hands on his knees, a muscle ticking in his jaw. "Did your husband know?"

"Ambrose never mentioned it. I doubt he would've acted even if he had."

"What did he do to make you desperate enough to flee your home? Why do you continue to fear him despite the hundreds of miles between you?"

His expression fierce, tension bristling along his body, Noah looked every inch the battle-hardened soldier he was at heart. He was ready to defend her against a faceless enemy.

"You don't understand how ruthless he can be. How determined."

"Tell me." His soft voice was at odds with his demeanor. "Help me understand."

Sucking in a fortifying breath, she told him about the

women whose lives he'd ruined. Most of them had been led down the road to destruction willingly, awed by his power, his harsh male beauty and convincing personality. There'd been rumors, though, that some hadn't been willing.

Chafing her arms, she stared at the aqua glass bowl on the coffee table. "I assumed I was safe in my in-laws' home. That Frank would never cross the line. And while Ambrose was alive, my encounters with him were annoying, yes, but not disturbing. Inappropriate remarks. Insisting on my company when I would rather have been left alone. My mother-in-law didn't help matters. She adores Frank. She encouraged me to go to museums and parks and parties with him. In her opinion, he was being the doting brother-in-law since my husband was often involved in business matters."

Noah made a sound of disgust. Shoving to his feet, he stalked across the room to stare out of a window. "I'm sorry you had to live like that. It couldn't have been easy to keep your guard up all the time." Swiveling around to meet her gaze, he said, "A husband is supposed to be a source of support and refuge. Yours failed to protect you from his own brother. I'll never understand that."

"Frank's behavior got bolder after Ambrose's death. He waited a month before proposing to me."

"Let me guess. He didn't take your rejection well."

Grace pressed her lips together and shook her head. "He promised me—threatened me, really—that I would ultimately become his wife." Her stomach roiled at the memory of his hot breath, his marble-smooth hands imprisoning her face as he forced his kiss on her. "He said I owed him and his parents, that I should be grateful they hadn't kicked me out on the streets after Ambrose's death. He said…" She pressed her hand against her middle. "He said if I didn't marry him, he'd make sure I'd never see my girls again."

"Did he hurt you? Physically, I mean."

"On three separate occasions, he discovered me in remote areas of the mansion and gardens. He kissed me despite my protests. The first time it happened, I went straight to my mother-in-law. She laughed it off, saying I was taking his advances too seriously. It was just a kiss. After the last time, when he attempted to do more, I made sure I always had a maid with me."

Noah passed a trembling hand over his face. Standing, she waited for the dizziness to pass before going to him. Capturing his wrists, she peered up into his turbulent blue eyes.

"I never intended to hurt you."

"Grace…"

"You don't know how many times I started to tell you the truth."

"At the welcome party for Mr. McAllister, when you told me about the man obsessed with your cousin, you were talking about yourself." There was no recrimination in his eyes, just quiet expectation.

"Yes. I—"

Pounding on the front door broke them apart. Noah strode into the hallway. Grace reached the entryway moments before the doctor.

The sight of James Johnson's white face speared fear into her heart. Never had she seen the cowboy so shaken.

"Noah. Grace." His gaze bounced between them.

"What is it?" Noah demanded. "Is Hannah okay? The baby? Do you need Doc?"

He shook his head, his eyes settling on Grace and begging forgiveness. "I'm sorry. The girls are gone."

"No." Anguish warred with shock. "Frank. It has to be Frank. H-he warned me…"

She weaved to the right. Noah's arm came around her, steadying her.

"You were watching the twins tonight?" he said. "Where are they?"

"I don't know." He threaded his hands anxiously in his longish black hair. "I heard the commotion in town and left to investigate. Once the fire had been extinguished, I returned home, only to find Hannah tied up and gagged. Ava was asleep in her bed, but the girls were gone. A stranger told Hannah to give Grace this."

Grace knew without looking at it who was responsible. Frank had promised to have her, one way or another, and he knew her biggest weakness.

"What did he look like?" Her voice shook. "Do you know?"

"Tall. Imposing. Black hair and dark eyes. Cold eyes, Hannah said."

Noah ripped open the envelope and scanned the contents. He blanched.

"Grace..." Horror gripped his features. "Your brother-in-law tracked you here. He has Jane and Abigail. If you don't meet him tomorrow morning at his requested spot alone, he'll take them away. You'll never see them again."

Chapter Twenty-Five

Noah would punish Frank Longstreet. He'd make him regret stepping foot on Kansas soil.

"I have to do what he says." Grace clutched the front of Noah's shirt, her eyes a touch wild. "Where am I to meet him? What time?"

Cupping her shoulders, he tried to control the fear and fury invading every part of his body. Grace needed him to be strong. The girls needed him to be levelheaded.

"He doesn't say. You're to go to the post office first thing tomorrow morning. He's left a missive for you there with instructions."

She was nodding, unaware that her fingernails were starting to dig into his skin. He covered her hands with his own and lightly squeezed.

"Okay. I'll do that. The girls will want their dolls. We'll need clothes."

"Grace. Listen to me."

Her gaze refocused on him.

"I can't let you do this."

"I have to." Her lower lip trembled. "I'll do anything to save my babies." Her voice broke, and she sagged against him, her body racked with sobs.

Noah held her, his heart rending in two at the thought

of Jane and Abigail out there in the night, frightened, confused and wanting their ma. Grace loved those girls more than life itself. He had to do everything in his power to return them to her safe and sound. *God, You are one who sees. You know where those precious girls are. Lead me to them, I beg You.*

Over her shoulder, he told Doc to fetch Tomasina. She could stay with Grace until he returned.

"You're going after them." James was pacing in the tight entryway. "I'll go with you."

Grace straightened and pulled away, her cheeks ravaged by tears. The stage makeup was smeared. "You can't. I know Frank. If he's paid someone to watch us and learns we're deviating from his orders, he'll take them away solely to punish me."

Fishing out a handkerchief, Noah handed it to her.

"James, I think it best if you stay with Hannah and Ava. But first, go fetch Will and Daniel. Have Will wake the postmaster and find that missive. I need to see it right away."

It was his only clue to Frank's general location. The blackguard wouldn't want to travel unnecessary distances with a pair of scared little girls in tow.

When they were alone, Noah grasped her hand and led her to the kitchen. He gently guided her into a chair at the table and put his own untouched cup of coffee in front of her.

"Drink."

Wrapping her hands about the cup, she stared at the contents but didn't lift it to her lips. "What if I lose them? I can't imagine what they're thinking right now." She looked on the verge of breaking down. "They must be so scared. He's their uncle, but they've always been intimidated by him."

Crouching beside her chair, he cupped her cheek. "We're not going to lose them, Grace. Not tonight. Not ever."

He knew it was a reckless promise to be making, but he fully intended on fulfilling it.

Frank Longstreet had gotten his way one time too many. It was going to stop.

Tomasina arrived five minutes later, alarmed but trying her best to hide it as she comforted Grace. Reassured she was in good hands, Noah grabbed his hat and made to leave, eager to start tracking Frank.

"Noah." Grace caught up to him and snatched his hand. "Be careful."

"Always."

She looked as if she had more to say, something urgent and important, but she shook her head. He had something momentous to say to her, too, but now wasn't the time. He had to be content with a quick kiss on her forehead and murmured encouragement.

Will intercepted him halfway to Eden Street. He was on horseback and leading Samson. He handed him a small envelope.

"Daniel's staying at the jail with Deputy Hanley," he told him. "I'm going with you."

Using Will's lantern to read by, Noah skimmed the lines on the paper. "The rendezvous point is an abandoned shack about a quarter of a mile east of the train terminus."

"Let's check it out. Maybe he plans to pass the night there."

Lighting his own lantern, Noah climbed into the saddle. "You sure you don't wanna wait with Tomasina and Grace? I know very little about this man, so I can't predict how he'll react."

"I should shoot you for suggesting such a thing," Will exclaimed. "Come on, we're wasting time." Nudging his mount's flank, he got a head start.

Noah urged Samson into motion, wishing there was time to fetch Wolf from the ranch. He'd made the decision to leave him at home for two reasons. First, he hadn't wanted him in the cross fire of their confrontation with Burrows. Second, he'd thought to offer Grace and the girls some protection.

With the moonlight to guide them, they raced through town, slowing near the tracks. This side of Cowboy Creek was rowdier, alive with more activity because of the cowboys and their late-night shenanigans. Following the tracks in silence, Noah pulled up sharply when his gaze hit on a small white object.

Sliding to the ground, he bent to retrieve it.

"What is it?" Will sidled closer.

Noah's chest squeezed as he fingered the white wooden duck. "This is Jane's. I carved it for her." Spinning in a circle, he frantically searched the tracks and grass. "There's nothing else here." Frustration underscored his words. "She must've dropped it."

"Let's keep looking."

For the first time, the endless prairie he'd grown to love had become an adversary, miles of uninhabited land where an unscrupulous snake like Frank could take refuge. As they ate up the distance between the town proper and the wooded section close to the shack, Noah prayed continuously, asking God to grant Grace peace and Jane and Abigail courage.

Will slowed his horse minutes later, and he pointed wordlessly to the lone shelter outlined in moonlight. Dismounting, they readied their weapons and walked the rest of the way. He didn't see a horse or wagon, but that didn't mean their quarry wasn't inside. Frank could've hidden it in the woods several minutes' walk from here.

Please Lord, let them be all right.

In silent agreement, they took up positions on either side of the door, guns raised. Noah pressed his ear to the wood. Nothing but stark silence greeted him—not even the scuffling of feet. He knew even before they busted inside that it would be empty.

Will holstered his weapon, his expression grim yet determined. "Let's check the woods."

Glad his friend was with him, Noah emerged first, his gaze on the darker portion of the prairie. The woods covered approximately three square miles. Did Grace's brother-in-law have the girls there? Or had he gone the opposite direction on the off chance someone would check his missive?

Noah matched Samson's pace to Will's animal's. His nerves were on edge.

Closer to the trees, they dismounted once more and tied their mounts to a low-slung branch. Several yards into the dense woods, Will threw out an arm. Noah stopped short as his friend plucked a shiny pink ribbon from a tree limb.

They exchanged a telling glance. Stuffing the ribbon in his pocket along with the duck, Noah couldn't help wondering if the girls had deliberately left him clues. The last book he'd read to them had been *Hansel and Gretel*, after all. Were they leaving him a trail like the fictional characters?

Their progress was slow. Too slow for his peace of mind. While he knew they couldn't risk alerting Frank to their presence, his mind and body demanded to rush ahead. He wanted those girls safe right this minute.

When something crunched beneath his boot, Noah picked up Jane's corn-husk doll and fought emotion clogging his throat. On a whim, he'd purchased one for each of the girls. Even though they'd brought expensive store-bought dolls from Chicago, they'd been delighted with these handmade ones.

Maybe their excitement had less to do with the gifts' worth and more to do with the fact you thought of them.

Inexplicably, the twins had taken a shine to him, despite his scars and beastly behavior. He wished he'd taken the time to tell them he'd taken a shine to them, too. He never thought he'd be a father. And then suddenly he'd had two adorable girls underfoot, gifting him with their sweet smiles and unconditional trust.

More than anything, he wanted to see them grow and mature into responsible young women who loved the Lord. Frank Longstreet didn't deserve to share the same air as them.

The distinct smell of smoldering ashes hit them at the same time. Will seized his arm and pointed to an opening in the trees. Although cloaked in shadows, he could just make out a figure too large to be a child. The man was pacing back and forth, his movements sporadic. Impatient.

"I have to use the necessary, Uncle Frank."

Noah tensed. *Abigail.*

"You used it not fifteen minutes ago," Frank snapped.

"I have to go, too." Jane's normally bright voice was tremulous.

In the moonlight, Will's furious expression mirrored Noah's feelings. Holstering his gun, Will gestured to the girls, indicating he'd see to getting them out of shooting range. That left Noah to ambush Frank.

He held up three fingers. Counted down.

His body primed for action, he stepped into the clearing, gun barrel leveled at Frank's back. "Game's over, Longstreet. Put your hands up and turn around."

The man spun on his heel, his fancy suit jacket flaring, and glared at them both. Disregarding Noah's order, he kept his hands at his sides. "You have no business here, sir. These are my nieces. As far as I'm aware, no one owns this land. We have a right to pass the night in these woods."

"Mr. Noah!" Jane's cry was eclipsed by Will, who took her and Abigail's hands and urged them to leave with him.

Abigail resisted. "No! I want Noah!"

Noah's chest constricted. "Go with Mr. Canfield, honey. Everything's going to be all right."

Frank did not react well.

"You're the man Grace has been living with?" he demanded, menace settling over his aristocratic features. "She always thought she was smarter than me. Hanging out with a lawman, I see. Perhaps I underestimated her."

He wasn't about to discuss her with the man who'd tormented her life. Itching to exact revenge for her sake, he recalled that justice was in the Lord's hands. Besides, he was duty bound to uphold the law. Those same laws that applied to everyone else applied to him, too.

"I'm the sheriff in these parts, and I said to put your hands in the air."

"Now, why would I do that?" Frank sneered, throwing his arms wide. Pale light glinted off his diamond tie pin. "I've done nothing wrong. Besides, you don't want to arrest me. Not if you value your position. I have friends in law and government with the power to finish you."

His arrogance astounded Noah. The man wielded his position and influence like a sword.

"Kidnapping is an arrestable offence, as is coercion."

"I'm their blood relation," he scoffed. "I can take them wherever I please."

"Not without their mother's permission, you can't. Frank Longstreet, you're going to be spending the foreseeable future in my jail. You have sixty seconds to submit before I put a bullet in you."

With an ungentlemanly growl, Frank pounced. Noah hit the ground. His bones jarred. The air whooshed from his lungs. His grip on his gun went slack. Frank landed a blow on Noah's jaw the same instant he grabbed for the weapon.

Noah hadn't survived bloody battles between the North and South to die at the hands of a spoiled, entitled swine.

He was leaving these woods alive. He would return the twins to their mother.

But then, all of a sudden, he didn't have a hold on the pistol. It slipped from his gloved hand. Skittered across the grass.

With a grunt of triumph, Frank lunged for it. Noah scrambled after him. He seized the other man's jacket collar and hauled him backward. He got an elbow in the nose for his efforts. Blood trickled into his mouth.

That one second of hesitation cost him. Suddenly, he was staring down the barrel of his own gun.

Frank laughed, a horrible, slightly maniacal sound that rent the night.

Please God, don't let that be the last sound I hear on this earth.

Frank was on his knees, panting, smoothing his mussed hair into place. Noah was on his back, no shelter in sight.

"Since you're not going to be around for the foreseeable future, lawman, let me fill you in on what's going to happen. After I dispense with you, I'm going to dispense with your friend. My nieces and I are going to spend the night here, as I planned, and we're going to wait for Grace to come to us. The four of us are going to return to Chicago, where Grace is going to accept my grand, romantic proposal. Our wedding will the event of the decade. After our honeymoon, which I will be sure to make very memorable, the girls will be carted off to boarding school so that Grace can devote her every minute to catering to my whims."

Rage unlike Noah had ever experienced took him in its hold. His thoughts blurred and melded into one—no way was the woman he loved more than his own life going to wind up with this creature.

"Let's make a deal." Adopting a humble air, Noah held up a hand as he slowly rose onto his knees, mimicking his foe's position.

"What type of deal would a lowly lawman like you have to offer someone like me?"

He nodded, gauging his options. "You know, you're right. I don't make deals with swine."

He threw his entire weight into Frank's shoulder. With the element of surprise on his side, Noah was able to close both hands around the gun. They wrestled for long moments. The gun blasted near his ear. A deafening, teeth-rattling blast.

His enemy emitted a surprised gasp before he fell backward, his head striking a tree stump.

Heart hammering, Noah surged to his feet, reholstering his gun before checking for a pulse. Still alive. From the faint light filtering through the treetops, he could make out the wound. Looked like the bullet had skimmed the top of his shoulder.

Searching the man's jacket pockets, he discovered a stitched handkerchief that he used to stem the blood.

"Noah?" Will called from some distance away. "You all right?"

"Fine. Where are the girls?"

"Safe. I heard the gunshot. Worried you were in trouble."

"Frank's unconscious. Can you give me a hand getting him on his horse?"

Will joined him and, in a matter of minutes, they had Frank slung over the saddle. Noah led him to where the girls were hunkered down. As soon as they saw him, they bolted to his side, wrapping their arms about his legs so tight he almost lost his footing.

Gratefulness flooded him as he returned their hugs.

"We were scared," Abigail whispered, trembling.

Noah swung her up into his arms. "You were very brave, sweetheart. Your ma and I are proud of you both. Now, how about we go and see her?"

Abigail nodded and buried her face in his chest. "Yes, please."

Will took Jane's hand. "Would you like to ride on my horse with me?"

"Yes, sir."

They made the trip back to town in silence. The girls were exhausted. Noah kept replaying the events of the past few hours, aware he'd come within seconds of dying. God had spared his life. Question was, what was he prepared to do in response?

Chapter Twenty-Six

The knock on Doctor Fletcher's door had a twofold effect on Grace. Dread mingled with anticipation. What would she find on the other side?

After fetching Tomasina, the doctor had stayed behind to observe the fire's damage and offer his services to anyone in need. Only Tomasina was there to keep her company. She followed on her heels.

Twisting the knob, Grace pulled the heavy door open inch by inch. The sight of Noah allowed her to breathe again, really breathe as she'd been unable to since he left. Handsome and rumpled, a new bruise on his unscarred jaw, he held a sleepy Abigail in his arms. Will stood to his left and slightly behind him, holding Jane with the ease of a natural born father.

With a small cry, Grace threw her arms around Abigail and Noah, tears of joy and relief flowing unchecked. "You brought them back to me. Thank you."

He barely had a chance to react before Abigail surged into her arms. "I want to go to bed, Momma."

Grace held her tight, showering kisses all over her hair and face. Tomasina joined Will. Grinning from ear to ear, she bussed her husband's cheek and patted a snoozing Jane's back.

"You did good, Daddy Canfield." Her wink indicated a private joke between the pair.

Noah's blue gaze held emotion she couldn't begin to decipher. "It's late. Time to get these two tucked into bed."

"You're welcome to stay at the hotel. Free of charge, of course," Will said.

"Thanks for the offer." Noah didn't take his eyes off Grace. "I'm going to round up a wagon and take my girls home."

Tomasina's eyes widened. Like Grace, she'd noted his phrasing. Did she dare hope there could be a future for them?

The men secured a wagon and, within fifteen minutes' time, the four of them—Noah, Grace and the girls—had bid the Canfields good-night and were riding through the tranquil prairie night, a canopy of twinkling stars and a fat white moon guiding their way. The air carried the hint of mint, and she knew the ranch was close. A multitude of questions rose up, demanding to be voiced. Where was Frank? Would Noah be staying in the barn or returning to the hotel like before? Had he forgiven her? Could he…did he…love her?

Afraid of the answers, she maintained her silence. Noah appeared lost in thought, as well. He must be as mentally and physically exhausted as she was.

At the cabin, he insisted on carrying the girls inside. Since they were already asleep, Grace decided to let them sleep in their clothing and to clean everything the next day. The thought gave her pause. What would the next day bring? She'd promised to purchase their train tickets and let Noah know the date of their departure. Was he still counting on that?

She closed the bedroom door and found him crouched by the fireplace, stroking Wolf's thick coat and talking to him as he would a human.

"Remember your job, buddy. You have to keep the girls safe."

Grace smiled when the big animal closed his golden eyes as if bored with the reminder.

"Are you returning to the hotel?"

He pivoted in her direction. With a final stroke of Wolf's head, he stood. He had shed his vest, and his gray shirt was open at the throat and bore signs of dirt and soot.

"I'm sleeping in the barn tonight."

What about after that? she longed to ask. Did he want her gone so he could have his room back?

Her gaze on his bruised cheek, she rounded the table to go closer. "Where's Frank?"

His lips thinned. "In a jail cell, making nice with Xavier Murdoch."

She boldly touched her fingertips to his cheek. "He did this to you?"

"It's nothing."

Sliding his torn sleeve up to his elbow, Grace discovered tiny cuts up and down his forearm. That he allowed her this examination surprised her. "How did you get these?"

"Couldn't get into the newspaper office, so I busted out a window."

He was still and quiet, his gaze watchful, his breathing steady and sure. She couldn't guess his mood or thoughts, couldn't determine if he liked having her close or wished she'd bid him good-night. Probably the latter.

Before she did so, though, she had some things to say, and she needed his anchoring touch to give her courage. Clasping his large hand between hers, she squared her shoulders and looked into his eyes.

"Noah, I can never repay you for everything you've done. Instead of turning us away as you had every right to do, you opened your home to us. You traded your comfortable bedroom for a barn loft. When I was sick, you took care of me and the girls without a word of complaint. You've provided for us, protected us. You saved our lives, Noah." Her voice wobbled. "And somewhere along the way, I fell in love with you."

His gaze felt like it was burning into her, searching, weighing, assessing. He waited so long to speak she assumed he was trying to figure out how to let her down gently.

"Actually, you can repay me."

"Oh." Her stomach dropped to her toes. "Certainly. Name the amount, and I'll go to the bank first thing in the—"

His mouth covered hers in an unexpected, hungry kiss. His hands came up to frame her face. The sensation of his fingertips in her hair and the slow slide of his thumbs across her cheeks made her light-headed. Grace steadied herself with her hands flat against his chest. Beneath her palm, his heart thudded as fast as her own. Seconds passed and the kiss gentled. The tenderness he displayed evoked a growing sense of wonder and joy.

Noah held nothing in reserve with this kiss. Before, she'd always sensed he wasn't fully present, his emotions under lock and key.

When he eased away, he looked deep into her eyes and smiled. That smile was like shafts of spring sunlight after months of winter gloom.

"You can probably guess I don't want your money," he murmured, still caressing her skin, running his fingers through her hair. "I want *you*, Grace."

The burst of happiness was all too brief. "How can you? After my lies?"

"I knew you weren't a malicious or devious person." He tapped his temple. "I knew that in here. But my pride had been blasted to bits. I'd been aware of little discrepancies along the way but hadn't put the pieces together, and I felt gullible. Not a good trait for a lawman. Here was a woman living beneath my roof that I cared about, deeply cared about, and yet I hadn't picked up on the fact she was running scared from a life that had threatened to destroy her."

"I cringed every time you called me Constance," she admitted.

His smile grew lopsided, lending him a boyish air. "I never thought the name suited you, you know. Grace suits you. A lovely name for a lovely human being." His thumb skimmed her earlobe, and prickles danced along her nape. How she adored his touch. "I wish I'd let you explain that first night. It would've saved us both some heartache. I'm sorry for not being understanding when you needed me to be. I almost lost you and the girls because of it."

"Of course you were hurt and angry." She cupped his scarred jaw, and he didn't flinch like the first time. "I don't blame you."

His expression turned fierce. "Frank's not going to hurt you ever again."

Grace trusted Noah. He'd proved his trustworthiness, his willingness to go to any lengths to protect her and her daughters. They were safe with him. She'd known that from the start, despite his bluster and attempts to keep them at bay. "I believe you."

"I love you, Grace Longstreet. I want you with me. Today. Tomorrow. Forever."

"Are you sure that's what you want?' she asked in a quavering voice. "An instant family?"

"Whether or not you agree to make it official, I already consider you my family. You, Jane and Abigail."

Sweeter words had never been spoken. Amazed at this gift God had blessed her with, at His mercy and tender care, Grace wrapped her arms around Noah's neck and burst into tears. His arms settled about her waist, and he nuzzled her hair.

"Hey, city girl, are those happy tears or sad tears?"

"Happy." It took a few moments to compose herself. He was patient, and apparently unconcerned with the moisture dampening his shirt. Easing her hold on him, she lifted her head and dashed the wetness from her cheeks.

His forehead furrowed. "You sure you're okay?"

"I'm ecstatic...and maybe a little overwhelmed." A little laugh escaped. "Noah, you make me feel protected and loved in a way I haven't since before my father died. I came out here expecting to have a businesslike marriage. The most I'd hoped for was mutual respect and, if I was fortunate, friendship. I never expected this." She lightly traced his eyebrows, bold cheekbones, chiseled mouth. "I never expected you."

Beneath her fingers, his lips curved into an affectionate smile. There were no more reservations, no more shadows in his eyes. "I'm not sure I know how to be a good husband or father, but I vow to love you and the girls and do right by you every day of my life."

"It's okay. We'll learn together." She kissed him tenderly. "I love you, Noah. I can't wait to be your wife."

Epilogue

Four Months Later

"I now pronounce you husband and wife. You may kiss the bride."

Noah had been waiting months for this exact moment, the moment he'd slide his ring on Grace's finger and seal their union. The days since he'd proposed had seemed to pass slowly and quickly all at the same time.

Releasing her slender hand, he framed her uplifted face. She was breathtaking, a vision in white, her hair arranged in an elegant sweep and adorned with white and orange blossoms. Her skin had a healthy flush. Her eyes shone with love. Her mouth held promise and secrets meant only for him.

As he lowered his head to kiss her for the first time as her husband, he admitted the wait had been worth it. The morning following his proposal, over a leisurely breakfast with the girls, they'd decided to set the date for October. Though unconventional, Noah had wanted them both to be counseled by Reverend Taggart. They'd spent hours with him, discussing the duties of a husband and wife, what God's expectations were for a family. For propriety's sake, Noah had lived in the hotel. He was eager to live under his own roof again. This time as Grace's husband and the girls' father.

He reluctantly kept the kiss brief. Beneath his touch, he could feel Grace's smile. He'd grown quite attached to that smile and intended to do whatever he could to keep it there.

In the distant fields, a cow lowed, and their guests broke into laughter, whistles and applause. Noah lifted his head and laughed, too.

"Still glad you chose our ranch for the ceremony?"

She nodded. "This is where we met and fell in love."

The twins stood nearby, arrayed like princesses in dainty white dresses with satin ribbons and flower crowns in their dark hair. Abigail giggled. Her dark brown eyes danced. Jane smiled, her dimples showing. They'd been as impatient as Noah and Grace for this day to arrive.

"Mr. and Mrs. Burgess, everyone," Reverend Taggart announced with a hearty clap.

Noah leaned close to her ear. "Should I make my announcement now or later?"

"Now would be good, before they have cake to lob at you."

"Right." Curving his arm about her waist and tugging her against his side, he held up his hand. The noise gradually petered out. "Ladies and gentlemen, we want to thank you for coming out to celebrate our special day."

His closest friends were seated on the first row of seats on loan from the hotel. In total, there were about forty people in attendance, including Amos and Opal Godwin with their newborn son. The expansive yard between the cabin and the creek had been transformed by Pippa and the hotel employees she'd bossed around. Tables swathed in white were loaded with silver trays piled high with meats, cheeses and fall vegetables. Pumpkins, squash and gourds, as well as cheery fall flowers set about the yard mimicked the trees' autumn foliage. Wolf remained in the shade of a distant cottonwood, content to observe from afar.

It reminded Noah of the days he'd chosen to be alone, always the outsider. He hadn't been content. He'd been lonely.

"Not so long ago, my friends thought it would be a good idea to spring a mail-order bride on me."

Will stood and, facing the crowd, swept an elegant bow. Daniel winked at Grace. Laughter rippled through the air.

Gazing down at his bride, Noah didn't care if the whole town witnessed how besotted he was with her. "Foolish man that I am, I didn't at first understand how wise my friends had been in bringing her here. Thank the Lord, I didn't succeed in running her off."

Grace's eyes grew moist. If he didn't want his new wife crying within minutes of their vows, he'd better get to the point.

Turning his attention to the others, he said, "Now that I have a wife and family to care for, I've decided to pass the sheriff's badge on to someone else."

Gasps and whispers replaced the good humor. Will, Daniel and Gideon weren't surprised because he'd discussed his decision with them at length.

"Hear me out, please. While I've appreciated the chance to be Cowboy Creek's sheriff, being a lawman is not my true calling. Ranching is in my blood. I can't give my all to both the town and this ranch. Grace and the girls are my priority now."

"Who you got in mind, Sheriff?" Old Horace hollered from the back row.

"It sure ain't gonna be you." Gus elbowed his friend.

Noah extended his hand to the young man seated on their right, just behind Will and Tomasina. "I suggest you choose Deputy Buck Hanley. He's got what it takes to make a fine sheriff."

The deputy's face registered humble surprise. He gave a deep nod to Noah.

Hanley had been instrumental in helping him sort Xavier and the gang members' transport to Lawrence. The younger man had also personally escorted Frank Longstreet to a larger jail in Illinois, where he was awaiting trial. Apparently Frank's influential friends weren't eager to extend help to a child kidnapper. And now that he was behind bars, a handful of young women had contacted the Chicago authorities with tales of his personal crimes against them. Grace didn't have to worry about her former brother-in-law bothering her again.

D. B. Burrows was still in their jail and would be there until Prudence arrived. Late last week, they'd received word from a sheriff on the opposite side of the state that they'd located her trying to board a train with a large sum of money. When she arrived, Noah would assist Hanley in the interview. As soon as they had court proceedings scheduled, he'd leave it in Hanley's capable hands.

Will stood and raised a hand. "While we're making announcements, I thought you'd like to know that Cowboy Creek has been chosen as the official county seat!"

The guests reacted with hoots and clapping.

"We can commemorate this momentous achievement tomorrow with a parade and town-wide picnic. Right now, we have a marriage to celebrate. Let's eat!"

After the guests took turns congratulating them and slowly formed a line for the food, Grace anchored her arm about Noah's lower back. "That went better than I thought it would."

"The announcement or the ceremony?"

"The announcement, silly." She laughed up at him. "I didn't have any doubts about the ceremony."

She'd supported his decision. Not surprising, since she was the first one to question his contentment with the job.

"Not a single one?" he teased, tapping her nose.

"Not a one. Well, there were a couple of times I thought you were going to kiss me before the reverend gave you permission."

"I don't need permission to kiss my bride," he mock growled, landing a possessive kiss square on her lips. The heat of her small hand on his chest where she'd slipped it beneath his suit lapel seared through the fine cotton shirt.

Love for this woman pushed out every dark shadow from his past, leaving only hope for the future. He couldn't wait for his family to meet her. They'd responded quickly to his letter, their relief almost leaping from the page. His father had expressed regret over the way they'd left things and asked if Noah would mind if they visited. He'd answered with a telegram, urging them to come at their earliest convenience. Two of his sisters were married, but the youngest one was still unwed and would be accompanying their parents. They'd be here in a matter of weeks, and he was already planning what all they'd do together.

"Are you hungry?" He caressed Grace's neck. "Want me to get you a plate?"

"I could eat." Her gaze assessing the festivities, she said, "And we wouldn't want to offend Pippa. She's gone to a lot of trouble."

The demonstrative actress, arrayed like a harvest queen herself, was herding guests to the tables, answering questions, giving pointers to the servers. Gideon stood talking with Daniel's father and Valentine Ewing, but his attention never left his new wife's side. They'd married in August and, much to the locals' dismay, were leaving in a week's time. Pippa and Gideon assured them they'd be back within six months' time. He'd worked a deal with the railroad to spend half of each year traveling and the other half working from their home in Cowboy Creek.

Noah noticed Will and Tomasina on the bank near the

water. She was leaning against him, her head buried in his shoulder. Lately, the normally vivacious redhead had been subdued. Wan, even.

"Why didn't Tomasina help?"

Grace's expression grew knowing. "She's been ill."

Concern flared. "Ill? Is it serious?"

"Very serious." But she was grinning. "She's expecting a baby."

Noah's gaze shot to Will. His friend had been quieter than usual, more intense, Noah realized. "I wonder why he hasn't said anything."

"Maybe he didn't want to detract from your big day."

"We have been busy, I suppose."

They'd turned his loft office into a bedroom for the girls. Jane and Abigail had taken great delight in their trips to the mercantile to order furniture and bedding. He'd surprised them with a hand-carved miniature of the cabin, complete with carved animals for them to play with. For the main living space, Grace had enlisted his help in choosing a sofa and chairs. His desk, bookshelves and cabinets were now in one corner of the living room.

"Let's go talk to them," he said.

By the time they reached the stream Daniel and Leah were there, already chatting with the couple. Leah's infant daughter, Evie, slept peacefully in her mother's arms. The baby had light blond hair and pink skin, and Daniel doted on her as much as he did Leah.

"I hear congratulations are in order." Noah clapped Will on the shoulder.

Tomasina blushed. That was a sight he hadn't seen before.

Will's smile held a mixture of pride and concern. "Thanks, old friend."

Daniel shook Will's hand. "I'm happy for you, Will. You, too, Tom," he tacked on, causing them all to chuckle.

"We would've told you sooner," Will explained, "but we wanted to wait until the sickness had passed and we were sure everything was progressing the normal way."

Tears shimmered in Tomasina's eyes. "The sickness may be starting to pass, but I can't stop crying! If the drovers could see me now…" She groaned.

Will dropped a kiss on her hair. "Emotional highs and lows are normal, remember?"

Leah touched her shoulder. "You know you can come to me with any questions or concerns. And I'll be happy to help when the baby's time arrives."

"Thank you, Leah." Tomasina managed a tremulous smile. "I appreciate that."

Abigail came running up, her rounded cheeks red and her lips forming a pout. Jane followed right behind her.

"Pa!" Abigail tugged on Noah's pant leg. "That mean boy over there won't leave us alone."

"What boy?" He frowned.

Jane pointed to a towheaded boy standing in line. "That one right there! Mr. Haggerman's grandson. He said my freckles look like the constellations." She looked furious. Her nose wrinkled. "What are constellations?"

Grace bent to Jane's level. After she'd explained, she said, "Your freckles are what make you unique. God made you exactly the way He wanted, and He doesn't make mistakes."

"I'm going to have a little chat with this boy," he grumbled.

She waylaid him. "Sweetheart, he's only eight."

"So?"

The girls ran off holding hands and, sticking out their tongues at the boy, went to observe the wedding cake.

Will and Daniel chuckled.

Grace hid a smile and shook her head. A thought struck him then.

Turning to Leah, he said, "How likely is it for a woman who's had one set of twins to have another?"

Grace gave him a playful swat. "Noah, really. Leah's a midwife. She can't predict something like that."

"She's right." Leah swayed from side to side as Evie started to squirm. "And besides, I haven't had experience with mothers of twins."

Noah considered the cabin. "You never know, city girl, we may have to add on a room or three."

"You could always live inside the barn," Daniel teased. "Plenty of space in there."

Will turned serious. Holding his wife close, he said, "I used to think the railroad and the cattle were the keys to making Cowboy Creek a success. I was wrong. It's the people who make our town what it is. And with new families being formed, like Noah and Grace's, babies being brought into the world, like Evie here and our little one on the way, we don't have to worry about out boomtown going bust."

"Profound words," Daniel agreed. "My father proposed to Valentine last night. She said yes. Looks like we'll have another wedding soon. Our latest bride train is due tomorrow. Who knows, maybe even Old Horace and Gus will make matches."

More laughter made it around their circle. Noah could hardly take in how much richer his life, and his town, had become. His plans had been small. Narrow. Limited. God, in His wisdom, had expanded those plans. He'd known what the town, and in particular Noah, had needed.

Uncaring they had an audience, Noah swept his bride into his arms for another kiss. "I love you, Grace Burgess."

"I love you, too." Her warm honey eyes were bright.

"You do know we're standing here watching you, right?" Tom demanded, a bit of her old fire reappearing.

Will's smile grew. "I don't know… I think he has the right idea, don't you, Daniel?"

Daniel stroked his chin. "Yep, I think he does."

As Daniel tugged Leah close and kissed her, Will did the same with his wife.

Noah laughed. "I can hardly wait to see what the future holds. Not just for me and Grace, but for all of us."

* * * * *

Dear Reader,

What fun Noah and Grace's story turned out to be! This was my first time writing about the years immediately following the Civil War. I learned a lot about the struggles and uncertainties people faced during that time. Writing about a scarred ex-soldier was an interesting challenge—Noah has to come to terms with his inner scars, as well as those visible on his body. A loner like him isn't the least bit pleased when his friends Will Canfield and Daniel Gardner order a mail-order bride specifically for him. Having the polished, winsome socialite and her twin daughters underfoot makes him question his decision to remain alone. In this story, the third installment of Cowboy Creek, we get to revisit the Kansas boomtown setting and the many beloved characters introduced in the previous two books. If you haven't yet, check out Daniel's story by Cheryl St. John and Will's story by Sherri Shackelford. I hope you enjoyed Noah and Grace's journey as much as I did.

If you'd like to learn more about this book and others, please visit my website at www.karenkirst.com. I'm also on Facebook, Goodreads and Twitter, @KarenKirst.

Many blessings,
Karen Kirst

REQUEST YOUR FREE BOOKS!

2 FREE INSPIRATIONAL NOVELS
PLUS 2 FREE MYSTERY GIFTS

Love Inspired HISTORICAL

*When a bachelor rancher abruptly gains custody
of his twin nieces, he needs all the help he can get.
But as he starts to fall for the girls' widowed caretaker,
can love blossom for this unexpected family?*

*Read on for a sneak preview of
STAND-IN RANCHER DADDY,
the heartwarming beginning of the series
LONE STAR COWBOY LEAGUE:
THE FOUNDING YEARS*

At last, CJ thought. Help was on the way.

With each step Molly took in his direction, he felt the tension draining out of him. She was a calming influence and the stability they all needed—not just Sarah and Anna, but CJ, too.

If she ever left him…

Not the point, he told himself.

She looked uncommonly beautiful this morning in a blue cotton dress with a white lace collar and long sleeves. The cut of the garment emphasized her tiny waist and petite frame.

He attempted to swallow past the lump in his throat without much success. Molly took his breath away.

If he were from a different family…

"Miss Molly," Anna called out. "Miss Molly, over here! We're over here."

Sarah wasn't content with merely waving. She pulled her hand free of CJ's and raced to meet Molly across the small expanse of grass. Anna followed hard on her sister's heels.

Molly greeted both girls with a hug and a kiss on the top of their heads.

"Well, look who it is." She stepped back and smiled down

at the twins. "My two favorite girls in all of Little Horn, Texas. And don't you look especially pretty this morning."

"Unca Corny picked out our dresses," Sarah told her.

"He tried to make breakfast." Anna swayed her shoulders back and forth with little-girl pride. "He didn't do so good. He burned the oatmeal and Cookie had to make more."

Molly's compassionate gaze met his. "Sounds like you had an…interesting morning."

CJ chuckled softly. "Though I wouldn't want to repeat the experience anytime soon, we survived well enough."

"Miss Molly, look. I'm wearing my favorite pink ribbon." Sarah touched the floppy bow with reverent fingers. "I tied it all by myself."

"You did a lovely job." Under the guise of inspecting the ribbon, Molly retied the bow, then moved it around until it sat straight on the child's head. "Pink is my favorite color."

"It's Pa's favorite, too." Sarah's gaze skittered toward the crowded tent. "I wore it just for him."

The wistful note in her voice broke CJ's heart. He shared a tortured look with Molly.

Her ragged sigh told him she was thinking along the same lines as he was. His brother always made it to church, a fact the twins had reminded him of this morning.

"Pa says Sunday is the most important day of the week," Sarah had told him, while Anna had added, "And we're never supposed to miss Sunday service. Not ever."

Somewhere along the way, the two had gotten it into their heads that Ned would show up at church today. CJ wasn't anywhere near as confident. If Ned didn't make an appearance, the twins would know that their father was truly gone.

Don't miss
STAND-IN RANCHER DADDY
by Renee Ryan, available July 2016 wherever
Love Inspired® Historical books and ebooks are sold.

www.LoveInspired.com

I was wondering if I could come by the house tomorrow. To go through your father's papers."

Lauren sighed.

Vic tamped down his immediate apology. He had nothing to feel bad about. He was just looking out for his brother's interests.

"Yes. Of course. Though—" She stopped herself there. "Sorry. You probably know better what you're looking for."

Vic shot her a glance across the cab of the truck. "I'm not trying to jeopardize your deal. When I first leased the ranch from your father, it was so that my brother could have his own place. And I'm hoping to protect that promise I made him. Especially now. After his accident."

"I understand," Lauren said, her smile apologetic. "I know what it's like to protect siblings."

"Are you the oldest?"

"Erin and I are twins, but I'm older by twenty minutes."

Lauren smiled at him. And as their eyes held, he felt it again. An unexpected rush of attraction. When her eyes grew ever so slightly wider, he wondered if she felt it, too.

He dragged his attention back to the road.

You're no judge of your feelings, he reminded himself, his hands tightening on the steering wheel as if reining in his attraction to this enigmatic woman.

He'd made mistakes in the past, falling for the wrong person. He couldn't do it again. He couldn't afford to.

Especially not with Lauren.

Don't miss
TRUSTING THE COWBOY
by Carolyne Aarsen, available July 2016 wherever
Love Inspired® books and ebooks are sold.

www.LoveInspired.com

LIEXP0616

"So you didn't like it here?" Vic asked. "Coming every summer?"

"I missed my friends back home, but there were parts I liked."

"I remember seeing you girls in church on Sunday."

"Part of the deal," Lauren said, a faint smile teasing her mouth. "And I didn't mind that part, either. The message was always good, once I started really listening. I can't remember who the pastor was, but what he said resonated with me."

"Jodie and Erin would attend some of the youth events, didn't they?"

"Erin more than any of us."

"I remember my brother Dean talking about her," Vic said. "I think he had a secret crush on her."

"He was impetuous, wasn't he?"

"That's being kind. But he's settled now."

Thoughts of Dean brought up the same problem that had brought him to the ranch.

His deal with Lauren's father.

"So, I hate to be a broken record," he continued, "but